Edward E. Hale

Stories of Adventure Told by Adventurers

Volume 1

Edward E. Hale

Stories of Adventure Told by Adventurers
Volume 1

ISBN/EAN: 9783337340025

Printed in Europe, USA, Canada, Australia, Japan

Cover: Foto ©Andreas Hilbeck / pixelio.de

More available books at **www.hansebooks.com**

STORIES OF ADVENTURE

TOLD BY ADVENTURERS.

By EDWARD E. HALE.

BOSTON:
ROBERTS BROTHERS.
1881.

PREFACE.

THIS volume is the third in a series suggested at the Librarians' Congress in Boston, in the summer of 1879. The three have been prepared in the wish to teach boys and girls how to use themselves the treasures, now at their hands, in public libraries. The public spirit, the munificence often, with which these libraries have been sustained ought to be loyally followed up by the friends of young people by careful effort to give them good habits in finding and enjoying the books they contain. It is not reasonable to throw on the librarians the work of introducing these books to young readers; but it is the duty of all those who are in any way charged with the interests of education to show to such readers how they can choose for themselves.

It will be seen, therefore, that my object is not to re-write the tales of adventure, here referred to, nor is it my wish to present them in such form as to satisfy the reader. Rather I have hoped that he may not be satisfied. I should be glad, as Sam Weller was, to make him wish for more, trusting that then, like Oliver Twist, he may go and ask for more.

The other volumes have been, "STORIES OF WAR, TOLD BY SOLDIERS," "STORIES OF THE SEA, TOLD BY SAILORS." The next, now in preparation, will be "STORIES OF DISCOVERY, TOLD BY DISCOVERERS."

EDWARD E. HALE.

Matunuck on the Hill, Rhode Island,
      July 16, 1881.

CONTENTS.

STORIES OF ADVENTURE.

I.

MARCO POLO.

A VERY bright and merry set of boys and girls have been invited, now for every winter for some years, to spend their Saturday afternoons with Col. Ingham, at his house at Jamaica Plain, near Boston. It is the old Lady Oliver house, which was built by some West Indian grandees before the Revolution, — from whose windows, indeed, they looked out to smile approval on the English troops, when, in the spring of 1775, they made their one " military promenade " out through Roxbury, and back through Dorchester into Boston, — the only time they ever went out to come safely back again.

The evenings of these young people at this house are generally spent in dancing or in round games around Col. Ingham's large tables ; but a habit has grown up, in which, if they choose, they may come as early as half-past three o'clock, and ask Col. Ingham questions about what they are reading, and burrow as much as they choose in the treasures of his curious library. The " Stories of the Sea," which has its place in this collection, were read aloud by these young people in successive visits of one winter, — much as they had dug out the "Stories of War," in a visit they made to the colonel at Little Crastis, on the Rhode Island seashore, the summer before.

After a summer and autumn crowded full with hairbreadth adventure, — stories of sea, indeed, and stories of land, though fortunately no worse stories of war than Blanche's encounter with a deaf conductor, and Bedford's somewhat doubtful encounters with quails and partridges at Quonochontaug, — the children gathered one dark afternoon at Col. Ingham's, with loud mutual felicitations, and with a cordial welcome from him. It was raining pitilessly out of doors; but rubber boots and gossamers had emancipated these girls, and the boys, of course, had to be out always, "weather or no."

"No Blue Hills to-day," said Uncle Fritz, laughing, as Blanche and May rubbed their little hands in front of his hickory fire.

"No," said Blanche, "the famous Alpine Club itself surrenders to this storm. And my sketch, Uncle Fritz, — what you called my grand study for a panorama, — will have to be finished with spring apple-blossoms on the right hand, to patch out the sombre chestnuts and oaks I had worked in so elaborately on the left hand; for we shall certainly have no more alpine clubs this fall."

The young people are fond of calling themselves the Alpine Club when they go to the Quarries or the Blue Hills or Nahant or the Brewsters or the Middlesex Fells or the Waverley Oaks or any of the other nice places within an easy excursion from Boston.

"Unless, indeed," said Col. Ingham, "unless we get a sleigh-ride some afternoon, and I send you up

to the top of the Blue Hills on snow-shoes. I did
not know how many of you might be here. I am not
jealous of Mr. Hale ; but when I found you were all
studying politics over at his house, I thought there
might be no time for story-telling. Have you prepared
your protocol for Count Bismarck, Blanche ? "

Blanche laughed. She said the more they read of one
thing, the more they wanted to read of another ; and
that, for her part, she found no one of Uncle Fritz's
rules so easy as that which bids her

CONFESS IGNORANCE.

Uncle Fritz's rules for talk are : —

TELL THE TRUTH.
DO NOT TALK ABOUT YOUR OWN AFFAIRS.
CONFESS IGNORANCE.
TALK TO THE PERSON WHO TALKS TO YOU.
DO NOT UNDERRATE HIM.
BE SHORT.[1]

All the boys and girls agreed with Blanche, as, indeed, they are apt to, for Blanche is as pleasant as she
is sensible ; and here are two qualities which do not
always travel together.

By this time almost all the " Alpine Club " had come.
The waterproofs were hung to drip and dry in the back
hall, under Flora Haggerty's care ; and in a great semi-
circle the young people sat round the hickory fire.
It was something about the " Stories of the Sea," which
had just been published by Roberts Brothers, which
started them on travels ; and how they would like to go
to Tahiti and New Zealand and all the wonderful
places !

[1] See " How to Do It," pp. 29–60.

Uncle Fritz told them of some college friends of his, who had planned landing in Arabia from Zanzibar, and then assuming Arab costumes, talking such Arabic as they could, and gradually making their way through Asia till they came out at Canton, on the eastern shore. They failed in this great plan only from the merest accident at the start.

"We know, to this hour, curiously little of Central Asia," he said. "There are regions of which Marco Polo's account is the only account we have to this day; and that is six hundred years old."

"And it was not true when it was new, was it?" asked Horace, laughing.

Uncle Fritz said that that was an old scandal. He said that Mandeville and Marco Polo had long been called the princes of liars, while people did not follow their example of travel; but in our times, their reputations are waking up to light again. In Marco Polo's case, he wrote almost wholly from memory, — from the mere fact that he wrote long after his return from the East; but later authorities have verified so much of his narrative that it is but fair to believe him when nothing can be proved against him.

Bertha confessed that she mixed him up very badly with Marco Paul, who travelled in Mr. Abbott's books.

They all laughed, because they knew what Bertha meant. "That was one of Jacob Abbott's quiet jokes. His books are wellnigh perfect in everything, and in nothing more perfect than in the choice of names. So he makes Marco Paul a traveller, on purpose that we may all remember the prince of the travellers of the Middle Ages."

Then Col. Ingham sent for the third volume of Irving's "Columbus," and for Col. Yule's recent edition of " Marco Polo," — a fascinating book, which should be in every public library. He told Bedford to go to the bookcase which had Columbus's bust on top, and look till he found them.

That is the case with the travels and geographies in it. Bedford knows it as well as he knows the bookshelves he has at home, which he made on his own work-bench in the laundry. Col. Ingham told Bedford he would find an account of Marco Polo in the Appendix ; and Bedford found it, and read aloud : —

IRVING'S ACCOUNT OF MARCO POLO.

Marco Polo was a native of Venice, who in the thirteenth century made a journey to the East, and filled all Christendom with curiosity by his account of the countries he had visited. He was preceded in his travels by his father Nicholas, and his uncle, Matteo Polo. These two brothers were of an illustrious family in Venice, and embarked, in the year 1260,[1] on a commercial voyage to the East. Having traversed the Mediterranean and the strait of Bosphorus, they stopped for a short time at Constantinople. From hence they proceeded by the Euxine to Armenia, where they remained for a year, entertained with great favor at the court of a Tartar prince. A war breaking out between their patron and a neighboring potentate, and the former being defeated, they were embarrassed how to extricate themselves from the country, and return home in safety. After various

---

[1] So Yule corrects Irving, who says 1250.

wanderings, they at length reached Bochara, in the Gulf of Persia, where they resided for three years. While here, there arrived an ambassador from one of the inferior Tartar powers, on his way to the court of the Great Khan. Finding that the two brothers were well acquainted with the Tartar tongue, he prevailed upon them to accompany him. After a march of several months, being delayed by snows and inundations, they arrived at the court of Cublai, otherwise called the Great Khan, which signifies king of kings, being the sovereign potentate of the Tartars. This magnificent prince received them with great distinction. He made inquiries about the countries and princes of the West, their civil and military government, and the manners and customs of the Latin nations.

.   .   .   .   .

After one return to the Levant they took a second journey, and this time took Marco Polo with them. He was gone twenty-four years. On their return, when they arrived at Venice, they were known by nobody. So many years had elapsed since their departure, without any tidings of them, that they were either forgotten or considered dead.

They repaired to their own house, which was a noble palace, afterwards known by the name of la Corte de la Milione. They found several of their relatives still inhabiting it ; but they were slow in recollecting the travellers, not knowing of their wealth, and probably considering them poor adventurers, returned to be a charge upon their families. The Polos, however, took an effectual mode of quickening the memories of their friends, and ensuring themselves a loving reception. They invited them all to a grand banquet. The guests were lost in astonishment, and could not comprehend the meaning of this masquerade, when, having dismissed all the attendants, Marco Polo brought forth the coarse Tartar dresses in which they had arrived. Slashing them in several places with a knife, and ripping open the seams and linings, there tumbled forth a vast quantity of precious jewels, such as rubies, sapphires, emeralds, and diamonds. The whole table glittered with inestimable wealth, which they had acquired from the munificence of the Grand Khan, and which they had conveyed in this portable form through the perils of their long journey.

The company, observes Ramusio, were out of their wits with amazement, and now clearly perceived what they had at first doubted, that these in very truth were those honored and valiant gentlemen, the Polos, and accordingly paid them great respect and reverence.

Some months after their return, Lampo Doria, commander of the Genoese navy, appeared in the vicinity of the island of Cuzzola, with seventy galleys. Andrea Dandolo, the Venetian admiral, was sent against him. Marco Polo commanded a galley of the fleet. His usual good fortune deserted him. Advancing the first in the line with his galley, and not being properly seconded, he was taken prisoner, and thrown in irons, and carried to Genoa. Here he was detained for a long time in prison, and all offers of ransom rejected. His imprisonment gave great uneasiness to his father and uncle, fearing that he might never return. Seeing themselves in this unhappy state, with so much treasure, and no heirs, they consulted together. They were both very old men ; but Nicolo, observes Ramusio, was of a galliard complexion.   It was determined he should take a wife, and he did so.

In the meanwhile, the fame of Marco Polo's travels had circulated in Genoa.   His prison was daily crowded with the nobility, and he was supplied with everything that could cheer him in his confinement.   A Genoese gentleman, who visited him every day, at length prevailed on him to write an account of what he had seen.   He had his papers and journals sent to him from Venice, and with the assistance of his friend produced the book which afterwards made such noise throughout the world.

"So, you see," said Uncle Fritz, "that the poor rich man wrote in prison, far away from home, and with such journals and notes as had escaped wars, shipwrecks, and travel."

Bedford and two of the girls seized on one volume of Col. Yule's book, — which is a recent edition of " Marco Polo," — and Laura and two of the boys seized on another.   There are very amusing and instructive pictures ; and the young people were delighted as they turned from chapter to chapter.   Meanwhile, Uncle Fritz was questioning the others about their summer travels ; and all the talk was running on adventure.

"This is a very good day for ' Marco Polo,'" said he ; " for what with Oregon, and Colorado Springs, and the Saguenay River, you have travelled about as far this summer as the Venetian gentlemen did in all those years.   Bedford, have you found nothing you can read to us ? "

And, after a minute's conference, Bedford selected and read —

HOW THE EMPEROR SENT MARK ON AN EMBASSY.

Now it came to pass that Marco, the son of Messer Nicolo, spéd wondrously in learning the customs of the Tartars as well as their language, their manner of writing, and their practice of war, — in fact, he came in brief space to know several languages, and four sundry written characters; and he was discreet and prudent in every way, insomuch that the emperor held him in great esteem. And so, when he discerned Mark to have so much sense, and to conduct himself so well and beseemingly, he sent him on an ambassage of his to a country which was a good six months' journey distant. The young gallant executed his commission well, and with discretion. Now, he had taken note on several occasions that, when the prince's ambassadors returned from different parts of the world, they were able to tell him about nothing except the business on which they had gone; and the prince, in consequence, held them for no better than fools and dolts, and would say, " I had far liever hearken about the strange things and the manners of the different countries you have seen than merely be told of the business you went upon," — for he took great delight in hearing of the affairs of strange countries. Mark, therefore, as he went and returned, took great pains to learn about all kinds of different matters in the countries which he visited, in order to be able to tell about them to the Great Kaan.

When Mark returned from his ambassage, he presented himself before the emperor; and, after making his report of the business with which he was charged, and its successful accomplishment, he went on to give an account, in a pleasant and intelligent manner, of all the novelties and strange things that he had seen and heard, insomuch that the emperor and all such as heard his story were surprised, and said, " If this young man live, he will assuredly come to be a person of great worth and ability."   And so, from that time forward, he was always entitled MESSER MARCO POLO ; and thus we shall style him henceforth in this book of ours, as is but right.

Then Bedford turned over to a place where Mary Long had put in a mark, and read —

OF THE GREAT COUNTRY OF PERSIA, WITH SOME ACCOUNT OF THE THREE KINGS.

Persia is a great country, which was in old times very illustrious and powerful ; but now the Tartars have wasted and destroyed it.   In Persia is the city of Saba, from which the three magi set out, when they went to worship Jesus Christ ; and in this city they are buried, in three very large and beautiful monuments, side by side. And above them there is a square building carefully kept.   The bodies are still entire, with the hair and beard remaining.   One of these was called Jasper, the second Melchoir, and the third Balthasar.   Messer Marco Polo asked a great many questions of the people of that city as to those three magi ; but never one could he find that knew aught of the matter, except that these were three kings, who were buried there in days of old.   However, at a place three days' journey distant, he heard of what I am going to tell you.   He found a village there which goes by the name of Cala Ataperistan, which is as much as to say, " The Castle of the Fire-worshippers " ; and the name is rightly applied, for the people there do worship fire, and I will tell you why. They relate that, in old times, three kings of that country went away to worship a prophet that was born; and they carried with them three manner of offerings, — gold and frankincense and myrrh, — in order to ascertain whether that prophet were God or an earthly king or a physician. " For," said they, " if he take the gold, then he is an earthly king ; if he take the incense, he is God ; if he take the myrrh, he is a physician." So it came to pass, when they had come to the place where the Child was born, the youngest of the three kings went in first, and found the Child apparently just of his own age; so he went forth again, marvelling greatly. The middle one entered next, and, like the first, he found the Child seemingly of his own age ; so he also went forth again, and marvelled greatly. Lastly, the eldest went in, and as it had befallen the other two, so it befel him ; and he went forth very pensive.

And when the three had rejoined one another, each told what he had seen ; and then they all marvelled the more. So they all agreed to go in all three together ; and on doing so, they beheld the Child with the appearance of its actual age, — to wit, some thirteen days. Then they adored, and presented their gold and incense and myrrh ; and the Child took all the three offerings, and then gave them a small closed box : whereupon the kings departed to return into their own land.

And when they had ridden many days they said they would see what the Child had given them. So they opened the little box ; and inside it they found a stone. On seeing this they began to wonder what this might be that the Child had given them, and what was the import thereof.   Now the signification was this: when they presented their offerings, the Child accepted all three ; and when they saw that, they had said within themselves that he was the True God, and the True King, and the True Physician.   And what the gift of the stone implied was that this Faith which had begun in them should abide firm as a rock.   For he well knew what was in their thoughts.   Howbeit they had no understanding at all of this signification of the gift of the stone, so they cast it into a well.   Then straightway a fire from heaven descended into that well wherein the stone had been cast.   And when the Three Kings beheld this marvel they were sore amazed, and it greatly repented them that they had cast away the stone ; for well they then perceived that it had a great and holy meaning.   So they took of that fire, and carried it into their own country, and placed it in a rich and beautiful church.   And there the people keep it continually burning, and worship it as a god ; and all the sacrifices they offer are kindled with that fire.   And if ever the fire becomes extinct they go to other cities round about, where the same faith is held, and obtain of that fire from them, and carry it to the church.   And this is the reason why the people of this country worship fire. They will often go ten days' journey to get of that fire.

The children were highly edified by finding this echo of the story of the wise men of the Bible, brought from the East, and asked Uncle Fritz if they might believe it, ever so little.   He told them that, till Mahomet's time, all these countries were more or less under the rule of Christian faith, though it were but limp faith, and stupid. It was quite possible that Messer Marco Polo might have found some legends there which he repeated here.

"But I think," said Uncle Fritz, "that if you are going to dip, before reading, you had better begin on Cublay Khan himself."

"Cublay Khan!" cried Fergus. "Are we to hear about Cublay Khan?"

"Why, what do you know about Cublay Khan?" cried Mary Long.

"Do you not remember, — 'Mustapha, Rubadub, Cublay Khan'?"

"I do not think you say it right. But hush! Horace is going to begin."

So Horace began : —

HOW NAYAN WAS BEATEN.

Now am I come to that part of our book in which I shall tell you of the great and wonderful magnificence of the Great Kaan now reigning, by name CUBLAY KAAN, — *Kaan* being a title which signifieth "the Great Lord of Lords," or Emperor. And of a surety he hath good right to such a title; for all men know for a certain truth that he is the most potent man, as regards forces and lands and treasure, that existeth in the world, or ever hath existed, from the time of our First Father, Adam, until this day.

"That was probably true," interrupted Col. Ingham.

All this I will make clear to you for truth, in this book of ours, so that every one shall be fain to acknowledge that he is the greatest lord that is now in the world, or ever hath been.   And now, ye shall hear how and wherefore.

.   .   .   .   .   .

There was a great Tartar chief, whose name was Nayan, a young man of thirty, lord over many lands and many provinces ; and he was uncle to the Emperor Cublay Kaan, of whom we are speaking. And when he found himself in authority, this Nayan waxed proud in the insolence of his youth and his great power ; for indeed he could bring into the field three hundred thousand horsemen, though all the time he was liegeman to his nephew, the Great Kaan Cublay, as was right and reason. Seeing, then, what great power he had, he took it into his head that he would be the Great Kaan's vassal no longer : nay, more, he would fain wrest his empire from him, if he could. So this Nayan sent envoys to another Tartar prince, called Caidu, also a great and potent lord, who was a kinsman of his, and who was a nephew of the Great Kaan, and his lawful liegeman also, though he was in rebellion, and at bitter enmity with his sovereign lord and uncle. Now, the message that Nayan sent was this : that he himself was making ready to march against the Great Kaan with all his forces, which were great, and he begged Caidu to do likewise from his side, so that by attacking Cublay on two sides at once with such great forces they would be able to wrest his dominion from him. And when Caidu heard the message of Nayan, he was right glad thereat, and thought the time was come at last to gain his object ; so he sent back answer that he would do as requested, and got ready his host, which mustered a good hundred thousand horsemen.

Now, let us go back to the Great Kaan, who had news of all this plot.

When the Great Kaan heard what was afoot, he made his preparations in right good heart, like one who feared not the issue of an attempt so contrary to justice. Confident in his own conduct and prowess, he was in no degree disturbed, but vowed that he would never wear crown again if he brought not those two traitorous and disloyal Tartar chiefs to an ill end. So swiftly and secretly were his preparations made that no one knew of them but his privy council, and all were completed within ten or twelve days. In that time he had assembled good three hundred and sixty thousand horsemen and one hundred thousand footmen, — but a small force, indeed, for him, and consisting only of those that were in the vicinity; for the rest of his vast and innumerable forces were too far off to answer so hasty a summons, being engaged under orders from him on distant expeditions to conquer divers countries and provinces. If he had waited to summon all his troops, the multitude assembled would have been beyond all belief; a multitude such as never was heard of, or told of, past all counting! In fact, those three hundred and sixty thousand horsemen that he got together consisted merely of the falconers and whippers-in that were about the court! And when he got ready this handful, as it were, of his troops, he ordered his astrologers to declare whether he should gain the battle, and get the better of his enemies. After they had made their observations they told him to go on boldly, for he would conquer and gain a glorious victory; whereat he greatly rejoiced. So he marched with his army; and after advancing for twenty days they arrived at a great plain, where Nayan lay with all his host, amounting to some four hundred thousand horse.   Now, the Great Kaan's forces arrived so fast and so suddenly that the others knew nothing of the matter ; for the Kaan had caused such strict watch to be made in every direction for scouts that every one that appeared was instantly captured.   Thus Nayan had no warning of his coming, and was completely taken by surprise, insomuch that, when the Great Kaan's army came up, he was asleep ; so thus you see why it was that the emperor equipped his force with such speed and secrecy.   Of the battle which the Great Kaan fought with Nayan, what shall I say about it?

When day had well broken, there was the Kaan, with all his host, upon a hill overlooking the plain where Nayan lay in his tent, in all security, without the slightest thought of any one coming thither to do him hurt. In fact, this confidence of his was such that he kept no videttes, whether in front or in rear ; for he knew nothing of the coming of the Great Kaan, owing to all the approaches having been completely occupied, as I told you. Moreover, the place was in a remote wilderness, more than thirty marches from the court, — though the Kaan had made the distance in twenty, so eager was he to come to battle with Nayan.   And what shall I tell you next? The Kaan was there on the hill, mounted on a great wooden bartizan, which was borne by four well-trained elephants ; and over him was hoisted his standard, so high aloft that it could be seen from all sides.   His troops were ordered in battles of thirty thousand men apiece, and a great part of the horsemen had each a foot-soldier, armed with a lance, set on the crupper behind him (for it was thus that the footmen were disposed of) ; and the whole plain seemed to be covered with his forces. So it was thus that the Great Kaan's army was arrayed for battle. When Nayan and his people saw what had happened, they were sorely confounded, and rushed in haste to arms. Nevertheless, they made them ready in good style, and formed their troops in an orderly manner. And when all were in battle array on both sides, as I have told you, and nothing remained but to fall to blows, then might you have heard a sound arise of many instruments of various music, and of the voices of the whole of the two hosts loudly singing.

For this is a custom of the Tartars, that before they join battle they all unite in singing and playing on a certain two-stringed instrument of theirs, a thing right pleasant to hear, and so they continue in their array of battle, singing and playing in this pleasing manner, until the great Naccara of the prince is heard to sound. As soon as that begins to sound the fight also begins on both sides ; and in no case before the prince's Naccara sounds dare any commence fighting.

So, then, as they were thus singing and playing, though ordered and ready for battle, the great Naccara of the Great Kaan began to sound, and that of Nayan also began to sound, and thenceforward the din of battle began to be heard loudly from this side and from that, and they rushed to work so doughtily with their bows and their maces, with their lances and swords, and with the arblests of the footmen, that it was a wondrous sight to see. Now might you behold such flights of arrows from this side and from that, that the whole heaven was canopied with them, and they fell like rain. Now might you see on this side and on that full many a cavalier and man-at-arms fall slain, insomuch that the whole field seemed covered with them. From this side and from that such cries arose from the crowds of the wounded and dying that had God thundered you would not have heard Him. For fierce and furious was the battle, and quarter there was none given; but why should I make a long story of it? You must know that it was the most parlous and fierce and fearful battle that has ever been fought in our day. Nor have there ever been such forces in the field in actual fight, especially of horsemen, as were then engaged; for, taking both sides, there were not fewer than seven hundred and sixty thousand horsemen, — a mighty force! — and that without reckoning the footmen, who were also very numerous. The battle endured with various fortune on this side and on that from morning till noon; but at last, by God's pleasure and the right that was on his side, the Great Kaan had the victory, and Nayan lost the battle and was utterly routed. For the army of the Great Kaan performed such feats of arms that Nayan and his host could stand against them no longer, so they turned and fled; but this availed nothing for Nayan, for he and all the barons with him were taken prisoners and had to surrender to the Kaan with all their arms.

Now you must know that Nayan was a baptized Christian, and bore the Cross on his banner, but this nought availed him, seeing how grievously he had done amiss in rebelling against his lord. For he was the Great Kaan's liegeman, and was bound to hold his lands of him like all his ancestors before him.

The scale of this fighting satisfied even Bedford, who is notorious for his passion for a good fight. Uncle Fritz told them that if they would look further they would see that military rockets were used in this battle, or something which resembled rockets more than cannon.

While they were talking, Horace and Fred looked further, and when there was a lull read —

And after the Great Kaan had conquered Nayan, as you have heard, it came to pass that the different kinds of people who were present, Saracens and idolaters and Jews, and many others that believed not in God, did gibe those that were Christians because of the Cross that Nayan had borne on his standard, and that so grievously that there was no bearing it. Thus they would say to the Christians: "See now what precious help this God's Cross of yours hath rendered Nayan, who was a Christian and a worshipper thereof." And such a din arose about the matter that it reached the Great Kaan's own ears. When it did so, he sharply rebuked those who cast these gibes at the Christians, and he also bade the Christians be of good heart, "for if the Cross had rendered no help to Nayan, in that It had done right well, nor could that which was good, as It was, have done otherwise; for Nayan was a disloyal and traitorous rebel against his lord, and well deserved that which had befallen him. Wherefore the Cross of your God did well in that It gave him no help against the right." And this he said so loud that everybody heard him. The Christians then replied to the Great Kaan: "Great King, you say the truth indeed, for our Cross can render no one help in wrong-doing, and therefore it was that It aided not Nayan, who was guilty of crime and disloyalty, for It would take no part in his evil deeds." And so thenceforward no more was heard of the floutings of the unbelievers against the Christians;

for they heard very well what the sovereign said to the latter about the Cross on Nayan's banner, and Its giving him no help.

POST HOUSES.

Now you must know that from this city of Cambaluc proceed many roads and highways leading to a variety of provinces, one to one province, another to another, and each road receives the name of the province to which it leads; and it is a very sensible plan, and the messengers of the emperor in travelling from Cambaluc, be the road whichsoever they will, find at every twenty-five miles of the journey a station which they call "Yamb," or, as we should say, the "Horse-Post-House." And at each of those stations used by the messengers there is a large and handsome building for them to put up at, in which they find all the rooms furnished with fine beds and all other necessary articles in rich silk, and where they are provided with everything they can want. If even a king were to arrive at one of these he would find himself well lodged.

At some of these stations, moreover, there shall be posted some four hundred horses standing ready for the use of the messengers; at others there shall be two hundred, according to the requirements, and to what the emperor has established in each case. At every twenty-five miles, as I said, or anyhow at every thirty miles, you find one of these stations on all the principal highways leading to the different provincial governments, and the same is the case throughout all the chief provinces subject to the Great Kaan; even when the messengers have to pass through a roadless tract where neither house nor hostel exists, still there the station-houses have been established just the same, excepting that the intervals are somewhat greater, and the day's journey is fixed at thirty-five to forty-five miles, instead of twenty-five to thirty. But they are provided with horses and all the other necessaries just like those we have described, so that the emperor's messengers, come they from what region they may, find everything ready for them.

And in sooth this is a thing done on the greatest scale of magnificence that ever was seen. Never had emperor, king, or lord such wealth as this manifests! For it is a fact that on all these posts taken together there are more than three hundred thousand horses kept up specially for the use of the messengers. And the great buildings that I have mentioned are more than ten thousand in number, all richly furnished as I told you. The thing is on a scale so wonderful and costly that it is hard to bring one's self to describe it.

But now I will tell you another thing that I had forgotten, but which ought to be told whilst I am on this subject. You must know that by the Great Kaan's orders there has been established between those post-houses, at every interval of three miles, a little fort, with some forty houses round about it, in which dwell the people who act as the emperor's foot-runners. Every one of those runners wears a great wide belt, set all over with bells, so that as they run the three miles from post to post their bells are heard jingling a long way off. And thus on reaching the post the runner finds another man similarly equipt, and all ready to take his place, who instantly takes over whatsoever he has in charge, and with it receives a slip of paper from the clerk, who is always at hand for the purpose ; and so the new man sets off and runs his three miles. At the next station he finds his relief ready in like manner; and so the post proceeds, with a change at every three miles. And in this way the emperor, who has an immense number of these runners, receives despatches with news from places ten days' journey off in one day and night; or, if need be, news from a hundred days off in ten days and nights, and that is no small matter! In fact, in the fruit season, many a time fruit shall be gathered one morning in Cambaluc, and the evening of the next day it shall reach the Great Kaan at Chandu, a distance of ten days' journey.

The clerk at each of the posts notes the time of each courier's arrival and departure; and there are often other officers, whose business it is to make monthly visitations of all the posts, and to punish those runners who have been slack in their work. The emperor exempts these men from all tribute, and pays them beside.

Moreover, there are also at those stations other men, equipt similarly with girdles hung with bells, who are employed for expresses when there is a call for great haste in sending despatches to any governor of a province, or to give news when any baron has revolted, or in other such emergencies; and these men travel a good two hundred or two hundred and fifty miles in the day, and as much in the night. I 'll tell you how it stands. They take a horse from those at the station, which are standing ready saddled, all fresh and in wind, and mount and go at full speed, as hard as they can ride, in fact. And when those at the next post hear the bells, they get ready another horse and a man equipt in the same way, and he takes over the letter or whatever it be, and is off full speed to the third station, where again a fresh horse is found all ready, and so the despatch speeds along from post to post, always at full gallop, with regular change of horses. And the speed at which they go is marvellous. By night, however, they cannot go so fast as by day, because they have to be accompanied by footmen with torches, who could not keep up with them at full speed.

Those men are highly prized; and they could never do it did they not bind hard the stomach, chest, and head with strong bands. And each of them carries with him a gerfalcon tablet, in sign that he is bound on an urgent express; so that if perchance his horse break down, or he meet with other mishap, whomsoever he may fall in with on the road, he is empowered to make him dismount and give up his horse. Nobody dares refuse in such a case; so that the courier hath always a good fresh nag to carry him.

Now all these numbers of post-horses cost the emperor nothing at all; and I will tell you the how and the why. Every city, or village, or hamlet that stands near one of these post-stations has a fixed demand made on it for as many horses as it can supply, and these it must furnish to the post. And in this way are provided all the posts of the cities, as well as the towns and villages round about them; only in uninhabited tracts the horses are furnished at the expense of the emperor himself.

How far all this was true, the children were then eager to know. But Uncle Fritz told them that, as to that, they must look at Col. Yule's very interesting notes. And while they clustered around him and Laura, who had the second volume, all looking at the maps and pictures, Ellen Mahony came in and said that tea was on the table.

Col. Yule's edition of Marco Polo was published by Murray, in London, in 1875. As has been said above, it should be in every public library which means to provide for intelligent readers.

II.

SIR JOHN MANDEVILLE AND THE CRUSADES.

COL. INGHAM was well pleased, when his boys and girls clustered round him the next Saturday, to find how many copies of " Marco Polo " they had found in different libraries, and how much of it they had read, in one reading-circle and another. They found in it manifold illustrations of the " Arabian Nights," which, in its best form, — Lane's translation, — is a favorite book in our little circle.

They began to understand what Uncle Fritz had meant, when he said that Marco Polo seemed accurate when he described what he saw, and that his exaggerations, or what people called his lies, came in when he was repeating stories which other people had told.

Esther asked him who Mandeville was, of whom he had said the same thing.

"Mandeville was an Englishman, — Sir John Mandeville, — who went to Constantinople, Egypt, Palestine, Armenia, and other countries of Western Asia a little less than two hundred years before Columbus sailed for America. The exact limits of his absence are said to be the years 1322 and 1356. It was as dark a time as there was in the Dark Ages. He was in the military service of one of the Eastern princes, and had a chance to see travellers from all lands, and to hear their stories. People told stories in the East then, just as they do now, and as I sometimes hope they will, one day, do hear again.

"For my part, when I am sitting in the rather dingy reading-room of a third-rate inn, in a fourth-rate town, waiting for my train, which is not to come till eleven at night, I should be very glad if a good story-teller would come in and sit down on a mat, and tell me either the story of Sindbad the Sailor or of Hiawatha and the Arrow-maker, or of his adventures in the Rebellion. When he passed his hat round, I should put in my five-cent piece much more willingly than I give it for the Torra-worra Tell-tale, which only gives me in brief the same news which I read in the Big Bow-wow the same morning.

"Well, Sir John Mandeville heard these stories told by story-tellers, just as you may hear them to-day in Cairo or in Damascus. Whether he wrote them down at once, I do not know ; but at some time or other he wrote them down, and now the whole is mixed up together, — what he saw himself with what travellers told him and with what story-tellers told him.

"So you may find bits of 'Arabian Nights' in Sir John Mandeville.

"There is so much of this that there came to be a time when people thought he had rather lie than to tell the truth.

"Indeed," said Uncle Fritz, "I can remember that at one time his name was spelled Man-Devil, as if he were quite outside of human nature ; but I believe there is now no doubt that this was his real name."

Esther said she remembered, in Catlin's "Indians," that he told of some chiefs who had been taken all

hrough the great cities, that they might understand the
ower of the whites, and, when they came back, were
wholly disgraced and degraded, because they told such
arge stories that nobody could believe they were true.

Uncle Fritz was well pleased with Esther's good
memory, and said it was just so with Sir John Mandeville.

Bob Edmeston brought the book, which is in a very
handy form.[1]   In Bohn's Library, it is included with
many other early journeys to Palestine.   The young
people knew the Antiquarian Library already.   And it
may be said to other young people, who have a little
money to spend for books, that in Bohn's various "Libraries" they get as much for their money — if they find
the book they want in the catalogue — as they can find
anywhere.

But the little book did not look as fascinating as the
elegant, large pages crowded with illustrations of Marco
Polo.

Uncle Fritz told Bob that when he was a man, and
had travelled all through Asia, he might edit an edition
of Sir John Mandeville, as elegant as Col. Yule's of
Marco Polo.

"You will have to be satisfied now," said he, "by looking for my pencil-marks.   Or turn to the end.   See what
I have noticed on the last page."

So they turned to the last page, and found that Uncle
Fritz had made an index of the things he liked in the
book.   This is always a good thing to do, — if the book
is your own, of course.   They read aloud the headings,
and came to " The Lady changed into a Dragon."

---

[1] In Bohn's Antiquarian Library.   It may be bought anywhere for
$1.25.

"That is the story in Morris's 'Earthly Paradise,'" said Uncle Fritz.   "Look a little further."   Esther read on, and he told her to turn back to the book, and read to them, when she found —

HOW ROSES FIRST CAME INTO THE WORLD.

From Hebron we proceed to Bethlehem in half a day, for it is but five miles ; and it is a very fair way, by pleasant plains and woods.   Bethlehem is a little city, long and narrow and well-walled, and on each side enclosed with good ditches.   It was formerly called Ephrata, as Holy Writ says, " Lo, we heard of it at Ephrata."   And towards the east end of the city is a very fair and handsome church, with many towers, pinnacles, and corners, strongly and curiously made, and within are forty-four great and fair pillars of marble ; and between the city and the church is the Field *Floridus*, — that is to say, the *field flourish-ed*.   For a fair maiden was blamed with wrong, and slandered, for which cause she was condemned to be burned in that place ; and as the fire began to burn about her, she made her prayers to our Lord that, as truly as she was not guilty, he would by his merciful grace help her, and make it known to all men.   And when she had thus said she entered into the fire, and immediately the fire was extinguished, and the fagots that were burning became red rose-bushes, and those that were not kindled became white rose-bushes, full of roses ; and these were the first rose-trees and roses, both white and red, that ever any man saw.   And thus was this maiden saved by the grace of God ; and therefore is that field called the field that God flourished, for it was full of roses.

Then Esther turned to another place which had struck
er eye, and read —

OF THE ROCKS OF ADAMANT.

In that island are ships without nails of iron or brass,
n account of the rocks of adamant (loadstones). For
hey are all abundant thereabout in that sea, that it is
narvellous to speak of ; and if a ship passed there that
ad either iron bands or iron nails, it would perish ; for
he adamant, by its nature, draws iron to it, and so it
vould draw it to the ship, because of the iron, that it
hould never depart from it.

"That," cried Bob Edmerton, "was what happened to
iindbad."
"Oh, no ; not to Sindbad !" said all the others.
Uncle Fritz confessed that he thought it was to
iindbad. This was a great triumph for the little
roop. "To think," said Tom Rising, "that we should
owl out Uncle Fritz on the 'Arabian Nights'! I
hought he knew the 'Arabian Nights' by heart." So
ie " Arabian Nights " (in Lane's version) was sent for,
nd Tom Rising read aloud from the story of " The
'hird Royal Mendicant."
"A royal mendicant," said Uncle Fritz, "is what was
alled a 'calendar,' when I was a boy."

'HE STORY OF THE THIRD ROYAL MENDICANT.

So he went aloft, and when he had come down he said
ɔ the captain, " I saw, on my right hand, fish floating
pon the surface of the water, and, looking towards the

midst of the sea, I perceived something looming in the distance, — sometimes black and sometimes white."

When the captain heard this report of the watch, he threw his turban on the deck, and plucked his beard, and said to those who were with him, " Receive warning of our destruction, which will befall all of us : not one will escape."　So saying, he began to weep ; and all of us, in like manner, bewailed our lot.　I desired him to inform us of that which the watch had seen.　The watch said, " To-morrow we shall arrive at a mountain of black stone, called loadstone : the current is now bearing us violently toward it, and the ship will fall in pieces ; for God hath given to the loadstone a secret property, by virtue of which everything of iron is attracted toward it. On that mountain is such a quantity of iron as no one knoweth but God, whose name be exalted ! for from times of old great numbers of ships have been destroyed by the influence of that mountain."

On the following morning we drew near to the mountain ; the current carried us toward it with violence, and when the ships were almost close to it, they fell asunder, and all the nails, and everything else that was of iron, flew from them toward the loadstone.　It was near the close of the day when the ship fell in pieces. Some of us were drowned, and some escaped ; but the greater number were drowned, and of those who saved their lives, none knew what became of the others, so stupefied were they by the waves and the boisterous wind.

After they had looked up the other passages, which are somewhat like this, in the Fifth Voyage of Sindbad the Sailor, they came back to Sir John Mandeville.　They found the story of the rich man Gathenabes, and his false Paradise, the same that is told of the King of the Assassins. This was in the mysterious land of Prester John. They found the happy story of the " Island of Bragman," which some men call the Land of Faith. Then they found the description of the Terrestrial Paradise, which poor Mandeville could not reach from the East Indies, better than poor Columbus could from the West.[1] They found about the country where the gentleman has such long nails that he may take nothing, nor handle anything.

Then they found — and this was a great relief to Sybil — that after all these travels, Sir John returned to Rome, and "was absolved of all that lay in my conscience of many grievous points." For notwithstanding Uncle Fritz's excuses for Sir John, Sybil was sadly afraid that he needed absolution for the master sin of lying; and if he ever repented of it, Sybil was glad.

Before she laid down the book she read one extract more.

OF THE GREAT CHAN OF CATHAY.

In this city (Caydon) is the seat of the Great chan,[2] in a very great palace, the fairest of the world, the walls of which are in circuit more than two miles; and within the walls it is all full of other palaces. And in the garden of the great palace there is a great hill, upon which is another palace, the fairest and richest that any man may devise. And all about the palace

---

[1] See "Stories of the Sea."

[2] We follow the spelling of the old English versions, even when they vary from each other.

and the hill are many trees bearing divers fruits. And
all about that hill are great and deep ditches, and
beside them are great fish-ponds on both sides; and
there is a very fair bridge to pass over the ditches.
And in these fish-ponds are an extraordinary number of
wild geese and ganders, and wild ducks and swans and
herons. And all about these ditches and fish-ponds is
the great garden, full of wild beasts, so that when the
Great chan will have any sport, to take any of the wild
beasts or the fowls, he will cause them to be driven,
and take them at the windows, without going out of his
chamber. Within the palace, in the hall, there are
twenty-four pillars of fine gold; and all the walls are
covered within with red skins of animals called pan-
thers, fair beasts and well-smelling; so that for the
sweet odor of the skins, no evil air may enter into
the palace.

The skins are as red as blood, and shine so bright
against the sun that a man may scarcely look at them.
And many people worship the beasts when they meet
them first in a morning, for their great virtue and for
the good smell that they have; and the skins they value
more than if they were plates of fine gold.

And in the middle of the palace is the mountour[1] of
the Great chan, all wrought of gold and of precious
stones and of great pearls; and at the four corners are
four serpents of gold; and all about there are made
large nets of silk and gold, and great pearls hanging all
about it. And under the mountour are conduits of
beverage that they drink in the emperor's court. And
beside the conduits are many vessels of gold, with which

---

[1] Mountour,—an old English rendering of the French *mountagnette*,
meaning a raised platform.

hey that are of the household drink at the conduit. The hall of the palace is full nobly arrayed, and full marvellously attired on all parts in all things that men apparel any hall with.

And first, at the head of the hall, is the emperor's throne, very high, where he sits at meat. It is of fine precious stones, bordered all about with purified gold and precious stones and great pearls. And the steps up to the table are of precious stones, mixed with gold. And at the left side of the emperor's seat is the seat of his first wife, one step lower than the emperor; and it is of jasper bordered with gold, and the seat of his second wife is lower than his first wife, and is also of jasper bordered with gold, as that other is. And the seat of the third wife is still lower by a step than the second wife's, for he has always three wives with him, wherever he is. And after his wives, on the same side, sit the ladies of his lineage, still lower, according to their ranks. And all those that are married have a counterfeit, made like a man's foot, upon their heads, a cubit long, all wrought with great, fine, and orient pearls, and above made with peacock's feathers, and of other shining feathers; and that stands upon their heads like a crest, in token that they are under man's foot, and under subjection of man. But the other ladies, that are unmarried, have none such. And after, at the right side of the emperor, first sits his eldest son, who shall reign after him, one step lower than the emperor, in such manner of seats as do the empresses; and after him, other great lords of his lineage, each of them a step lower than the other, according to their rank. The emperor has his table alone by himself, and each of his wives has also her table by herself. And his eldest son, and the other lords also, and the ladies, and all that sit with the emperor, have very rich tables, alone by themselves. And under the emperor's table sit four clerks, who write all that the emperor says, be it good or evil; for all that he says must be held good; for he may not change his word nor revoke it.

At great feasts men bring, before the emperor's table, great tables of gold, and thereon are peacocks of gold, and many other kinds of different fowls, all of gold, and richly wrought and enamelled; and they make them dance and sing, clapping their wings together, and making great noise; and whether it be by craft or by necromancy I know not, but it is a goodly sight to behold. But I have the less marvel because they are the most skilful men in the world in all sciences and in all crafts; for in subtilty, malice, and forethought they surpass all men under heaven; and, therefore, they say themselves that they see with two eyes, and Christians see with but one, because they are more subtle than they. . . .

Nevertheless the truth is this, — that Tartars, and they that dwell in Greater Asia, came of Cham, but the emperor of Cathay was called not Cham, but Chan; and I shall tell you how. It is but little more than eight score years since all Tartary was in subjection and servage to other nations about; for they were but herdsmen, and did nothing but keep beasts, and lead them to pastures. But among them they had seven principal nations that were sovereigns of them all, of which the first nation or lineage was called Tartar; and that is the most noble and the most praised. The second lineage is called Tanghot; the third, Eurache; the fourth, Valair; the fifth, Semoche; the sixth, Megly; the seventh, Coboghe. Now it befell that of the first

lineage succeeded an old worthy man, and was not rich,
who was called Changuys. This man lay one night in
bed, and he saw in a vision that there came before him
a knight, armed all in white, and he sat upon a white
horse, and said to him, "Chan, sleepest thou? The
immortal God hath sent me to thee; and it is his will
that thou go to the seven lineages, and say to them that
thou shalt be their emperor; for thou shalt conquer the
lands and the countries that are about; and they that
march upon you shall be under your subjection, as you
have been under theirs; for that is God's immortal will."

Changuys arose, and went to the seven lineages and
told them what the white knight had said. And they
scorned him, and said that he was a fool; and so he
departed from them, all ashamed. And the night following, this white knight came to the seven lineages
and commanded them, on behalf of the immortal God,
that they should make this Changuys their emperor,
and they should be out of subjection, and they should
hold all other regions about them in servage, as they
had been to them before. And next day they chose
him to be their emperor, and set him upon a black
chest, and after that lifted him up with great solemnity,
and set him in a chair of gold, and did him all manner
of reverence; and they called him Chan, as the white
knight called him. And when he was thus chosen,
he would make trial if he must trust in them or not,
and whether they would be obedient to him; and then
he made many statutes and ordinances, that they call
Ysya Chan.

The first statute was, that they should believe in and
obey immortal God, who is almighty, and who would
cast them out of servage; and they should at all

times call to him for help in time of need. The second statute was that all manner of men that might bear arms should be numbered, and to every ten should be a master, and to every hundred a master, and to every thousand a master, and to every ten thousand a master. After, he commanded the principals of the seven lineages to leave and forsake all they had in goods and heritage, and from thenceforth to be satisfied with what he would give them of his grace. And they did so immediately. After this .he commanded the principals of the seven lineages, that each should bring his eldest son before him, and with their own hands smite off their heads without delay. And immediately his command was performed.

And when the Chan saw that they made no obstacle to perform his commandment, then he thought that he might well trust in them ; and he commanded them presently to make them ready, and to follow his banner. And after this, the Chan put in subjection all the lands about him. Afterwards it befel on a day, that the Chan rode with a few companies to behold the strength of the country that he had won, and a great multitude of his enemies met with him ; and to give good example of bravery to his people, he was the first that fought, and rushed into the midst of his enemies, and there was thrown from his horse, and his horse slain. And when his people saw him on the earth, they were all discouraged, and thought he had been dead, and fled every one ; and their enemies pursued them, but they knew not that the emperor was there. And when they were returned from the pursuit, they sought the woods, if any of them had been hid in them ; and many they found and slew.

So it happened that as they went searching toward
e place where the emperor was, they saw an owl sitting
ı a tree above him; and then they said amongst them
at there was no man there, because they saw the bird
ere, and so they went their way; and thus the emper-
escaped death. And then he went secretly by night,
l he came to his people, who were very glad of his
ming, and gave great thanks to immortal God, and to
at bird by which their lord was saved; and, therefore,
ove all fowls of the world, they worship the owl; and
ıen they have any of its feathers, they keep them full
eciously instead of relics, and bear them upon their
ads with great reverence; and they hold themselves
essed, and safe from all perils, while they have these
athers on them, and therefore they bear them upon
eir heads. After all this the Chan assembled his
ople, and went against those who had assailed him
fore, and destroyed them, and put them in subjec-
ın and servage.

At this moment in the reading supper was announced;
.t Clem begged them to wait a minute, while he read
ıy Sir John Mandeville did not tell about Paradise.
Blanche said that there was no need of explaining
at; but Clem persevered.

"Of Paradise I cannot speak properly, for I was not
ere."

"That," said Horace, is like Cousin: 'I say nothing
Buddhism, because I know nothing about it.'"

"If only everybody would be as thoughtful!" said
ncle Fritz. And Clem continued, though he was
"eady losing his audience:—

"It is far beyond, and I repent not going there, but

I was not worthy." "I should think not," interrupted Blanche. "But as I have heard say of wise men beyond, I shall tell you with good will. Terrestrial Paradise, as wise men say, is the highest place of the earth, and it is so high that it nearly touches the circle of the moon there, as the moon makes her turn. For it is so high that the flood of Noah might not come to it that would have covered all the earth of the world all about, and above and beneath, except Paradise. And this Paradise is inclosed all about with a wall, and men know not whereof it is; for the wall is covered all over with moss, as it seems, and it seems not that the wall is natural stone. And that wall stretches from the south to the north; and it has but one entry, which is closed with burning fire, so that no man that is mortal dare enter."

"So they were well rid of Mandeville," said Blanche, laughing; and she and Clem went in to their supper.

III.

BERTRANDON IN PALESTINE.

WHEN the children met him the next week, Uncle Fritz said that as they had gone so far east in their two afternoons, they would do well to look over some of the accounts of the Crusaders' expeditions.

The boys were well pleased at this suggestion. Some of them knew Froissart, and all of them had read Ivanhoe," and "The Talisman," and "Count Robert of Paris."

So Uncle Fritz sent again for the "Travels in Palestine," in the same volume of Bohn's Antiquarian Library, and Bedford first, and Esther afterward, read the exacts he had marked for them from

BERTRANDON DE LA BROCQUIÈRE.

To animate and inflame the hearts of such noble men as may be desirous of seeing the world, and by the order and command of the most high, most powerful, and my most redoubted lord, Philip, by the grace of God Duke of Burgundy, Lorraine, Brabant, and Limbourg, Count of Flanders, Artois, and Burgundy, Palatine of Hainault, Holland, Zealand, and Namur, Marquis of the Holy Empire, lord of Friesland, Salines, and Mechlin, I, Bertrandon de la Brocquière, a native of the duchy of Guienne, lord of Vieux-Chateau, counsellor and first esquire-carver to my aforesaid most redoubted lord, after bringing to my recollection every event, in addition to what I had made an abridgment of in a small book by way of memorandums, have fairly written out this account of my short travels, in order that if any king or Christian prince should wish to make the conquest of Jerusalem, and lead thither an army overland, or if any gentleman should be desirous of travelling thither, they may be made acquainted with all the towns, cities, regions, countries, rivers, mountains, and passes, in the different districts, as well as the lords to whom they belong, from the duchy of Burgundy to Jerusalem.

The route hence to the holy city of Rome is too well known for me to stop and describe it. I shall pass lightly over this article, and not say much until I come to Syria. . . . Gaza, situated in a fine country near the sea, and at the entrance of the desert, is a strong town, although uninclosed. It is pretended that it formerly belonged to the famous Samson. His palace is still shown, and also the columns of that which he pulled down; but I dare not affirm that these are the same. Pilgrims are harshly treated there; and we also should have suffered had it not been for the governor, a man about sixty years of age, and a Circassian, who heard our complaints and did us justice.

Thrice were we obliged to appear before him; once, on account of the swords we wore, and the two other times for quarrels which the Saracen moucres sought to have with us. Many of us wished to purchase asses; for the camel has a very rough movement, which is extremely fatiguing to those unaccustomed to it. An ass is sold at Gaza for two ducats; but the moucres not only wanted to prevent our buying any, but to force us to hire asses from them, at the price of five ducats, to St. Catherine's. This conduct was represented to the governor. For myself, who had hitherto ridden on a camel, and had no intention of changing, I desired they would tell me how I could ride a camel and an ass at the same time. The governor decided in our favor, and ordered that we should not be forced to hire any asses from the moucres against our inclinations.

We here laid in fresh provisions necessary for the continuance of our journey; but, on the eve of our departure, four of my companions fell sick, and returned to Jerusalem. I set off with the five others, and we came to a village situated at the entrance of the desert, and the only one to be met with between Gaza and St. Catherine's. We thus travelled two days in the desert, absolutely without seeing anything deserving to be related. Only one morning I saw, before sunrise, an animal running on four legs, about three feet long, but scarcely a palm in height. The Arabians fled at the sight of it, and the animal hastened to hide itself in a bush hard by. Sir Andrew and Pierre de Vandrei dismounted, and pursued it sword in hand, when it began to cry like a cat on the approach of a dog. Pierre de Vaudrei struck it on the back with the point of his sword, but did it no harm, from its being covered with scales like a sturgeon. It sprang at Sir Andrew, who, with a blow from his sword, cut the neck partly through, and flung it on its back with its feet in the air, and killed it. The head resembled that of a large hare; the feet were like the hands of a young child, with a pretty long tail, like that of the large green lizard. Our Arabs and interpreter told us it was very dangerous.

At the end of the second day's journey I was seized

with such a burning fever that it was impossible for me to proceed. My four companions, distressed at this accident, made me mount an ass, and recommended me to one of our Arabs, whom they charged to reconduct me, if possible, to Gaza. This man took a great deal of care of me, which is unusual in respect to Christians. He faithfully kept me company, and led me in the evening to pass the night in one of their camps, which might consist of fourscore and some tents, pitched in the form of a street. These tents consist of two poles stuck in the ground by the bigger end, at a certain distance from each other, and on them is placed another pole cross-way, and over this last is laid a thick coverlid of woollen, or coarse hair. On my arrival, four or five Arabs, who were acquainted with my companion, came to meet us. They dismounted me from my ass, and laid me on a mattrass which I had with me, and then, treating me according to their method, kneaded and pinched me so much with their hands, that from fatigue and lassitude I slept, and reposed for six hours. During this time no one did me the least harm, nor took anything from me. It would, however, have been very easy for them to do so; and I must have been a tempting prey, for I had with me two hundred ducats, and two camels laden with provision and wine.

I set out on my return to Gaza before day; but when I came thither, I found neither my four companions who had remained behind nor Sir Sanson de Lalaing: the whole five had returned to Jerusalem, carrying with them the interpreter. Fortunately I met with a Sicilian Jew, to whom I could make myself understood; and he sent me an old Samaritan, who, by some medicines which he gave me, appeased the great heat I endured. Two days after, finding myself a little better, I set off in company with a Moor, who conducted me by a river on the seaside. We passed near Ascalon, and thence traversed an agreeable and fertile country to Ramlé, where I regained the road to Jerusalem. On the first day's journey I met on the road the governor of that town, returning from a pilgrimage, with a company of fifty horsemen, and one hundred camels, mounted principally by women and children, who had attended him to his place of devotion. I passed the night with them, and the morrow, on my return to Jerusalem, took up my lodgings with the Cordeliers, at the Church of Mount Sion, where I again met my five comrades. On my arrival I went to bed, that my disorder might be properly treated ; but I was not cured, or in a state to depart, until the 19th of August. During my convalescence I recollected that I had frequently heard it said that it was impossible for a Christian to return overland from Jerusalem to France. I dare not, even now, when I have performed this journey, assert that it is safe. I thought, nevertheless, that nothing was impossible for a man to undertake who has a constitution strong enough to support fatigue, and has money and health. It is not, however, through vain boasting that I say this ; but with the aid of God and his glorious Mother, who never fail to assist those who pray to them heartily, I resolved to attempt the journey. I kept my project secret for some time, without even hinting it to my companions. I was also desirous, before I undertook it, to perform other pilgrimages, especially those to Nazareth and Mount Tabor. I went, in consequence, to make Nanchardin, principal interpreter to the sultan, acquainted with my intentions, who supplied me with a sufficient interpreter for my journey.   I thought of making my first pilgrimage to Mount Tabor, and everything was prepared for it ; but when I was on the point of setting out, the head of the convent where I lodged dissuaded me, and opposed my intentions most strongly. The interpreter, on his side, refused to go, saying that in the present circumstances I should not find any person to attend me ; for that the road lay through the territories of towns which were at war with each other, and that very lately a Venetian and his interpreter had been assassinated there. I confined myself, therefore, to the second pilgrimage, in which Sir Sanson de Lalaing and Humbert wished to accompany me.

The principal monk at Jerusalem was so friendly as to accompany us as far as Jaffa, with a Cordelier friar of the Convent of Beaune. They there quitted us, and we engaged a bark from the Moors, which carried us to the port of Acre. This is a handsome port, deep and well inclosed. The town itself appears to have been large and strong, but at present there do not exist more than three hundred houses, situated at one of its extremities, and at some distance from the sea.

With regard to our pilgrimage, we could not accomplish it. Some Venetian merchants whom we consulted dissuaded us, and from that time we gave it up. They told us, at the same time, that a galley from Narbonne was expected at Baruth ; and my comrades being desirous to take that opportunity of returning to France, we consequently followed the road to that town. . . . It is two days' journey from Baruth to Damascus. The Mohammedans have established a particular custom for Christians all through Syria, in not permitting them to enter the towns on horseback. None that are known to be such dare do it; and in consequence, our moucre made Sir Sanson and myself dismount before we entered any town. Scarcely had we arrived in Damascus than about a dozen Saracens came round to look at us. I wore a broad beaver hat, which is unusual in that country; and one of them gave me a blow with a staff, which knocked it off my head on the ground. I own that my first movement was to lift my fist at him, but the moucre, throwing himself between us, pushed me aside, and very fortunately for me he did so; for in an instant we were surrounded by thirty or forty persons, and if I had given a blow I know not what would have become of us. I mention this circumstance to show that the inhabitants of Damascus are a wicked race, and consequently care should be taken to avoid any quarrels with them. It is the same in other Mohammedan countries. I know by experience that you must not joke with them, nor at the same time seem afraid; nor appear poor, for then they will despise you; nor rich, for they are very avaricious, as all who have disembarked at Jaffa know to their cost. Damascus may contain, as I have heard, one hundred thousand souls. The town is rich, commercial, and after Cairo the most considerable of all in the possession of the sultan. To the north, south, and east is an extensive plain; to the west rises a mountain, at the foot of which the suburbs are built. A river runs through it, which is divided into several canals. The town only is inclosed by a handsome wall, for the suburbs are larger than the town.

I have nowhere seen such extensive gardens, better fruits, nor greater plenty of water. This is said to be so abundant that there is scarcely a house without a fountain. The governor is only inferior to the sultan in all Syria and Egypt; but as at different times some governors have revolted, the sultans have taken precautions to restrain them within proper bounds.

Damascus has a strong castle on the side toward the mountain, with wide and deep ditches, over which the sultan appoints a captain of his own friends, who never suffers the governor to enter it. It was, in 1400, destroyed and reduced to ashes by Tamerlane. Vestiges of this disaster now remain, and toward the gate of St. Paul there is a whole quarter that has never been rebuilt. There is a khan in the town appropriated as a deposit and place of safety to merchants and their goods. It is called Kahn Berkot, from its having originally been the residence of a person of that name. For my part, I believe that Berkot was a Frenchman, and what inclines me to this opinion is, that on a stone of the house are carved fleur-de-lis, which appear as ancient as the walls. Whatever may have been his origin, he was a very gallant man, and to this day enjoys a high reputation in that country. Never during his lifetime, and while he was in power, could the Persians or Tartars gain the smallest portion of land in Syria. The moment he learned that one of their armies was advancing he instantly marched to meet it, as far as the river, beyond Aleppo, that separates Syria from Persia. . . . The people of Damascus are persuaded that, had he lived, Tamerlane would never have carried his arms thither. Tamerlane, however, did honor to his memory, for when he took the town and ordered it to be set on fire, he commanded the house of Berkot to be spared, and appointed a guard to prevent its being hurt by the fire, so that it subsists to this day. The Christians are hated at Damascus. Every evening the merchants are shut up in their houses by persons appointed for this purpose, who, on the morrow, come to open their gates when it may please them.

.   .   .   .   .

I was shown the place without the walls of Damascus where St. Paul had a vision, was struck blind, and thrown from his horse. He caused himself to be conducted to Damascus, where he was baptized, but the place of his baptism is now a mosque. I saw also the stone from which St. George mounted his horse when he went to combat the dragon. It is two feet square, and they say, that when formerly the Saracens attempted to carry it away, in spite of all the strength they employed, they could not succeed.

Having seen Damascus, Sir Sanson and myself returned to Baruth, where we found Sir Andrew, Pierre de Vaudrei, Geoffroi de Toisi, and Jean de la Roe, who had come thither, as Jacques Cœur had told us. The galley arrived from Alexandria two or three days afterward, and during this short interval we witnessed a feast celebrated by the Moors in their ancient manner. It began in the evening at sunset. Numerous companies, scattered here and there, were singing and uttering loud cries. While this was passing, the cannons of the castle were fired, and the people of the town launched into the air, very high and to a great distance, a kind of fire, larger than the largest lantern that I ever saw lighted. They told me they sometimes made use of such at sea to set fire to the sails of an enemy's vessel. It seems to me that as it is an easy thing to be made, and of little expense, it may be equally well employed to burn a camp or a thatched village, or in an engagement with cavalry to frighten the horses. Curious to know its composition, I sent the servant of my host to the person who made this fire, and requested him to teach me the method. He returned for answer that he dared not, for that he should run great danger were it known ; but, as there is nothing that a Moor will not do for money, I offered him a ducat, which quieted his fears; and he taught me all he knew, and even gave me the moulds in wood, with the other ingredients, which I have brought to France.

The evening before the embarkation, I took Sir Andrew de Toulongeon aside, and, having made him promise that he would not make any opposition to what I was about to reveal to him, I informed him of my design to return home overland. In consequence of his promise he did not attempt to hinder me, but represented all the dangers I should have to encounter, and the risk I should run of being forced to deny my faith in Jesus Christ. I must own that his representations were well founded, and of all the perils he had menaced me with there was not one I did not experience, except denying my religion. He engaged his companions to talk with me also on this subject, but what they urged was vain. I suffered them to set sail and remained at Baruth. . . . I was lodged at the house of a Venetian merchant, named Paul Barberico, and as I had not entirely renounced my two pilgrimages to Nazareth and Mount Tabor, in spite of the obstacles which it had been said I should meet with, I consulted him on this double journey. He procured for me a moucre, who undertook to conduct me, and bound himself before him to carry me safe and sound as far as Damascus, and to bring him back from thence a certificate of having performed his engagement, signed by me. This man made me dress myself like a Saracen. The Franks, for their security in travelling, have obtained permission from the sultan to wear this dress when on a journey. I departed with my moucre from Baruth on the morrow after the galley had sailed, and we followed the road to Seyde that lies between the sea and the mountains. These frequently run so far into the sea that travellers are forced to go on the sands, and at other times they are three quarters of a league distant. After an hour's ride I came to a small wood of lofty pines, which the people of the country preserve with care. It is even forbidden to cut down any of them, but I am ignorant of the reason for such a regulation. Further on was a tolerably deep river, which my moucre said came from the valley of Noah, but the water was not good to drink. It had a stone bridge over it, and hard by was a kahn, where we passed the night.

.   .   .   .   .

The mountain near Sur forms a crescent, the two horns advancing as far as the sea; a league farther we came to a pass, which forced us to travel over a bank, on the summit of which is a tower. Travellers going to Acré have no other road than this, and the tower has been erected for their security. From this defile to Acre the mountains are low, and many habitations are visible, inhabited, for the greater part, by Arabs. Near the town I met a great lord of the country, called Fancardin; he was encamped on the open plain, carrying his tents with him. . . . From Nazareth I went to Mount Tabor, the place where the transfiguration of our Lord and many other miracles took place. These pasturages attract the Arabs, who come thither with their beasts, and I was forced to engage four additional men as an escort, two of whom were Arabs. The ascent of the mountain is rugged, because there is no road: I performed it on the back of a mule, but it took me two hours. . . . To the east of Mount Tabor, and at the foot of it, we saw the Tiberiade, beyond which the Jordan flows. To the westward is an extensive plain, very agreeable from its gardens, filled with date-palm trees, and small tufts of trees planted like vines, on which grows the cotton. At sunrise these last have a singular effect, and, seeing their green leaves covered ·with cotton, the traveller would suppose it had snowed on them.

I descended into this plain to dinner, for I had brought with me chickens and wine. My guides conducted me to the house of a man, who, when he saw my wine, took me for a person of consequence, and received me well. He brought me a porringer of milk, another of honey, and a branch loaded with dates. They were the first I had ever seen.

I noticed also the manner of manufacturing cotton, in which men and women were employed. Here my guides wanted to extort more money from me, and insisted on making a fresh bargain to reconduct me to Nazareth. It was well I had not my sword with me, for I confess I should have drawn it, and it would have been madness in me and in all who shall imitate me. The result of the quarrel was, that I was obliged to give them twelve drachms of their money, equivalent to half a ducat. The moment they had received them, the whole four left me, so that I was obliged to return alone with my moucre. We had not proceeded far on our road when we saw two Arabs, armed in their manner, and mounted on beautiful horses, coming towards us.

The moucre was much frightened; but, fortunately, they passed us without saying a word. He owned that, had they suspected I was a Christian, they would have killed us both without mercy, or, at the least, have stripped us naked.

Each of them bore a long and thin pole, shod at the ends with iron; one of them was pointed, the other round, but having many sharp blades a span long. Their buckler was round, according to their custom, convex at the centre, whence came a thick point of iron; and from that point to the bottom it was ornamented with a long silken fringe. They were dressed in robes, the sleeves of which, a foot and a half wide, hung down their arms; and instead of a cap they had a round hat, terminated in a point of rough crimson wool, which, instead of having the linen cloth twisted about it, like other Moors, fell down on each side of it, the whole of its breadth.

    .   .   .   .   .

I met, near Damascus, a very black Moor, who had ridden a camel from Cairo in eight days, though it is usually sixteen days' journey. His camel had run away from him; but with the aid of my moucre, we recovered it. These couriers have a singular saddle, on which they sit cross-legged; but the rapidity of the camel is so great that, to prevent any bad effects from the air, they have their heads and bodies bandaged. This courier was the bearer of an order from the sultan. A galley and two galliots of the prince of Tarentum had captured, before Tripoli in Syria, a vessel from the Moors; and the sultan, by way of reprisal, had sent to arrest all the Catalonians and Genoese who might be found in Damascus and throughout Syria.

This news which my moucre told me did not alarm me; I entered the town boldly with other Saracens, because, dressed like them, I thought I had nothing to fear. This expedition had taken up seven days. On the morrow of my arrival I saw the caravan return from Mecca. It was said to be composed of three thousand camels; and, in fact, it was two days and as many nights before they all entered the town. This event was, according to custom, a great festival. The governor of Damascus, attended by the principal persons of the town, went to meet the caravan, out of respect to the Alcoran, which it bore. This is the book of law which Mohammed left to his followers. It was enveloped in a silken covering, painted over with Moorish inscriptions; and the camel that bore it was, in like manner, decorated all over with silk. Four musicians, and a great number of drums and trumpets, preceded the camel, and made a loud noise. In front and around were about thirty men, some bearing crossbows, others drawn swords, others small harquebuses,[1] which they fired off every now and then. Behind this camel followed eight old men, mounted on the swiftest camels, and near them were led their horses, magnificently caparisoned, and ornamented with rich saddles, according to the custom of the country. After them came a Turkish lady, a relation of the grand seignior, in a litter borne by two camels with rich housings.

The caravan was composed of Moors, Turks, Barbaresques, Tartars, Persians, and other sectaries of the false prophet, Mohammed. These people pretend that, having once made a pilgrimage to Mecca, they cannot

---

[1] This is an early mention of portable fire-arms in the East; they were at this time novelties in Europe.

be damned. Of this I was assured by a renegado slave, a Bulgarian by birth, who belonged to the lady I have mentioned. He was called Hayauldoula, which signifies, in the Turkish language, "Servant of God," and pretended to have been three times at Mecca. I formed an acquaintance with him, because he spoke a little Italian, and often kept me company in the night as well as in the day. In our conversations I frequently questioned him about Mohammed, and where his body was interred. He told me he was at Mecca; that the shrine containing the body was in a circular chapel, open at the top, and that it was through this opening the pilgrims saw the shrine; that among them were some who, having seen it, had their eyes thrust out, because, they said, after what they had just seen, the world could no longer offer them anything worth looking at. There were, in fact, in this caravan two persons, the one of sixteen and the other of twenty-two or twenty-three years old, who had thus made themselves blind.

    •   •   •   •   •

The distance from Mecca to Damascus is forty days' journey across the desert. The heat is excessive; and many of the caravan were suffocated. According to the renegade slave, the annual caravan to Medina should be composed of seven hundred thousand persons; and when this number is incomplete, God sends his angels to make it up. As I was incessantly hearing Mohammed spoken of, I wished to know something about him; and for this purpose, I addressed myself to a priest in Damascus, attached to the Venetian consul, who often said mass in his house, confessed the merchants of that nation, and, when necessary, regulated their affairs. Having confessed myself to him, and settled my worldly concerns, I asked him if he were acquainted with the doctrines of Mohammed. He said he was, and knew all the Alcoran. I then besought him, in the best manner I could, that he would put down in writing all he knew of him, that I might present it to my lord the Duke of Burgundy. He did so with pleasure; and I have brought with me his work.

    .   .   .   .   .

In regard to the pilgrims that go to Mecca, the grand Turk has a custom peculiar to himself, — at least, I am ignorant if the other Mohammedan powers do the same, — which is, that when the caravan leaves his states he chooses for it a chief, whom they are bound to obey as implicitly as himself. The chief of this caravan was called Hoyarbarach; he was a native of Bursa, and one of its principal inhabitants. I caused myself to be presented to him, by mine host and another person, as a man that wanted to go to that town to see a brother. They entreated him to receive me into his company, and to afford me his security. He asked if I understood Arabic, Turkish, Hebrew, the vulgar tongue, or Greek. When they replied that I did not, he answered, "Well, what can he pretend to do?" However, representations were made to him that, on account of the war, I dared not go thither by sea; and that, if he would condescend to admit me, I would do as well as I could. He then consented; and, having placed his two hands on his head and touched his beard, he told me, in the Turkish language, that I might join his slaves, but he insisted that I should be dressed just like them.

I went, after this interview, with one of my friends, to the market, called the Bazaar, and bought two long white robes that reached to my ankles, a complete turban, a linen girdle, a fustian pair of drawers to tuck the ends of my robe in ; two small bags, the one for my own use, the other to hang on my horse's head while feeding him with barley and straw ; a leathern spoon, and salt ; a carpet to sleep on ; and, lastly, a paletot of a white skin, which I lined with a linen cloth, and which was of service to me in the nights. I purchased also a white tarquais (a sort of quiver) complete, to which hung a sword and knives ; but as to the tarquais and sword, I could only buy them privately ; for if those who have the administration of justice had known of it, the seller and myself would have run great risks. The Damascus blades are the handsomest and best of all Syria, and it is curious to observe their manner of burnishing them. This operation is performed before tempering, and they have, for this purpose, a small piece of wood, in which is fixed an iron, which they rub up and down the blade, and thus clear off all inequalities, as a plane does to wood. They then temper and polish it. This polish is so highly finished, that, when any one wants to arrange his turban, he uses his sword for a looking-glass. As to its temper, it is perfect ; and I have nowhere seen swords that cut so excellently. There are made at Damascus, and in the adjoining country, mirrors of steel that magnify objects like burning glasses. I have seen some that, when exposed to the sun, have reflected the heat so strongly as to set fire to a plank fifteen or six-teen feet distant.

I bought a small horse that turned out very well. Before my departure I had him shod at Damascus, and thence, as far as Bursa, which is near fifty days' journey, so well do they shoe their horses, that I had nothing to do with his feet, excepting one of the fore ones, which was pricked by a nail, and made him lame for three weeks.

.　　　.　　　.　　　.　　　.

The men of fortune carry with them, when they ride, a small drum, which they use in battle, or in skirmishes, to rally their men. It is fastened to the pommel of their saddles, and they beat on it with a piece of flat leather. I also purchased one, with spurs and vermilion-colored boots, which came up to my knees, according to the custom of the country. As a mark of my gratitude to Hoyarbarach I went to offer him a pot of green ginger, but he refused it, and it was by dint of prayers and entreaties that I prevailed on him to accept it. I had no other pledge for my security than what I have mentioned, but I found him full of frankness and good-will — more, perhaps, than I should have found in many Christians. God, who had protected me in the accomplishment of this journey, brought me acquainted with a Jew of Caiffa, who spoke the Tartar and Italian languages, and I requested him to assist me in putting down in writing the names of everything I might have occasion to want for myself and my horse while on the road. On our arrival, the first day's journey, at Ballec I drew out my paper to know how to ask for barley and chopped straw, which I wanted to give my horse. Ten or twelve Turks near me, observing my action, burst into laughter, and coming nearer to examine my paper seemed as much surprised at our writing as we are with theirs. They took a liking to me, and made every effort to teach me to speak Turkish. They were never weary of making me often repeat the same thing, and pronounced it so many different ways that I could not fail to retain it ; so, when we separated, I knew how to call for everything necessary for myself and horse. During the stay of the caravan at Damascus, I made a pilgrimage, about sixteen miles distant, to our Lady of Serdenay. To arrive there we traversed a mountain a full quarter of a mile in length, to which the gardens of Damascus extend. We then descended into a delightful valley, full of vineyards and gardens, with a handsome fountain of excellent water. Here, on a rock, has been erected a small castle, with a church of green monks, having a portrait of the Virgin painted on wood, whose head has been carried thither miraculously, but in what manner I am ignorant. It is added that it always sweats and that this sweat is an oil. All I can say is, that when I went thither I was shown at the end of the church, behind the great altar, a niche formed in the wall, where I saw the image, which was a flat thing, and might be about one foot and a half high by one foot wide. I cannot say whether it is of wood or stone, for it was entirely covered with clothes. The front was closed with an iron trellis, and underneath was the vase containing the oil. A woman accosted me, and with a silver spoon moved aside the clothes, and wanted to anoint me with the sign of the cross on the forehead, the temples, and breast. I believe this was a mere trick to get money, nevertheless I do not mean to say that Our Lady may not have more power than this image.

    .   .   .   .   .

I returned to Damascus, and, on the evening of the departure of the caravan, settled my affairs and my conscience as if I had been at the point of death; for suddenly I found myself in great trouble. I have before mentioned the messenger whom the sultan had sent with orders to arrest all the Genoese and Catalonian merchants found within his dominions. By virtue of this order my host, who was a Genoese, was arrested, his effects seized, and a Moor placed in his house to take care of him. I endeavored to save all I could for him; and that the Moor might not notice it, I made him drunk. I was arrested in my turn, and carried before one of their cadies, who are considered as somewhat like our bishops, and have the office of administering justice. This cadi turned me over to another cadi, who sent me to prison with the merchants, although he knew I was not one; but this disagreeable affair had been brought on me by an interpreter, who wanted to extort money from me, as he had before attempted on my first journey hither. Had it not been for Antoine Mourrourzin, the Venetian consul, I must have paid a sum of money; but I remained in prison; and, in the mean time, the caravan set off. The consul, to obtain my liberty, was forced to make intercession, conjointly with the governor of Damascus, alleging that I had been arrested without cause, which the interpreter well knew.

The governor sent for a Genoese, named Gentil Imperial, a merchant employed by the sultan to purchase slaves for him at Caiffa. He asked me who I was, and my business at Damascus. On my replying that I was a Frenchman returning from a pilgrimage to Jerusalem, he said they had done wrong to detain me, and that I might depart when I pleased.

I accordingly set off, accompanied by a moucre, whom I had first charged to carry my Turkish dress out of the town, because a Christian is not permitted to wear a white turban there. At a short distance a mountain rises, on which I was shown a house said to have been that of Cain! During the first day we travelled over mountains, but the road was good. On the second day we entered a fine country, which continued cheerful until we came to Balbeck. My moucre there quitted me, as I had overtaken the caravan. It was encamped near a river, on account of the great heat of these parts ; the nights are nevertheless very cold, which will scarcely be believed, and the dews exceedingly heavy. I waited on Hoyarbarach, who confirmed the permission he had granted me to accompany him, and recommended me not to quit the caravan.

On the morrow morning, at eleven o'clock, I gave my horse water, with oats and straw, according to the custom of our countries. This time the Turks said nothing to me ; but at six o'clock in the evening, when, having given him water, I was about fastening the bag, that he might eat, they opposed it and took off the bag ; for they will not suffer their horses to eat but during the night, and will not allow one to begin eating before the rest, unless when they are at grass. The captain of the caravan had with him a mameluke of the sultan, who was a Circassian, and going to Caramania in search of a brother. This man, seeing me alone and ignorant of the language of the country, charitably wished to serve me as a companion, and took me with him ; but, as he had no tent, we were often obliged to pass the nights under trees in gardens. It was then that I was obliged to learn to sleep on the ground, to drink nothing but water, and to sit cross-legged. This posture was at first painful, but it was still more so to accustom myself to sit on my horse with such very short stirrups, and I suffered so much that, when I had dismounted, I could not remount without assistance ; but after a little time this manner seemed even more convenient than ours.

That same evening I supped with the mameluke ; but we had only bread, cheese, and milk. I had, when eating, a table-cloth, like the rich men of the country. These cloths are four feet in diameter, and round, having strings attached to them, so that they may be drawn up like a purse. When they are used they are spread out ; and when the meal is over, they are drawn up with all that remains within them, without their losing a crumb of bread or a raisin. But I observed that, whether their repast had been good or bad, they never failed to return thanks aloud to God.

Balbeck is a good town, well inclosed with walls, and tolerably commercial. In the centre is a castle, built with very large stones. At present it contains a mosque, in which, it is said, there is a human skull with eyes so enormous that a man may pass his head through their openings. I cannot affirm this for fact, as none but Saracens may enter the mosque. . . . As my companion, the mameluke, and myself had no tent, we fixed our quarters in a garden. There we were joined by two Turcomans of Satalia, returning from Mecca, who supped with us. These men, seeing me well clothed and well mounted, having a handsome sword and well-furnished tarquais, proposed to the mameluke, as he afterwards owned when we separated, to make away with me, considering that I was but a Christian and unworthy of being in their company. He answered that, since I had eaten bread and salt with them, it would be a great crime ; that it was forbidden by law ; and that, after all, God had created the Christians as well as the Saracens. They, however, persisted in their design ; and as I testified a desire of seeing Aleppo, the most considerable town in Syria after Damascus, they pressed me to join them.   I was ignorant of their intention, and accepted their offer ; but I am now convinced they only wanted to cut my throat.   The mameluke forbade them to come any more near us, and by this means saved my life.

We set out from Balbeck two hours before day, and our caravan consisted of from four to five hundred persons, with six or seven hundred camels and mules ; for it had great quantities of spicery.   I will describe the order of its march.   The caravan has a very large drum ; and the moment the chief orders the departure, three loud strokes are beaten.   Every one then makes himself ready, and when prepared, joins the file without uttering a word.   Ten of our people would, in such cases, make more noise than a thousand of theirs.

Thus they march in silence, unless it be at night, or that any one should sing a song celebrating the heroic deeds of their ancestors.   At the break of day, two or three, placed at a great distance from each other, cry out and answer one another, as is done from the towers of the mosques at the usual hours.   In short, a little before and after sunrise, devout people make their customary prayers and oblations.   To perform these oblations, if they be near a rivulet, they dismount, and with feet naked, they wash their whole bodies.   Should there be no rivulet near, at the usual time for these ceremonies, they pass their hands over their bodies.   The last among them washes, and then turns to the south, when all raise two fingers in the air, prostrate themselves, and kiss the ground thrice ; they then rise up and say their prayers.   Persons of rank, to avoid failing in their performance, always carry, when they travel, leathern bottles full of water, which are suspended under the bellies of camels or horses, and are generally very handsome.

.   .   .   .   .

The Turks bear well fatigue and a hard life ; they are not incommoded, as I have witnessed, during the whole journey, by sleeping on the ground like animals. They are of a gay, cheerful humor, and willingly sing songs of the heroic deeds of their ancestors. Any one, therefore, who wishes to live with them must not be grave or melancholy, but always have a smiling countenance. They are also men of probity, and charitable toward each other. I have often observed, that should a poor person pass by when they are eating, they would invite him to partake of their meal, which is a thing we never do.

IV.

GEOFFREY OF VINSAUF.

THE children were talking, at their next meeting, of the curious question, what makes one book interesting while another is dull.

"You can almost tell," said Hester, "when you open a book, whether it will be entertaining. It seems as if there were something in the look of the page."

Uncle Fritz set them to guessing what were the easiest books for foreigners to read, in learning English. He told them that "The Vicar of Wakefield" is one of the books given to all beginners. This is because the English style is so simple.

"What makes books interesting to young people," he said, "and, for that matter, to old people, is human incident; and the more life-like this incident, — nay, the more detail in it, within certain limits, of human affairs, — the more will it interest the average reader."

Blanche said that she was on the top of Mt. Washington once, when Mr. Alger happened to be there. When he saw how she pointed out every chimney-smoke and every shed or barn, which relieved the wide spread of uninhabited forest, he told her it was the "human pathos" which gave interest to the scene.

That is an admirable observation, and the expression is worth remembering.

"Do you remember," said Uncle Fritz, "how much interest you took in Plutarch's Lives? That is because they are all crowded with personal anecdotes of the men he describes. In these bits of real life we see the men. It is as you look on a street at night, when there is a flash of lightning. You see the comers and goers for that instant, and, when another flash comes, you see them again. For the moment you see them well.

"Now our modern school of biography is very apt to drag us through the book, and yet not let us see the man once plainly. 'Whether Mr. Smith were descended from Reginald Smythe, who crossed with the Conqueror, or from Thomas the smith, who held the forge at the manor of Shoebury, is not well known. The family first appears on the American registers in the person of John Smith, who, with his wife Mary, crossed in the Cat, Jones, master, in 1629,' and so on, and so on.

"Ah me! I have read miles of such biographies.

"It is just so with histories and books of travel," continued Uncle Fritz. "If the man will tell you something about some real people, you will read. But if he says, 'The army this day advanced through an open country,' or 'The fleet this day lay by, waiting for orders,' you skip, if you dare, because 'army' and 'fleet' do not interest you as Richard and Saladin do."

Alice said she supposed this was the reason why novels are pleasanter reading than the dull histories.

Uncle Fritz smiled his approval, because he saw that the girl had listened intelligently so far; and Alice said that they had been reading Scott's novel of "The Talisman" aloud, as they met to make baby-clothing in their "Lend-a-Hand Club." They had just come to the loss of the banner, and they wanted terribly to look forward and see what happened to the brave Scot.

"While you are waiting," said Uncle Fritz, "suppose we take down the true story of the Siege of Acre." So he sent Fanchon for the book, which proved to be the next volume of Bohn's Antiquarian Library to that which had the travels of Sir John Mandeville.

Uncle Fritz gave it to Alice to read about the Siege of Acre. But, as she looked for that, she came to some earlier passages first, describing the start for the Third Crusade ; and once and again the children recognized scraps which Sir Walter Scott had used.

The book is by Geoffrey of Vinsauf. It is called the Itinerary of Richard I. As you will see, it has no lack of personal anecdote, or "human pathos."

Saladin had got possession of nearly all the kingdom, and everything succeeded to his wishes. Elated with his proud triumphs, he talked in magnificent terms of the law of Mahomet, and pointed to the result of his enterprise as a proof that it was superior to the law of Christ. These insolent vaunts he often threw out in the presence of the Christians, one of whom, well known to him for his loquacity, on a certain occasion, inspired by the Almighty, turned him into ridicule by the following reply : "God, who is the Father of the faithful, judging the Christians worthy of reproof for their crimes, has chosen thee, O prince, as his agent in this matter. Thus, sometimes, a worldly father in anger seizes a dirty stick out of the mire, wherewith when he has chastised his erring sons he throws it back among the filth where he found it."

Whilst these things were done in Palestine the Arch-

bishop of Tyre had embarked on shipboard, and already
reported to Christendom the news of this great calamity,[1]
and the affliction of so small a kingdom was felt as a
calamity over many countries. Fame had carried to the
ears of all the kings and of all the faithful, that the
inheritance of Christ was occupied by the heathen.
Some were affected to tears by the news, and some were
stimulated to vengeance. First of all, Richard, the brave
Earl of Poitou, assumed the cross to avenge its wrongs,
and took the lead of all, inviting others by his example.
His father Henry, King of England, was now declining
in years; yet the young man was not deterred by either
his father's advanced age, or his own right to the throne,
or the difficulties of so long a voyage; no arguments
could deter him from his purpose. The Almighty, to
reward the valor of this brave man, whom he had chosen
to be the first inciter of the others, reserved him, after
the other princes were dead or returned to their own
country, to achieve his great work.

Some time after, Philip, King of France, and Henry,
King of England, took the cross at Gisors, followed by
the nobles of both kingdoms, with numbers of the
clergy and laity, — all with equal aspirations, bent upon
the same design. So great was the ardor of this new
pilgrimage, that it was no longer a question of who
would take the cross, but who had not yet taken it.
Several persons sent a present of a distaff and wool to
one another, as a significant hint that whosoever declined the campaign would degrade himself as much as
if he did the duties of a woman: wives urged their hus-
bands, mothers their sons, to devote themselves to this

---

[1] The news of Saladin's victories in Tyre, Antioch, Acre, etc.

noble contest; and they only regretted that the weakness
of their sex prevented themselves from going also. The
renown of this expedition spread so extraordinarily,
that many migrated from the cloister to the camp, and,
exchanging the cowl for the cuirass, showed themselves
truly Christ's soldiers, in quitting their libraries for the
study of arms. The prelates of the churches publicly
preached to one another the virtue of abstinence, ad-
monishing all men that, laying aside all extravagance
in dress, they should refrain from their accustomed
luxuries.

It was agreed also, both among nobles and bishops,
by common consent, that to maintain the pilgrims that
were poor, those who remained at home should pay
tithes of their property; but the flagitious cupidity of
many took advantage of this to lay heavy and undue
exactions upon their subjects. . . . In process of time,
Frederic, the Roman emperor, assumed the insignia of
the holy pilgrimage, and displayed, both outwardly in
his dress, and inwardly in his heart, the form of a true
pilgrim. So great a king, whose empire was bounded
on the north by the Northern Ocean, on the south by
the Mediterranean Sea, whose glory was augmented by
continual victories, whose fortune had experienced no
check, resigns every pleasure and blandishment of the
world, and humbly girds on his sword to fight for
Christ. His bravery, especially in his declining years,
is no less to be wondered at than praised; for though
he was an old man and had sons, whose age and valor
seemed better fitted to military service, yet esteeming
them insufficient, he took upon himself the charge of de-
fending Christianity; but when his sons urged him to
let them discharge the task which he had undertaken,

either in his stead or in his company, he left his eldest
son to govern his empire, and the younger, whom he
had created Duke of Suabia, he took with him on the
expedition; and because the imperial majesty never
assails any one without sending a defiance, but always
gives notice of war to his enemies, a herald is dis-
patched from the emperor to Saladin, calling upon him
to give full satisfaction to Christendom, which he has
injured, or failing to do so, to prepare himself for war.

.   .   .   .   .   .

The princes of all the empire followed him, and when
they were met at Mayence, according to the imperial
edict, all of them joined with one acclaim in taking the
vow of so noble a pilgrimage. . . .

Thus, then, led by the Holy Spirit, they flocked together on every side; and whoever could have seen so
many nations and princes under one commander must
have believed that the ancient glory of Rome was not
yet departed.

In this army of Christ were pontiffs, dukes, earls,
marquises, and other nobles without number; for if we
were to recapitulate their names and territories, the
writer would become tedious, his reader be disgusted,
and his plan of brevity be overthrown. It was determined by a prudent council that no one should go on
this expedition whose means could not provide him
with supplies for one year. A large number of carriages were constructed for the use of the pilgrims who
should be sick, that they might neither give trouble to
the sound, nor be left behind and perish. It had long
been a question whether the mass of the army should
proceed by sea or land. But it seemed that any number of ships, however large, would be insufficient to

transport so great a multitude. The emperor, therefore, urging on the task which he had undertaken, determined to march through Hungary; and so, though he was the last sovereign who took the vow of pilgrimage, he was the first to carry it into effect. . . . Our army, having entered the territories of the Turks, experienced no hostility during several days. The sultan wished by his forbearance to allure them into the heart of his dominions, until want of food and the asperities of the road should give him ·more ready means of annoying them. That nefarious traitor had seized the rugged mountain-tops, the thickets of the woods, and the impassable rivers; and whilst he professed to observe the treaty which he had made, he opposed arrows and stones to our passage. This was the market and the safe-conduct which he had promised us. Such is the faith that must be placed in the unbelievers; they always esteem valor and treachery as equally praiseworthy towards an enemy.

Moreover, they avoid, above all things, coming to close quarters and fighting hand to hand; but they shower their arrows from a distance; and with them it is no less glory to flee, than to put their enemies to flight. They attack both extremities of the army, at one time the rear, at another time the van; that, if by any chance they can be separated, they may attack either the one or the other by itself. Night brought with it neither sleep nor rest; for a terrific clamor disturbed the army on every side. A shower of javelins pierced through their tents; numbers of them were slain asleep, and the enemy hung on them so incessantly that for six weeks they ate their meals under arms and slept under arms, without taking off their coats of mail. At the same time they were assailed by such violent hunger and thirst, that when they lost their horses by the chances of war, it was to them a consolation and source of delight to feed on horse-flesh and drink the blood; in this manner, by the ingenuity which necessity teaches, they found out an additional use for the animals on which they rode.

There was a place between high rocks which was rendered so difficult to pass by reason of the steep ascent and the narrowness of the paths that when the first division of the army, led by the emperor's son, had passed through, the Turks suddenly rushed from their ambush on the last division, and in their confidence of victory, attacked them with lance and sword. The alarming news was carried to the duke, who returned with headlong haste upon his march, eagerly retracing all the difficulties which he had a little before rejoiced at having surmounted. His rage heeded not danger; his cavalry were made to gallop where, before, they could not even walk. In this manner, whilst he was anxiously and incautiously seeking for his father on every side, and incessantly shouting his father's name, his helmet was struck off by a stone, and his teeth knocked out, yet still he remained immovable and unshaken. . . . At last, after many severe attacks, the army arrives at Iconium, where that wicked traitor had shut himself within the walls of the city. Our soldiers pitched their tents at no great distance, uncertain what new disasters the morrow might bring with it.

It was now about the end of Whitsuntide, and that same night so violent and sudden a storm burst upon them that its fury was felt even within the camp. In the morning, when the clouds were dispersed, the sky became clear, and behold! the Turkish army appear around on every side, with trumpets, drums, and horrid clang, ready to attack. They had never before been seen in such multitudes, nor could they have been conceived to have been so numerous. All this multitude had been roused to arms by the sultan's son, Melkin, who wished to anticipate his father-in-law Saladin's victory, and, trusting in the number and valor of his men, was confident of success. Meanwhile the sultan had ascended a lofty tower, where he sat in expectation, eying the country beneath him, and the armies that were ready to engage; and hoping in a short time to see accomplished what his sanguine mind had promised. The emperor, seeing some of his men alarmed at the unusual multitude of the enemy, displayed the confidence of a noble chieftain, and raising his hands to heaven, gave thanks to God, in the sight of all, that the inevitable necessity was at length arrived for that combat which had so long been deferred by the flight of the enemy.

At these words all were inspired with fresh ardor as they looked on the emperor's placid countenance, and one old man, weak though he was, supplied an incentive of valor to many who were young and strong. What God is so great as our God? All that multitude, who were so sure of victory that they brought chains with them rather than swords, were overthrown in a moment, and at once the city was taken and occupied, and the enemy without vanquished; everywhere were blood and death and heaps of slain; their number impedes their flight, and they fall by those very means on which they had counted for triumph. The battle is now fought hand to hand; the bows are snapped asunder; the arrows no longer fly, and they have scarcely room to wield their swords. Thus everything is thrown into confusion by the multitude, and what our enemies intended for our ruin turns out to our greater glory; the flying war, which had been waged among brambles and the gorges of rocks, is now carried on in a fair and open field; the Christians satiate their fury, which had so often been put forth in vain. The Turks experience, against their will, how well their enemies can fight hand to hand whom they had so often provoked at a distance. This splendid victory was not granted unworthily by the Divine excellence to His faithful servants; for they observed chastity in the camp and discipline when under arms; in all, and above all, was the fear of the Lord; with all was the love of their neighbor; all were united in brotherly affection as they were also companions in danger. . . .

The victorious army now enters the Armenian territories; all rejoice at having quitted a hostile kingdom, and at their arrival in the country of the faithful. But, alas! a more fatal land awaits them, which is to extinguish the light and joy of all. On the borders of Armenia there was a place, surrounded on one side by steep mountains, on the other side by the river Selesius. Whilst the sumpter-horses and baggage were passing this river the victorious emperor halted. He was indeed an illustrious man, of stature moderately tall, with red hair and beard; his hair was partly turning gray, his eyelids were prominent and his eyes sparkling; his cheeks short and wide; his breast and shoulders broad; in all other respects his form was manly. There was in him, as is read of Socrates, something distinguished and awful; for his look denoted the firmness of his mind, being always immovably the same, neither clouded by grief, nor contracted by anger, nor relaxed by joy.

He so much reverenced the native language of Germany that although he was not ignorant of other languages yet he always conversed with ambassadors from foreign countries by means of an interpreter.

This great man having halted some time, in consequence of the sumpter-horses crossing the river, became at last impatient of delay, and wishing to accelerate the march he prepares to cross the nearest part of the stream, so as to get in front of the sumpter-horses and be at liberty to proceed.[1] O sea! O earth! O heaven! The ruler of the Roman empire, ever august, in whom the glory of ancient Rome again flourished, its honor again lived, and its power was augmented, was overwhelmed in the waters and perished. If the mountains of Gilboa, where the brave ones of Israel were slain, deserved to be deprived of the dew and rain, what imprecations may we not deservedly utter upon this fatal river, which overthrew a main pillar of Christendom? There were some who said that the place had been marked by a fatality from ancient times, and that the nearest rock had long borne upon it these words inscribed, " Here the greatest of men shall perish." The lamentable report of his death was spread around, and filled all with dismay. If we search all the traditions of history and the fictions of romance, concerning the sorrows of mothers, the sighs of brides, or the distresses of men in general, the present grief will be found to be without example, never before known in any age, and surpassing all tears and lamentations. There were

---

[1] This was the river of Kalycadnus in Seleucia. The estimate given of Frederic I. by Geoffrey is confirmed by other history.

many of the emperor's domestics present, with some of
his kinsmen and his son, but it was impossible to distinguish them amid the general lamentation, with which
all and each lamented the loss of their father and their
lord. This, however, was a consolation to all, and they
all returned thanks for it to Divine Providence, that he
had not died within the territories of the infidels.

.   .   .   .   .

In the mean time Christ's soldiers, who had been conveyed by sea to the succor of the Holy Land, were
laying siege to Acre. That the order of the siege may
be better understood, we will relate it from the beginning. Guy, King of Jerusalem, after he had been a
year in captivity at Damascus, was released by Saladin,
on the strict promise that he should abjure his kingdom,
and, as soon as possible, go into exile beyond the sea.
The clergy of the kingdom determine to release the
king from the bond of his oath; both because what is
done under compulsion deserves to be annulled, and
because the bands of the faithful who were on their
way would find in him a head and a leader. It was
right, indeed, that art should overreach, and that the
treachery of the tyrant should be deceived by its own
example. . . . But God so ordered it that the counsel
of Belial was brought to nought; for the tyrant was
baffled in his hopes of retaining the kingdom, and the
king was released by the sentence of the clergy from the
enormity of his promise. . . . Thus, then, when numbers had flocked together to meet the king at Tripoli,
the minds of all were inspired with bravery, so that they
not only strove to keep what they had retained, but also
to recover what they had lost.

After a while the king assembled his army and proceeded to Tyre ; but, demanding admittance, was refused by the marquis, though the city had been committed to his custody on the condition that it should be restored to the king and the heirs of the kingdom. Not content with this injury he adds insult to the breach of faith, for whenever the king's messenger, or any of the pilgrims, endeavored to enter the town, they were treated harshly, and were in his sight no better than Gentiles and publicans. But the Pisans, who possessed no small part of the city, would not be induced to consent to his perfidy, but with commendable rebellion stood up for the king's rights. The marquis directed not only insults but civil war against them, and they, prudently withdrawing for a time, retired with others from the city to the army. The troops had pitched their camp in an open plain, but none of them were allowed to enter the city, even to buy provisions, and they all found an enemy where they had hoped to find an ally. Whilst these events were going on the marquis was afflicted by a complaint to which he had long been subject ; but, as it chanced to assail him this time with greater violence than usual, he conjectured that he had taken poison. Upon this he issued a harsh edict against physicians who make potions ; innocent men were put to death on false suspicions, and those whose province it was to heal others now found the practice of their art lead to their own destruction. The king was urged by many to attack the city, but he prudently dissembled his own wrong, and hastily marched with all the army he could collect to besiege the town of Acre.

There were seven hundred knights, and others more numerous still, collected out of all Christendom ; but if we were to estimate the whole army, its strength did not amount altogether to nine thousand men. At the end of August, on St. Augustin's day, two years after the city had been taken, they bravely commenced that long and difficult siege, which was protracted during two years longer before the city surrendered. The Turks, from the battlements of the walls, beheld the army approach, but without knowing who they were, or for what they came. When they learnt the truth they feared not their approach, and treated their intentions with derision. The men of Pisa, who chose to proceed by sea, as shorter and easier, approached Acre in due order in their ships and bravely occupied the shore; where they had no sooner secured a station than they formed the siege on the side towards the sea with equal courage and perseverance. The king, with the rest of his army, fixed his tents on a neighboring hill, commonly called Mount Turon, from which, by the eminence of the ground, he overlooked the approach both by sea and land. This hill was higher on the eastern side of the city; and, as it allowed the eye to rove freely round, it gave a prospect over the plain on all sides, far and wide. On the third day after their arrival the Christians made an assault upon the town; and deeming it tedious to await the effect of engines for throwing stones, together with other machines, they trusted to the defence of their shields alone, and carried scaling-ladders to mount the walls. That day would have put a happy termination to the toil of so many days, if the malice of the ancient enemy and the arrival of false information had not frustrated their achievement when it was almost completed, for it was reported that Saladin was at hand, and our men returned with speed to the camp, but when they perceived that it was only a small body that had come in advance they expressed indignation rather than complaint that the victory had been snatched from them. They were, indeed, few that had come, but fear had reported that an innumerable multitude was at hand; for it is not unusual that things should be magnified through terror.

The sultan, at this time, was besieging the castle of Belfort, and when he heard what was going on he marched in haste with a large army to Acre. Our men, unequal to cope with him, kept themselves within the limits before described. The Turks assailed them perseveringly, both morning and evening, trying every means to penetrate to the hill-top; and thus those who came to besiege others were now besieged themselves. In this position, then, were our men when the Morning Star visited them from on high; for, behold! fifty ships, such as are commonly called coggs, having twelve thousand armed men on board, are seen approaching, — a grateful sight to our men on account of the strait which they were in. Grateful is that which comes when prayed for, more grateful still is that which comes contrary to our hope, but grateful beyond all is that which comes to aid us in the last necessity; yet ofttimes we suspend our belief concerning a thing we so much long for, and cannot credit what we so much desire. Our army, from the top of the hill, see the reinforcements coming, and dare not hope for an event so joyful, and the new comers, also, look upon the camp as an object of suspicion. When, however, they came nearer and saw the ensigns of the Christian faith, a shout is raised on both sides; their joyful feelings find vent in tears; they eagerly flock together and leap into the waves to go and meet them. O happy fleet, which, sailing from the Northern Ocean, and encountering a voyage never before tried, passed over so many seas, so many coasts, so many dangers, and came from Europe, along the shores of Africa, to succor Asia in her distress ! The crews of these ships were Danes and Frisons, men inured to labor by the rigors of the north, and having three qualities good in war, — large limbs, invincible minds, and devout fervor for the faith. . . . To Acre, then, they came ; and, having pitched their camp between the city and Mount Turon, they turned their invincible prowess to the destruction of the enemy, whom they assailed, not by frequent skirmishes, but by one continued conflict ; for their prodigal valor and reckless fury exposed them to so many dangers that afterwards, when the city was taken, hardly a hundred men remained alive out of the twelve thousand.

.   .   .   .   .

At a season of calm, when Easter was close at hand, the marquis at our request returned from Tyre, with a large equipment and supplies of men, arms, and provisions. For by the provident care of the chiefs, the king and marquis were pacified on the pretext that the marquis should have possession of Tyre, Berytus, and Sidon, and on condition that he should be faithful and strenuous for the interests of the king and his kingdom.

.   .   .   .   .

At length the towns-people liked not their privation of liberty, and determined to try the issue of a sea-fight. They, therefore, led forth their galleys by twos, and keeping good order they rowed into the offing to meet and attack those that were coming ; our men prepared to meet them as they came on, and since there was no means of getting away, prepared to face them with greater resolution. On the other hand our men got on board our war-ships, and straining to the left by an oblique course, retreated to a distance and gave the enemy free means of egress. The sea was perfectly tranquil and calm, as if it favored the battle, and the rippling wave impeded neither the shock of the attacking ship nor the stroke of the oars. As they closed, the trumpets sounded on both sides. A terrific clang is roused, and the battle is commenced by the throwing of missiles. Our men implore the Divine assistance and ply their oars strenuously, and dash at the enemy's ships with their beaks. Soon the battle began ; the oars become entangled and they fight hand to hand, having grappled each others' ships together, and they fire the decks with burning oil, which is vulgarly called Greek fire. That kind of fire, with a detestable stench and livid flames, consumes both flint and steel ; it cannot be extinguished by water, but is subdued by the sprinkling of sand, and put out by pouring vinegar on it. But what can be more dreadful than a fight at sea ? what more savage where such various fates await the combatants ? Some are tortured by the burning flames ; some, falling overboard, are swallowed by the waves ; others, wounded, perish by the enemy's weapons. One galley, unskilfully managed by our men, exposed its flank to the foe ; and being set on fire received the Turks as they boarded her on all sides. The rowers in their fright fell into the sea ; but a few soldiers, impeded by their heavy armor, and restrained by ignorance of swimming, took courage from desperation, and commenced an unequal fight ; and trusting in the Lord's valor, a few of them overcame numbers ; and having slain the foe, they brought back the half-burnt vessel in triumph. Another ship was boarded by the enemy, who had driven the combatants from the upper deck, while those who were below strove to escape by the help of their oars. Wondrous and terrible was the conflict; for, the oars being pulled different ways, the galley was drawn first one way, then the other, as the Turks drove it; yet our men prevailed, and the enemy, who rowed on the upper deck, being overcome and thrust down by the Christians, yielded. In this naval contest the enemy lost both the galley and a galleon, together with their crews; and our men, unhurt and joyful, gained a glorious triumph.

Having drawn the captured galley on shore, they gave it up to be plundered by both sexes, who came to meet them. On this, our women, dragging the Turks by the hair, after treating them shamefully, beheaded them. . . . A like sea-fight was never seen, — so destructive in its issue, accomplished with so much danger, and completed with so much cost. In the mean time the Turkish army from without, though deeply bewailing our victory, persisted in making attacks upon our men who were within the trench, endeavoring either to fill up the completed portion, by casting back the earth, or to slay those who resisted. Our men sustaining their attack, though with difficulty, fight under great disadvantages, for they seemed unequal to contend against so countless a multitude, — for the numbers of the assailants continually increased, and we had to take precautions on the side of the city lest they also should rush in and assault us. There was amongst the assailants a fiendish race, very impetuous and obstinate; deformed in nature, as they were unlike to the others in character; of a darker appearance, of vast stature, of

exceeding ferocity, having on their heads red coverings
instead of helmets; carrying in their hands clubs bristling with iron teeth, which neither helmet nor coat of
mail could withstand; and they had a carved image of
Mahomet for a standard. So great was the multitude
of this evil race, that as fast as one party was thrown
to the earth, another rushed forward over them. Thus,
by their constant attacks, they confounded our men so
much that we doubted which way to turn ourselves; for
as there was neither security nor rest, we were distressed
on all sides; at one time guarding ourselves from sallies
of the besieged from the city, at another from the incessant attacks of the enemy from without; and again
from the side of the sea, where their galleys were lying
in wait to convey the Turks into the city as they arrived,
or to intercept the succors which were coming to us, the
Christians. At length, by favor of the Divine mercy,
our adversaries were driven back and repulsed.

    .   .   .   .   .

Meanwhile, according to the various events of war,
as has been said, success changing from one side to the
other, there occurred manifold incidents, not less wonderful than to be wondered at, which seem worthy of
our notice. . . . Amongst those who were carrying
earth to make a mound in the ditch for assaulting the
town more easily was a woman who labored with great
diligence and earnestness, and went to and fro unceas-
ingly, and encouraged others unremittingly, in order
that the work might be accomplished; but her zeal put
an end to her life and labors; for while a crowd of all
sexes and ages were constantly coming and going to
complete the work in question, and while the aforesaid
woman was occupied in depositing what she had brought,

a Turk, who had been lying in wait for her, struck her a mortal blow with a dart. As she fell to the ground, writhing with the violence of her pain, she entreated her husband and many others who had come up to assist her, with tears in her eyes, and very urgently, saying, "By your love for me, my dearest lord, by your piety as my husband, and the faith of our marriage contracted of old, permit not my corpse to be removed from this place; but I pray and beseech you, that since I can do nothing more towards the fulfilment of the work, I may deem myself to have done some good, if you will allow my lifeless body to be laid in the trench instead of earth, for it will soon be earth." Oh, zeal of woman, worthy of imitation! for she ceased not, even dead, to help those who labored, and in her death continued to show her zeal in the cause!

There were two friends, comrades in misfortune as well as in war, so needy and distressed that the two possessed only one piece of money, commonly called an angevin, and with that only they wished to purchase something to eat; but what could they do? It was a mere trifle, and worth little, even if there had been abundance of all sorts of good things; and they had nothing else but their armor and clothing. They considered for a long time very thoughtfully what they should buy with that one little piece, and how it could be done to ward off the pressing evil of the day. They at last came to the resolution of buying some beans, since nothing was to be bought of less value; with difficulty, therefore, they obtained, after much entreaty, thirteen beans for their dinner, one of which, on returning home, they found consumed by maggots, and therefore unfit for eating. Upon this, by mutual agreement, they went a long distance in search of the seller, who consented, not without difficulty and after much supplication, to give them a whole bean in exchange.

  .   .   .   .   .

On the Saturday before the festival of the blessed apostle Barnabas, in the Pentecost week, King Richard [1] landed at Acre with his retinue, and the earth was shaken by the acclamations of the exulting Christians. The people testified their joy by shouts of welcome and the clang of trumpets. The day was kept as a jubilee, and universal gladness reigned around, on account of the arrival of the king, long wished for by all nations. The Turks, on the other hand, were terrified and cast down by his coming; for they perceived that all egress and return would be at an end, in consequence of the multitude of the king's galleys. The two kings conducted each other from the port, and paid one another the most obsequious attention. Then King Richard retired to the tent prepared for him, and forthwith entered into arrangements about the siege; for it was his most anxious care to find out by what means, artifice, and machines they could capture the city without loss of time.

No pen can sufficiently describe the joy of the people on the king's arrival, nor tongue detail it. The very calmness of the night was thought to smile upon them with a purer air; the trumpets clanged, horns sounded, and the shrill intonations of the pipe, and the deeper notes of the timbrel and harp, struck upon the ear; and soothing symphonies were heard, like various notes

---

[1] His father, Henry I. of England, had died since Richard joined the Crusades.

blended into one; and there was not a man who did not, after his own fashion, indulge in joy and praise, — either singing popular ballads to testify the gladness of his heart, or reciting the deeds of the ancients, stimulating by their example the spirit of the moderns. Some drank wine, from costly cups, to the health of the singers, while others, mixing together, high and low, passed the night in constant dances. And their joy was heightened by the taking of Cyprus by King Richard, — a place so useful and necessary to him, and one which would be of the utmost service to the army. As a further proof of the exultation of their hearts, and to illume the darkness of the night, wax torches and flaming lights sparkled in profusion, so that night seemed to be usurped by the brightness of day, and the Turks thought the whole valley was on fire.

By the conjunction of the retinue of two kings an immense army of Christians was formed. With the King of France, who had arrived on the octaves of Easter, there came the Count of Flanders, the Count of St. Paul, William de Garlande, William des Barres, Drogo d'Amiens, William de Mirle, and the Count of Perche; and with them also came the marquis, of whom we have before spoken, and who aspired to be King of Jerusalem. But why should we enumerate them singly? There was not a man of influence or renown in France who came not, then or afterwards, to the siege of Acre; and on the following day of Pentecost, King Richard arrived with an army, the flower of war, and upon learning that the King of France had gained the good-will and favor of all by giving to each of his soldiers three *aurei* a month, not to be outdone or equalled in generosity, he proclaimed by mouth of herald, that whosoever was in his service, no matter of what nation, should receive four statute *aurei* a month for his pay. By these means his generosity was extolled by all, for he outshone every one else in merit and favors, as he outdid them in gifts and magnificence. "When," exclaimed they, "will the first attack take place by a man whom we have expected so long and anxiously, — a man, by far the first of kings, and the most skilled in war throughout Christendom? Now let the will of God be done, for the hope of all rests on King Richard!"

. . . . .

The King of France first recovered from his sickness and turned his attention to the construction of machines and petrariæ, suitable for attacks, and which he determined to ply night and day, and he had one of superior quality, to which they gave the name of "Bad Neighbor." The Turks also had one they called "Bad Kinsman," which by its violent casts often broke "Bad Neighbor" in pieces, but the King of France rebuilt it, until by constant blows he broke down part of the principal city wall, and shook the tower Maledictum. On one side, the petraria of the Duke of Burgundy plied; on the other, that of the Templars did severe execution; while that of the Hospitallers never ceased to cast terror among the Turks. Besides these, there was one petraria, erected at the common expense, which they were in the habit of calling the "petraria of God." Near it there constantly preached a priest, a man of great probity, who collected money to restore it at their joint expense, and to hire persons to bring stones for casting. By means of this engine a part of the wall of the tower Maledictum was at length shaken down, for about two poles' length. The Count of Flanders had a very choice petraria of large size, which after his death King Richard possessed; besides a smaller one, equally good. These two were plied incessantly, close by a gate the Turks used to frequent, until part of the tower was knocked down. In addition to these two, King Richard had constructed two others of choice material and workmanship, which would strike a place at an incalculable distance. He had also built one put together very compactly, which the people called "Berefred," with steps to mount it, fitting most tightly to it; covered with raw hides and ropes, and having layers of most solid wood, not to be destroyed by any blows, nor open to injury from the pouring thereon of Greek fire, or any other material. He also prepared two mangonels, one of which was of such violence and rapidity that what it hurled reached the inner rows of the city market-place. These engines were plied day and night, and it is well known that a stone sent from one of them killed twelve men with its blow. The stone was afterwards carried to Saladin for inspection; and King Richard had brought it from Messina, which city he had taken. Such stones, and flinty pieces of the smoothest kind, nothing could withstand; but they either shattered in pieces the object they struck, or ground it to powder.

The city of Acre, from its strong position, and its being defended by the choicest men of the Turks, appeared difficult to be taken by assault. The French had hitherto spent their labor in vain in constructing machines and engines for breaking down the walls with the greatest care; for whatever they erected, at a great expense, the Turks destroyed with Greek fire or some devouring conflagration. Amongst other machines and engines which the King of France had erected for breaking down the walls, he had prepared one, with great labor, to be used for scaling it, which they called a "cat," because like a cat it crept up and adhered to the wall. He had also another made of strong hurdle-twigs, put together most compactly, which they used to call a "cercleia," and under its covering of hides the King of France used to sit, and employ himself in throwing darts from a sling; he would thus watch the approach of the Turks, above on the walls, by the bat-tlements, and hit them unawares. But it happened one day that the French were eagerly pressing forward to apply their cat to the walls, when, behold! the Turks let down upon it a heap of the driest wood, and threw upon it a quantity of Greek fire, as well as upon the hurdle they had constructed with such toil, and then aimed a petraria in that direction, and all having forth-with caught fire, they broke them in pieces by the blows from their petraria. Upon this the King of France was enraged beyond measure, and began to curse all those who were under his command; and rated them shame-fully for not exacting condign vengeance of the Saracens, who had done them such injuries. In the heat of his passion, and when the day was drawing in, he published an edict, by voice of herald, that an assault should be made upon the city on the morrow. . . . There hap-pened a wonderful event, not to be passed over in silence. There was a man of renown for his tried valor and excellence, named Alberic Clements, who, when he saw the French toiling to very little purpose, exerted his strength in the vehemence of his ardor, exclaiming, "This day I will perish, or, if it please God, I will enter into the city of Acre." With these words he boldly mounted the ladder; and as he reached the top of the wall the Turks fell on him from all sides and killed him. The French were on the point of following him, but were overwhelmed by the pressure of numbers which the ladder could not hold, and some were bruised to death, and others dragged out much injured. The Turks shouted with the greatest joy and applause when they saw the accident, for it was a very severe misfortune. They surrounded and overcame Alberic Clements, who was left alone on the top of the wall, and pierced him with innumerable wounds. He thus verified what he had before said, — that he would die a martyr if he was unable to render his friends assistance by entering Acre. The French were much discouraged by his loss, and ceasing the assault gave themselves up to lamentation and mourning on account of his death, for he was a man of rank and influence and great valor.

Not long after the French miners, by their perseverance, undermined the tower Maledictum, and supported it by placing beams of wood underneath. The Turks also, digging in the same direction, had reached the same part of the foundations; on which they entered into a mutual treaty of peace that the Turks should depart uninjured, and some of the Christians whom they held captive were, by agreement, in like manner set at liberty. On discovering this the Turks were very much chagrined, and stopped up the passages by which they had gone out. . . . What can we say of this race of unbelievers who thus defended their city? They must be admired for their valor in war, and were the honor of their whole nation, and had they been of the right faith they would not have had their superiors as men throughout the world. Yet they dreaded our men, not without reason, for they saw the choicest soldiers from the ranks of all Christendom come to destroy them ; their walls in part broken down, in part shattered, the greater portion of their army mutilated, some killed, and others weakened by their wounds. . . .

Meanwhile, the petrariæ of the Christians never ceased, day and night, to shake the walls, and when the Turks saw this they were smitten with wonder, astonishment, terror, and confusion ; and many, yielding to their fears, threw themselves down from the walls by night, and without waiting for the promised aid, very many sought, with supplications, the sacrament of baptism and Christianity. There was little doubt, and with good reason as to their merits, that they presumptuously asked the boon more from the pressure of urgent fear than from any divine inspiration ; but there are different steps by which men arrive at salvation.

Saladin, perceiving the danger of delay, at length determined to yield to the entreaties of the besieged ; he was, moreover, persuaded by his admirals and satraps, and his influential courtiers, who had many friends and kinsmen amongst the besieged. The latter alleged also that he was bound to them by his promise made on the Mahometan law, that he would procure for them an honorable capitulation at the last moment, lest, perchance, made prisoners at discretion, they should be exterminated or put to an ignominious death, and thus the law of Mahomet, which had been strictly observed by their ancestors, be effaced by its dependence on him ; and, nevertheless, very much would be derogated from his name and excellence if the worshippers of Mahomet should fall into the hands of the Christians. They also begged to remind Saladin of the fact that they, a chosen race of Turks, in obedience to his com-mands, had been cooped up in the city and withstood the siege for so long a time ; they reminded him too that they had not seen their wives and children for three years, during which period the siege had lasted ; and they said it would be better to surrender the city than that people of such merit should be destroyed. The princes persuading the sultan to this effect that their latter condition might not be worse than their former one, he assented to their making peace on the best terms they could, and they drew up a statement of what appeared to them the most proper terms of treaty. On the messengers bringing back the resolution of Saladin and his satraps the besieged were filled with great joy, and forthwith the principal men of the city went to the kings, and, through their interpreters, offered to surrender unconditionally the city of Acre, the Cross, and two hundred and fifty noble Christian captives ; and when they perceived this did not satisfy them they offered two thousand noble Christian captives, and five hundred of inferior rank, whom Saladin would bring together from all parts of his kingdom, if they would let the Turks depart from their city, with their shirts only, leaving behind them their arms and property ; and, as a ransom for themselves, they would give two hundred thousand Saracenic talents. As security for the performance of these conditions they offered to deliver up, as hostages, all the men of noble or high rank in the city. After the two kings had considered with the wisest of the chiefs the opinion of all was for accepting the offer and consenting to the conditions, that on taking the oath for security and subscribing the terms of peace they might quit the city without carrying anything with them, having first given up the hostages. . . .

And when the day came that the Turks, so renowned
for their courage and valor, most active in the exercise
of war, and famous for their magnificence, appeared on
the walls ready to leave the city, the Christians went
forth to look at them, and were struck with admiration
when they remembered the deeds they had done. They
were also astonished at the cheerful countenances of
those who were thus driven almost penniless from their
city, their demeanor unchanged by adversity; and those
who but now had been compelled by sheer necessity to
own themselves conquered, and betake themselves to
supplication, bore no marks of care, as they came forth,
nor any signs of dejection at the loss of all they possessed — not even in the firmness of their countenances,
for they seemed to be conquerors by their courageous
bearing; but the form of superstitious idolatry and the
miserable error of sinfulness threw a stain upon their
warlike glories. At last, when all the Turks had departed, the Christians, with the two kings at their head,
entered the city without opposition, through the open
gates, with dances and joy and loud vociferations,
glorifying God and giving Him thanks, because He had
magnified His mercy to them, and had visited them, and
redeemed His people.

.   .   .   .   .

On the Wednesday before the feast of St. Mark the
Evangelist, the king and his army set out to Gadida to
protect the city, but found no one there, for the enemy
had taken to flight when they heard of his coming. On
their way back the king attacked a fierce boar, which,
hearing the noise of the party passing by, had come out
and stood in the way. The fierce animal, foaming at
the mouth with rage, and with his shaggy hair bristling

up, and his ears erect, seemed to be collecting all his strength and fury to receive or make an attack. He did not move from his place when the king shouted; nay, when the king made a circuit round him, he also turned himself in his astonishment round in a circle, and kept himself in the same place which he had first occupied. The king, now making use of his lance for a hunting spear, moved on to pierce him; and the boar, turning a little to one side, prepared to meet him. The animal was of enormous size and terrible aspect, and the lance which was boldly thrust against his broad breast broke in two, from not being strong enough to bear the force of both, as they were closing with each other. The boar, now rendered furious by his wound, rushed with all his might upon the king, who had not an inch of room, or a moment of time to turn away; so putting spurs to his horse he fairly leapt over the animal, unharmed, though the boar tore away the hinder trappings of his horse, but the activity of the latter frustrated the blow, and the part of the lance which was fixed in the animal's breast prevented him from coming to closer quarters. They then made a simultaneous attack on each other, and the boar made a rapid movement, as if to close with the king; but he, brandishing his sword, smote him with it as he passed, and stunned him with the blow; then wheeled round his horse, and, cutting the boar's sinews, he consigned the animal to the care of his huntsmen.

It also happened . . . that while the king was staying there (at Betnoble) they were much comforted by news which was brought to the king; for a devout man, the abbat of St. Elie, whose countenance bespoke holiness, with long beard and head of snow, came to the king and told him that a long time ago he had concealed a piece of the Holy Cross, in order to preserve it, until the Holy Land should be rescued from the infidels and restored entirely to its former state, and that he alone knew of this hidden treasure, and that he had often been pressed by Saladin, who had tried to make him discover the Cross by the most searching inquiries, but that he had always baffled his questioners by ambiguous replies, and deluded them with false statements; and that on account of his contumacy, Saladin had ordered him to be bound, but he persisted in asserting that he had lost the piece of the Cross during the taking of the City of Jerusalem, and had thus deluded him notwithstanding his anxiety to find it. The king, hearing this, set out immediately, with the abbat and a great number of people, to the place of which the abbat had spoken; and having taken up the piece of the Holy Cross with humble veneration, they returned to the army; and, together with the people, they kissed the Cross with much piety and contrition.

.   .   .   .   .

In the mean time our men, having by God's grace escaped destruction, the Turkish army returned to Saladin, who is said to have ridiculed them by asking where Melech Richard was, for they had promised to bring him a prisoner. "Which of you," continued he, "first seized him, and where is he? why is he not produced?" To whom one of the Turks that came from the furthest countries of the earth, replied: "In truth, my lord, Melech Richard, about whom you ask, is not here; we have never heard since the beginning of the world that there ever was such a knight, so brave, and so experienced in arms. In every deed at arms he is ever foremost; in deeds he is without a rival, the first to advance, and the last to retreat; we did our best to seize him, but in vain, for no one can escape from his sword; his attack is dreadful; to engage with him is fatal, and his deeds are beyond human nature."

V.

HERNANDO CORTES'S LETTERS.

ALL this talk about Asia interested the children in the old geography of Asia. They could see, by the map in Col. Yule's book, how very vague the notion of the eastern shore of Asia was. Marco Polo had sailed down that shore ; in fact, he came home that way.

"But," said Tom Rising, "he knew no more about it than I knew of Cape Ann and the Isle of Shoals, after I went from Boston to Mount Desert in a steamer."

"Exactly," said Horace Feltham, "but you knew that there was no land where you sailed over water, and Marco Polo knew the same."

Then Uncle Fritz showed them a droll old map of the world made by Fra Mauro, from the results of Marco Polo's discoveries. The southeast shore of Asia had a very suspicious curve, and Africa and Hindostan and the other peninsulas were all squeezed into the same curve. He explained to the children that this was done so that the whole of the three Continents, which we call the Eastern Hemisphere, might be brought up on one round plate, with Jerusalem for the centre.

"And this was the Asia that Columbus was looking for," said Tom Rising.

"Yes, and this was the Asia Columbus thought he had found.

"He thought so, probably, till he died, and for a generation other men thought so. It seems certain now that the coast of our own United States was put down on the maps before it was really discovered. It is doubtful how far the Cabots traced it. It is wellnigh certain that the supposed discovery by the Verrazzani was all a lie. They found people living stark naked early in March in the latitude of our New Jersey; they found odorous palms and laurels in the same place at the same time; wild roses and lilies in bloom. This is indeed 'a lie with a circumstance.'

"But all the same the coast of the United States was on the maps, without any Cape Cod, without any Hudson River, without any Chesapeake Bay. It is now supposed that, after Florida was discovered on the south, and the regions around Newfoundland on the north, the geographers were so certain that this was the Asiatic coast of Marco Polo, that they drew it boldly in."

When Uncle Fritz had explained this to the children, he made Sybil trace the true eastern line of Asia, and compare it with the true eastern line of America, and they were surprised and amused to see how much they resembled each other.

"When Cortes discovered California," said Uncle Fritz, "he gave it that name because in a romance of that time, called Esplandian, there was an island called California, inhabited by Amazons, in the east of Asia. Cortes thought he had struck the east of Asia. He thought California was an island, and so he put California down on the map. And it has stayed there long after everybody forgot the romance, — except Don Quixote, and me."

Some of the children said they liked Cortes better than they did Pizarro.

"And well you may," said Uncle Fritz. "Neither of them were Christian gentlemen of the type of the nineteenth century. But Cortes was, in every regard, much more of a man than Pizarro. And, of all the numerous accounts of his marvellous adventures, none are better written than those by himself."

"If only," cried Clem Waters, "he had written in English ! I am always groaning about that."

This was a constant complaint of Clem's. But Uncle Fritz told him that in this case his difficulty was solved. Cortes's letters to the sovereign have now all been translated. They were found in one receptacle or another, in different depositories in Europe, for Charles V. was here or there or everywhere. But now six of them have been found, and have been translated."

He sent Bob for the different editions of Cortes's letters to the sovereign, and, partly guided by Uncle Fritz's marks and suggestions, the children read the following passages : —

EXTRACT FROM CORTES'S THIRD AND FOURTH LETTERS.

The next day, after mass, I sent a messenger to the town of Vera Cruz to carry the good news that the Christians were alive, and that I had entered the city, which was quiet. The messenger returned in half an hour after his departure, covered with bruises and injuries, crying aloud that all the Indians of the city were in arms, and that they had raised the bridges ; and soon after an attack was made upon us by so great a multitude of people on all sides, that neither the streets nor the roofs of the houses were visible on account of the crowd, from whom proceeded the most violent outcries and terrible shouts that could be conceived. Stones thrown by slings fell in such numbers upon the garrison that it seemed as if they came down like rain from the clouds; and darts and arrows were so thick that the houses and squares were filled with them, and almost prevented our walking about. I sallied forth at two or three different points, where they were engaged stoutly with our men; and at one time, when a captain had led forth two hundred men, they fell upon them before he had time to form them in order, and killed four of their number, besides wounding the captain and several others. I was also wounded, and many of the Spaniards who were with me engaged in another quarter. We destroyed few of the enemy, because they took refuge beyond the bridges, and did us much injury from the roofs of houses and terraces, some of which fell into our possession and were burned. But they were so numerous and strong, and so well defended and supplied with stones and other arms, that our whole force was not sufficient to take them, nor to prevent the enemy from attacking us at their pleasure.

The attack on the fortress or garrison was made with such violence that they succeeded in setting fire to several parts of it, and a considerable portion of it was burned without our being able to prevent it, until we cut away the walls and levelled a portion of the building with the ground, by which we obstructed the progress of the fire and extinguished it. And had it not been for the great caution that I used in posting musketeers, archers, and several pieces of artillery, they would have

scaled our walls in broad daylight without our being
able to resist them.   Thus we fought all that day until
the darkness of night enveloped us, and even then they
continued to assail us with noises and alarms till daylight.   That night I directed the breaches caused by the
fire to be repaired, together with all other parts of the
garrison that seemed to require it; and I arranged
the quarters, determining who were to remain in them
the next day, and who were to be engaged without; at the
same time I caused suitable care to be taken of the
wounded, who amounted to more than eighty in number.   As soon as it was daylight, the enemy renewed
the combat with still greater vigor than the day before,
for the number of them was so immense that there was
no need of levelling the guns, but only to direct them
against the mass of Indians.   And although the fire-
arms did much injury, for we played off thirteen arquebuses besides matchlocks and cross-bows, they produced
so little impression that their effect scarcely seemed to
be felt ; since where a discharge cut down ten or twelve
men, the ranks were instantly closed up by additional
numbers, and no apparent loss was perceived.   Leaving
in the garrison a sufficient force for its defence, and as
large as I could spare, I sallied forth with the rest, and
took from the enemy several bridges, setting fire to a
number of houses and destroying the people who defended them ; but they were so numerous, that although
we did them much injury, the effect was still impercep-
tible.   Our men were compelled to fight all day long
without cessation, while the enemy were relieved at intervals by fresh forces, and still had a superabundance
of men.   But we had none of our Spanish force killed
on this day, although fifty or sixty were wounded, and

we continued the contest till night, when we withdrew wearied into the garrison. Seeing the great mischief done us by the enemy in wounding and slaying our people, while they were either unharmed, or if we caused them any loss, it was immediately repaired by their great numbers, we spent all that night and the next day in constructing three engines of timber, each of which would contain twenty men, covered with thick plank to protect them from the stones that were thrown from the terraces of houses. The persons to be conveyed in the machines were musketeers and archers, together with others provided with spades, pickaxes, and bars of iron, to demolish the barricades erected in the streets and pull down the houses. While we were building these machines, the enemy did not cease their attacks; and so resolute were they, that when we sallied forth from our quarters they attempted to enter them, and we had trouble enough to resist their progress. Montezuma, who was still a prisoner (together with his son and many other persons of distinction, who had been secured at the beginning of operations), now came forward and requested to be taken to the terrace of the garrison, that he might speak to the leaders of his people and induce them to discontinue the contest. I caused him to be taken up, and when he reached a battlement projecting from the fortress, and sought an opportunity to address the people who were fighting in that quarter, a stone thrown by some one of his own subjects struck him on the head with so much force that he died in three days after. I then gave his dead body to two Indians who were amongst the prisoners, and taking it upon their shoulders they bore it away to his people; what afterwards became of it I know not. The war, however, did not cease, but increased in violence and desperation every day. On the same day a cry was heard in the quarter where Montezuma had been wounded, some of the enemy calling to me to approach there, as certain of their captains wished to confer with me. I accordingly did so, and we passed amongst them ; when, after a long parley, I asked them to discontinue their attacks, since they had no good reason for it, having received many benefits from me, and having always been treated well. Their answer was, that I must depart and leave the country, when the war would immediately cease ; otherwise they were all resolved to die, or to destroy us. This they did, as it appeared, to induce me to leave the fortress, that they might cut us off at pleasure on our departure from the city, when we were between the bridges. I answered them that they need not suppose I asked for peace from fear, but that I was pained to be under the necessity of injuring them and destroying so fine a city as theirs. They replied that they should not cease their attacks until I departed from the city.

After the engines were completed, immediately on the following day, I sallied forth to gain possession of certain terraces and bridges ; and placing the engines in front, they were followed by four pieces of artillery, with many bowmen and shield-bearers, and more than three thousand native Tlascalans, who had come with me as auxiliaries, subordinate to the Spanish troops. Having reached a bridge, we brought the engines near to the walls of the terraces, together with scaling ladders, by means of which we ascended them. But the multitude of people was so great that defended the bridge and the terraces, and such showers of heavy stones were thrown from above, and the movements of the engines were disconcerted, and a Spaniard killed and many others wounded, without our being able to make any progress, although we struggled hard for it, and fought from morning till mid-day, when we returned sad enough to our quarters.

The enemy were so much encouraged by this unsuccessful movement on our part, that they advanced almost to our doors, and took possession of the great temple, to the loftiest and most considerable tower of which nearly five hundred Indians, apparently persons of rank, ascended, taking with them a large supply of bread, water, and other provisions, and a great quantity of stones. Most of them were armed with lances of large size, having points formed of flint, broader and not less sharp than ours; and from this position they did much mischief to the people in the garrison, as it was very near. The Spanish soldiers attacked this tower two or three times, and attempted to ascend it; but it was very lofty, and the passage up difficult on account of its having more than a hundred steps, and those above were well supplied with stones and other means of defence, and favored by our not having succeeded in gaining possession of the neighboring terraces; in consequence of these circumstances, every time our soldiers attempted the ascent, they came rolling down, many of them severely wounded; and the other portions of the enemy's force, seeing this, took courage, and penetrated to the very garrison without fear. Being sensible that if they continued their assaults while in possession of the tower, besides doing us much harm, they would be encouraged in the prosecution of the war, I sallied forth from the garrison, although lame in my left hand from a wound I had received in the engagement on the first day; and having tied a shield to my arm, I advanced to the tower, attended by a number of Spanish soldiers, and caused it to be surrounded at its base by a sufficient number of men, as was quite practicable. This precaution was not a useless one, as the troops stationed around the tower were attacked on all sides by the enemy, who increased in numbers to favor those within; in the mean time I began to ascend the stairs, followed by certain Spaniards. While they who were above disputed the ascent with great courage, and even overturned three or four of my followers, by the aid of God and his glorious Mother, for whose house this tower had been designated, and whose image had been placed in it, we succeeded in ascending, and engaged with the enemy on the upper area, until I compelled them to leap down to a lower terrace that surrounded it, one pace in width. Of these terraces the tower had three or four, about sixteen feet one above the other. Some of the enemy fell to the very bottom, who, besides the injury received from the fall, were slain by the Spanish soldiers stationed around the base. Those who remained on the upper terraces fought so desperately that we were more than three hours engaged with them before they were all despatched; thus all perished, not one escaping. And your sacred Majesty may be assured that so arduous was the attempt to take this tower, that if God had not broken their spirits, twenty of them would have been sufficient to resist the ascent of a thousand men, although they fought with the greatest valor, even unto death. I caused this tower and the others within the temple to be burned, from which they had removed the images we had placed in them.

The fierceness of the enemy was somewhat abated by the capture of this position; and while they relaxed their exertions throughout the city to a considerable degree, I directed my attention to the neighboring terrace, and called to the chiefs who had before conferred with me, but were now somewhat dismayed by what they had witnessed. They immediately appeared, when I said to them that they saw their inability to maintain their ground; that we should every day do them much injury, destroy many lives, burn and lay waste the city; and that we should persevere until nothing was left of it or them. They answered, that they were well aware much harm would befall them, and that many of them would lose their lives; but that they were still determined to make an end of us, even if they should all perish in the attempt; that I might see how the streets, public squares, and terraces were filled with people, who were so numerous that they had made a calculation that if twenty-five thousand of them should fall to one of ours, we would be first exterminated, so small was our number compared with theirs; that all the causeways leading to the city had been destroyed (which was so far true that only one of them remained), and thus we had no way of escape but by water; that they knew well we had few provisions and but little fresh water, and that ere long we should perish with hunger, even if they did not kill us. They were, indeed, quite right in saying that had we nothing else to contend with, hunger and want would soon put an end to our lives. We exchanged many other words, each party sustaining his own side. As soon as it was dark, I sallied forth with a number of Spaniards, and as I found the people were taken by surprise, we obtained possession

of one street, in which we burned more than three hundred houses. While the enemy were assembling in that
quarter in its defence, I speedily turned into another
street, where I also burned several houses, especially
certain terraces that adjoined our quarters, from which
we had experienced much annoyance. Thus the events
of that night struck great terror into the enemy; and
during the same night I caused the engines, that had
created confusion in our ranks the day before, to be repaired and got in readiness.

The next morning, in order to follow up the victory
God had granted us, I sallied forth at break of day
into the same street where they had routed us the day
before, and I found the enemy not less prepared for
defence than they were on the former occasion. But
as our lives and honor were now at stake, and as that
street led to a causeway that remained unbroken,[1] extending to the main land, although interrupted by eight
bridges very large and high, and the street itself was
filled with lofty terraces and towers; we put forth so
much resolution and spirit that, with the aid of our
Lord, we secured that day four of the bridges, and
burned all of the terraces, houses, and towers, as far as
the last of these bridges. They had erected during the
previous night, on all the bridges, many strong breastworks of unburnt bricks and clay, so that neither the
guns nor the crossbows made any impression on them.
We filled up the space occupied by the four bridges with
the unburnt bricks and the earth from the breastworks,
together with a great quantity of stones and timber
from the burnt houses, although this was not effected

---

[1] This is the street to Tacuba, now a village on solid ground, which was
then covered entirely by the lakes.

without danger, and many Spaniards were wounded.
The same night I used much precaution in guarding
the bridges, lest the enemy should succeed in recovering
them.

The next day in the morning I made another sally
from our quarters, and God gave us again success and
victory, although the enemy appeared in great numbers,
and defended the bridges, protected by strong en-
trenchments and ditches which they had formed during
the night; we took them all, and covered them up; and
some of our horsemen followed at the heels of the fugi-
tives in the heat of victory, and pursued them to the
main land.   While I was employed in repairing the
bridges and filling them up, messengers came to me in
great haste, reporting that the enemy had attacked the
garrison, and at the same time had sued for peace,
several of their leaders being in waiting to see me.   I
immediately went with two horsemen to see what they
wanted.   These men assured me that if I would engage
not to punish them for what they had done, they would
raise the blockade, replace the bridges that had been
destroyed, and restore the causeways, and that hereafter
they would serve your Majesty as they had before done.
They also requested that I would bring them a priest of
theirs whom I had taken prisoner, who was, as it were,
the commander-in-chief of their religion.   He came and
addressed them, and brought about an arrangement
between me and them; and it appeared that they immediately despatched messengers to inform the captains
and the people who were in the camp that the attacks
on the garrison and all other offensive operations
should cease.   Upon this being done we took leave of
them, and I went to the garrison to procure some food.

While I was beginning to take some refreshment, information was brought me in great haste that the Indians had attacked the bridges which we had taken the same day, and had killed certain Spaniards. God only knows with what feelings I received this intelligence, since I had thought that we had nothing more to trouble us after having gained the possession of the avenue leading out of the city. I mounted in the greatest possible haste, and galloped the whole length of the street, followed by a few horsemen; and without stopping a moment I dashed in amongst the Indians, and put them to flight whilst I regained the bridges, and pursued them to the main land. As the infantry were wearied, wounded, and panic-struck, they did not follow me, and I saw the dangerous situation in which I was placed from being unsupported by them. On this account, after having passed the bridges, when I sought to return I found them in possession of the enemy, and sunk to a great depth where we had filled them up; and both sides of the causeway were covered with people, on the land and water, who galled us with stones and arrows to such a degree that if God had not been pleased to interpose mysteriously in our behalf, it would have been impossible for us to escape thence; and, indeed, it was rumored amongst the people in the city that I was dead. When I reached the last bridge next the city I found all the cavalry that had accompanied me fallen in, and one horse without a rider; and as in this situation I could not pass, I rushed alone against the enemy, and thus opened a passage by which the horsemen could extricate themselves. After this I found the bridge free and passed over, although with some trouble, as I had to leap my horse in one place nearly six feet from one side to the other; but as I and my horse were well protected by armor the enemy did us no harm more than to cause our bodies a little pain.

Thus the enemy that night came off victorious, having regained four of the bridges. The other four I left well guarded, and returned to the garrison, where I constructed a bridge of timber that could be carried by forty men. Seeing the dangerous situation in which we were now placed, and the very serious injury that the Indians were doing us every day; and fearing that they would also destroy the remaining causeway, as they had done the others, and when that was effected death would be our inevitable fate; and moreover, having been often entreated by all my companions to abandon the place, the greater part of whom were so badly wounded as to be disabled from fighting, I determined to quit the city that night. I took all the gold and jewels belonging to your Majesty that could be removed and placed them in one apartment, where I delivered it in parcels to the officers of your Highness, whom I had designated for this purpose in the royal name; and I begged and desired the alcaldes, regidores, and all the people, to aid me in removing and preserving this treasure; I gave up my mare to carry as much as she could bear; and I selected certain Spaniards, as well my own servants as others, to accompany the gold and the mare, and the rest the magistrates above mentioned and myself distributed amongst the Spaniards, to be borne by them. Abandoning the garrison, together with much wealth belonging to your Highness, the Spaniards and myself, I went forth as secretly as possible, taking with me a son and two daughters of Muteczuma[1] and Cacamacin, cacique of Aculuacan, with

---

[1] This is always the spelling in Cortes's letters.

his brother, whom I had appointed in his place, and several other governors of provinces and cities that I had taken prisoners.

Arriving at the bridges (now broken up) which the Indians had left, the bridge that I carried was thrown over where the first of them had been, without much difficulty, as there was none to offer resistance, except some watchmen who were stationed there, and who uttered so loud cries, that before we had arrived at the second an immense multitude of the enemy assailed us, fighting in every direction, both by land and water. I sallied across with great speed, followed by five horsemen and a hundred foot, with whom I passed all the (broken) bridges swimming, and reached the main land. Leaving the people who formed this advance party, I returned to the rear, where I found the troops hotly engaged; it is incalculable how much our people suffered, as well Spaniards as our Indian allies of Tascaltecal, nearly all of whom perished, together with many native Spaniards and horses, besides the loss of the gold, jewels, cotton cloth, and many other things we had brought away, including the artillery. Having collected all that were alive, I sent them on before, while with three or four horse and about twenty foot that dared to remain with me, I followed in the rear, incessantly engaged with the Indians, until we at length reached a city called Tacuba (Tlacopan), beyond the causeway, after encountering a degree of toil and danger, the extent of which God only knows. As often as I turned against the enemy, I met a shower of arrows and darts and stones, and there being water on both sides, they assailed us without exposing themselves, and without fear; for when we attacked them on the causeway, they immediately leapt into the water, receiving little hurt, except some few, who, when the multitude was so great as to trample upon one another, fell and perished. Thus with great labor and fatigue I brought off all this portion of our force without any of the Spaniards or Indians being wounded or slain, except one of the horse that had gone with me to the rear, where they fought with no less fury than in front or on the flanks, although the hottest part of the fight was in the extreme rear, where our men were constantly exposed to fresh attacks from the inhabitants of the city.

Having reached the city of Tacuba, I found all our people gathered together in the square, not knowing where to go; I gave immediate directions to march into the country, before the inhabitants should collect in greater numbers in the city, and that they should take possession of the terraces, as the enemy would be likely to do us much injury from them. Those who had led the van, saying that they knew not in which direction to leave the city, I bade them remain with the rear, while I took command of the van until I had led them out into the open fields, where I waited till the rest came up. When the rear arrived, I saw that they had suffered some loss, and that they had left on the road much gold, which the Indians had seized. I remained there until all our people had arrived, closely pursued by the enemy. I kept the enemy at bay until the infantry had taken possession of a hill on which there was a tower with a strong building, which they took without suffering any loss, and I maintained my position, not suffering the enemy to advance, until the hill was taken;[1] and God

1 Called the hill of Muteczuma, on which is now a celebrated sanctuary of the Lady de los Remedios.

only knows the toil and fatigue with which it was accom-- plished; for of twenty-four horses that remained to us, there was not one that could move briskly, nor a horse- man able to raise his arm, nor a foot-soldier unhurt who could make any effort. When we had reached the build- ing, we fortified ourselves in it; and the enemy invested it, remaining till night without allowing us an hour of rest.

In this defeat it was ascertained that one hundred and fifty Spaniards lost their lives, together with forty- five mares and horses, and more than two thousand Indians, our auxiliaries; amongst the latter were the son and daughters of Muteczuma, and the other caciques whom we had taken prisoners. The same night[1] about midnight, thinking that we were not perceived, we sallied forth from the building very secretly, leaving in it many lighted fires, without knowing our route, nor where to go, except that one of the Tascaltecal Indians who guided us promised to lead us to his country, if the enemy did not embarrass the route. But guards had been stationed around who noticed our movements, and gave the alarm to the multitudes of people dwelling in that vicinity, of whom great numbers were collected, who pursued us until daylight, when five horsemen who went before as runners attacked some squadrons of people on the road, and killed a number of them; these fled, supposing that there was a greater number of horse and foot than ap- peared. When I saw that the number of the enemy was increasing on all sides, I made a disposition of our force, and out of those remaining unhurt I formed squadrons, and placed them in front and rear, and on the flanks; I put the wounded in the centre; and I also arranged

---

[1] This is the night known as the sorrowful night, *la noche triste.*

the position of the horse. During the whole of that day we were engaged in fighting in every direction, so that during the whole night and day we did not advance more than three leagues. It pleased our Lord when the night came to show us a tower and a good house on a hill, where we entrenched ourselves ; and that night the enemy left us undisturbed, except that near the dawn of day there was a sudden alarm that only sprung from the constant apprehension we all had of the multitude of people that was continually at our heels.

"You see," said Uncle Fritz, "that it was not all sunshine with Cortes. Now you shall read something of his resource as an explorer."

EXTRACT FROM CORTES'S FIFTH LETTER.

One day the idea struck me that by following down the river of that village I might perhaps come to the other large river that empties itself in the sweet gulfs, where I had left my brigantine, as well as my boats and canoes. I consulted the matter with some of the prisoners of that village, and they all seemed to agree in saying that the two rivers communicated ; but as they did not understand us well, and they spoke a language totally different from those we had hitherto met, no great reliance could be placed in their information. Through signs, however, and aided by a few words in that language which I understood, I begged that two of them should accompany ten of my Spaniards, and show them the meeting of the two rivers. This they promised to do, adding that the place was near at hand, and that they would be back on the next day. And so it was, for God permitted that after marching two leagues through very fine orchards, full of cacao and other fruit trees, they should guide my men to the banks of that large river, which they said communicated with the gulf, where my shipping was. They even went so far as to say that the river's name was Apolochic, and that they had often navigated it. On their return, the next day, I asked them how many days it would take a canoe to go down the river to the gulfs, and having answered me that five days were sufficient to accomplish the journey, I determined upon sending thither two Spaniards, accompanied by one of the guides, who offered to take them by cross-roads known to him to the very spot on the gulf where my ships were. I gave my men instructions to have the brigantine, boats, and canoes taken to the mouth of that large river, and that, leaving the vessel behind, they should try with one of the canoes and a boat to ascend the river to the spot where the other one joined it. This being done, and the men despatched on their errand, I ordered four rafts to be constructed with pieces of timber and very large bamboos, capable of supporting forty faneagues or bushels of dried maize, and ten men each, without counting a quantity of beans, peppers, and cacao, which each Spaniard afterwards threw into it for his own private supply. The rafts being made, after eight days' hard work, and the provisions placed on them, the Spaniards I had sent to the brigantine came to me and said that, after ascending the river during six consecutive days, they had found it impossible for the boat to go on, and had left it behind with ten Spaniards to guard it ; that, prosecuting their journey with the canoe, they had arrived at a place, about one league down the river, where, worn out by fatigue, and unable to use their oars, they had left it hidden among the bushes; that on their way up the river they had met Indians, and fought occasionally with them, and although they were then few in number, they had reason to fear that they would come back in force, and wait for their return. I immediately sent people to look out for the canoe, and bring it alongside of the rafts; and having placed on these all the provisions we had collected, chose among my people those who were most capable of directing those rafts, and avoiding by means of great poles the many floating timbers and gigantic trees with which the bed of the river was covered, and which rendered the navigation extremely dangerous. The remainder of my people, under a captain appointed for the purpose, I sent to the gulf by the same route which we had followed in coming up to Chacujal, with instructions that if they arrived before me they were to wait at the place of our landing until I should come for them, and that if, on the contrary, I was before them on the spot, I would not move until they came. As to myself, I embarked in the canoe with only two cross-bow men, the only ones disposable in all my suite. Though the journey I was about to undertake was exceedingly dangerous, owing to the impetuosity and strength of the current, as well as the almost certainty that the Indians would wait for us on our passage, I nevertheless preferred this route by water to the other by water, because our stock of provisions went this way, and I could thus watch better over it. And so, trusting myself in the hands of God, our Saviour, I began descending the river with such rapidity, owing to the strength and violence of the current, that in less than three hours' navigation we came to the spot where the boat had been left. Here we attempted to lighten the rafts by putting part of their cargo in the boat, but it was found impracticable, for no human effort could stop the rafts, driven on as they were by a rapid current. I then embarked in the boat, and gave orders that the canoe, well fitted with good oars, should go in front of the rafts, in order to see whether any Indians lay in ambush, or whether we came to any dangerous pass in the river; I myself remaining behind with the boat ready to give assistance to the rafts, as it was clear to me that, in case of need, I might more easily help from the rear than if placed in the van. In this order we went down that river, until about sunset, when one of the rafts struck violently against a piece of timber that held fast to the bottom. So strong was the shock, that the raft was almost entirely submerged, and although the violence of the waters at that spot made it float again, half its cargo was lost. Three hours later in the night, I heard in front of us the shouting of some Indians, but not choosing to leave the rafts behind, I did not go forward to ascertain what it might be. The shouting, however, ceased, and we heard no more of it for some time. A little later in the night I again heard the shouts, at what seemed to me a shorter distance; but I could not ascertain the fact, for the canoe went, as I have said, in front, and then three of the rafts, and I followed in the rear with the fourth, which, owing to the accident sustained, could not go so fast.

In this manner we proceeded for some length of time, until we came to a turning of the river, where the current was so strong that, notwithstanding all our efforts, rafts and boat were cast on shore.

Some time before this, hearing no longer those alarming shouts, confidence had returned to my people, and I myself, taking off my helmet — for I was ill with fever at the time — had laid my head on my hand to see if I could rest. It was soon, however, ascertained that the shouting we had heard in the distance came from that particular spot, for the Indians, who knew the river well, as inhabiting its banks, and being almost born on it, had followed us for some time along the shore, knowing very well that we should be cast by the current on the very spot where they were waiting in ambush for us. No sooner, therefore, did the canoe and rafts reach the place where the Indians lay concealed than we were assailed by a volley of arrows from the shore that wounded almost every man on board ; though, knowing that most of us remained still behind, the attack of the Indians was by no means so strong or furious as the one they afterwards made on us. Thus assailed, the people in the canoe attempted to come back and give me notice of the danger, but they never succeeded in porting the helm, owing to the strength of the current. When, however, it came to our turn to strike the land, the Indians gave a most terrific shout, and assailed us with such a volley of arrows and stones that not one man on board escaped without a wound. I, myself, was struck by a stone on the head, the only part of my body that was unarmed, having taken off my steel cap some time before. God, however, permitted that at the spot where this happened the banks of the river should be high and the waters deep. To this circumstance we owed our salvation ; for the night being dark, some of the Indians who attempted to leap upon the rafts and boat fell into the water, and I believe that a good number of them were drowned in this way. The current itself soon extricated us from the danger, so that a few minutes after this we scarcely heard their shouts.

The rest of the night passed without encounter of any sort, though from time to time we still heard in the distance, or from the sides of the river, the Indian war-cries.

The shores, I observed, were covered with villages and plantations, and there were, besides, many fine orchards with cacao and other fruit trees.

At dawn of day we were five leagues from the mouth of that river that empties itself into the gulf, and where the brigantine was waiting for us, and about the hour of noon we arrived on the spot, so that in four-and-twenty hours we ran no less than twenty long leagues down that river.

Having given orders that the provisions on the rafts should be transferred immediately to the brigantine, I was informed, to my great disappointment, that most of the maize was wet, and that if I could not have it dried I ran a risk of losing the whole stock, whereby all the trouble we had in procuring it would have proved in vain. I immediately caused the dry maize to be put aside and stored in the brigantine, and as to that which had been spoilt by water, I had it thrown into the two boats and in two canoes, and sent it in haste to the village for the purpose of drying; the shores of that gulf being so swampy and low that there was no spot, however small, where the operation could be effectually carried on. My men, therefore, went away with the boats and canoes, but I gave them orders to send the same back to me, the brigantine and one remaining canoe being sufficient to convey all my people. Soon after their departure I set sail in the brigantine, and steered towards the place where it was agreed that I should wait for the people coming from Chacujal by

land. I waited for them three days, at the end of which
they all arrived in good spirits, and with no other loss
but that of a Spaniard, who having eaten of some herbs
he saw in the fields died almost immediately after.
They also brought with them an Indian, whom they had
surprised and taken prisoner near the place where I left
them. This Indian was dressed differently and spoke
a language unknown in these parts. I had already
begun to interrogate him by signs, when a man was
found among the prisoners who said he understood a
little of his dialect. In this manner we learned that he
was a native of Teculutlan. No sooner did I hear that
name pronounced than I recollected having heard it
repeated on other occasions, and when I returned to
the village I consulted certain memoranda of mine,
where I actually found that name written as being that
of a place across the country, between which and the
Spanish establishments in the South Sea, governed by
Pedro de Alvarado, one of my captains, there was only
a distance of seventy-eight leagues. The above memoranda further stated that the village of Teculutlan
had been visited by Spaniards, and as the Indian bore
also testimony to the fact, I was very much pleased at
receiving such intelligence.

My people being all congregated together, and the
boats not having yet returned, we consumed all the dry
grain we had in store, and embarked on board the brigantine, though, the vessel being so very small, we had
the greatest difficulty to move. It was my idea to cross
the gulf to that village where we had landed at first,
because I recollected that the maize plantations were
very fine and in full grain, though not sufficiently ripe
for our cutting. Five-and-twenty days had elapsed since

that time, and it was to be hoped that a good deal of it was dry enough for us to keep ; and it so happened ; for being one morning in the middle of the gulf we saw the boats and canoes coming towards us, and, having sailed altogether in that direction, recognized the place where the village was. Immediately after landing, all my people, Spaniards as well as Indians, besides forty native prisoners, went straight forward to the village, where they found several maize plantations in the finest possible condition. The natives, if there were any at the place, not having shown themselves or made any opposition, my men reaped as much of that maize as they could, every man of us, Christian or Indian, making that day three journeys, fortunately very short, from the village to the ship, loaded with as much grain as he could carry. The brigantine being filled as well as the boats, I went to the village myself, leaving there all my people engaged in that most providential harvest ; I afterwards sent to them the two boats, and one more belonging to a vessel from New Spain, and that had been lost in those waters, and four canoes. In these vessels all my people embarked, after having, as I said before, brought sufficient provision to last us all for many a day. It was, indeed, a most providential supply, and one that compensated us for all our past troubles ; for had we not found it at that moment we should all have perished through hunger.

"How much of the Cortes wonders do you believe, Uncle Fritz ? "

This was Horace Feltham's question.

Uncle Fritz said that there were two sets of opinions about it. For himself, when Cortes squarely said that

a thing was thus and so, he took it as probably true,
with due allowance for a man's praise of his own
achievements, and for Spanish and travellers' exaggera-
tion.

But a great deal of what you find in the received accounts of the conquest must be set down as belonging
to the same school of romance as in the same days
wrote tales of chivalry or lives of saints. Especially
where men do not tell what they saw themselves must
you be careful when you are dealing with these Spanish
authorities.

VI.

FRA MARCO AND CORONADO.

WHEN the children came in the next week they found Col. Ingham's large study-table cleared from books and papers, and quite covered with a display of earthenware.

Blanche asked if there were to be an æsthetic wedding; she told him his table seemed to be covered with wedding presents.

"I do not know how the young brides would like my crockery," said the colonel, laughing, "but you see I could fit out any of you." There was a gigantic soup-tureen, pitchers of grotesque shapes, curious water-bottles for travellers to carry at their sides, and every sort of cup, of saucer, and tall vases. The material of some was black; of the tureen and most of the larger objects yellow ware, painted with quaint pictures of beasts and of birds and sometimes of men.

He bade them see how closely these things resembled the pottery dug from the western mounds, which he had shown them when they went with him to the Peabody Museum in Cambridge; and, at a nod from him, Tom Rising took down the first volume of Bryant's History, which is really "Gay's," and which is for young people the best history of the United States. Here they found pictures of earthenware from the mounds, and the chil-

dren engaged eagerly in comparing them with specimens on the table.

Over the sofa was thrown a great rug, woven or knit in black and white wool, and smaller rugs or mats of the same size hung over the chairs.

" Are they from the mounds, Uncle Fritz?"

" These are not," said he ; " these are all modern, so far as I know. My friend, Mr. Cargill, who is an officer of the Atchison Railroad, has lent them to me that I might show them to you. You know, or you ought to know, that they are, just now, pressing their connection with the Pacific. Through New Mexico and Arizona, their roads pass quite near to the pueblos, as they are called, of these industrious Indians, who, under different names, have always held those valleys. They are people who believe in the 'Together' The necessity of uniting to irrigate the land holds them together. They live in these houses, two, three, or four stories high, of which Mr. Cargill has lent us these pictures."

And then Uncle Fritz showed them some beautiful photographic views of the "pueblos," or villages. "Pueblos," which originally means "peoples," is the name which the Spaniards of Mexico give to any such town.

" By keeping together in these towns, which are almost fortresses, they have defied the roving Indians, like the Camanches and the Apaches, since Cortes's day. Indeed, the Spaniards found them an even match."

Then the children found that Col. Ingham had laid out for them the original records, which are still rare, of the first Spanish explorations. Eager for more gold, the viceroy Mendoça sent, as early as 1540, an expedition to discover this country under Coronado. It was

a party of three hundred Spaniards with eight hundred
native Mexicans.

They were tempted to it by the lying stories of Father
Marco, who is one of the princes of lying.

"Four Spaniards, one of whom was a negro, named
Stephen, had crossed the continent from the Gulf of
Mexico, after the failure of Narvaez. You will find
about them in the first volume of the Popular History
there, Bryant's. Father Marco got hold of the negro,
and, under his guidance, went north from the then
settled parts of Mexico. When he came home he told
a grand rigmarole about these pueblos, which probably
looked then very much as they look now.

"Here is a part of his letter in your dear old Hakluyt."

Blanche read aloud what Uncle Fritz had marked for
her.

Thus I travelled three days' journey through towns
inhabited by the same people, of whom I was received
as I was of those which I had passed, and came into a
town of reasonable bigness, called Vacupa, where they
showed me great courtesies, and gave me great store of
good victuals, because the soil is very fruitful, and may
be watered. This town is forty leagues distant from the
sea, and because I was so far from the sea, it being two
days before Passion Sunday, I determined to stay there
until Easter, to inform myself of the islands, whereof I
said before that I had information; and so I sent certain
Indians to the sea by three several ways, whom I commanded to bring me some Indians of the sea-coast and
some of those islands, that I might receive information
of them; and I sent Stephen Dorantez, the negro,

another way, whom I commanded to go directly northward, fifty or threescore leagues, to see if by that way
he might learn any news of any notable thing which we
sought to discover. And I agreed with him that if he
found any knowledge of any peopled and rich country
which were of great importance, that he should go no
farther, but should return in person, or should send me
certain Indians with that token which we were agreed
upon, that if it were but a mean thing he should send
me a white cross one handfull long ; and if it were any
great matter, one of two handsfull long ; and if it were
a country greater and better than Nueva Espana, he
should send me a great cross. So the said Stephen
departed from me on Passion Sunday after dinner, and
within four days after the messengers of Stephen returned unto me with a great cross as high as a man, and
they brought me word from Stephen that I should forth-
with come away after him, for he had found people
which gave him information of a very mighty Province,
and that he had certain Indians in his company which
had been in the said Province, and that he had sent me
one of the said Indians. This Indian told me that it
was thirty days' journey from the town where Stephen
was, into the first city of the said Province, which is
called Cevola. He said also that there are seven great
cities in this Province, all under one Lord ; the houses
are made of lime and stone, and are very great ; and
the least of them with one loft overhead, and some of
them two and three lofts, and the house of the lord of
the Province of four, and that all of them joined one
into the other in good order, and that in the gates of
the principal houses there are many Turkish stones
(Turquoise stones) cunningly wrought, whereof he said

they had there a great many; also that the people of
this city are very well dressed, and that beyond this
there are other provinces, all which are much greater
than these seven cities. . . . I deferred my departure
to follow Stephen Dorantez, because I thought he
would stay for me, and also to attend the return of my
messengers whom I had sent to the sea, and who returned to me Easter Day, bringing with them certain
inhabitants of the sea-coast, and of two of the islands;
of whom I understood that the islands mentioned were
scarce of victuals, as I had learned before, and that they
are inhabited by people who wear shells of pearls upon
their foreheads, and they say that they have great pearls
and much gold. They informed me of thirty-four islands,
and that they traffic with one another upon rafts. This
coast stretches northward as is to be seen. These Indians of the coast brought me certain targets made of
cowhides very well dressed, which were so large that
they covered them from head to foot, with a hole in the
top to look out of; they are so strong that a cross-bow
(as I suppose) will not pierce them. . . .

Having considered the former report of the Indians
and the evil means which I had to prosecute my voyage
as I desired, I thought it not good to wilfully loose my
life as Stephen did, and so I told them that God would
punish those of Cevola, and that the Viceroy, when he
understood what had happened, would send many Christians to chastise them, but they would not believe me,
for they said that no man was able to withstand the
power of Cevola; and herewithal I left them and went
aside two or three stones east, and when I returned I
found an Indian of mine which I had brought from
Mexico, called Marcus, who wept and said to me:

"Father, these men have consulted to kill us, for they say that through your and Stephen's means their fathers are slain, and that neither man nor woman of them shall remain unslain." Then again I divided among them certain other things which I had to appease them, whereupon they were somewhat pacified, though they still showed great grief for the people which were slain. I requested some of them to go to Cevola to see if any other Indian had escaped, with intent that they might learn news of Stephen, which I could not obtain at their hands. When I saw this I said to them that I purposed to see the city of Cevola, whatever came of it. They said that none of them would go with me. At the last, when they saw me resolute, two of the chief of them said they would go with me; with whom and with my Indians and interpreters I followed my way till I came within sight of Cevola, which is situated on a plain at the foot of a round hill, and makes sure to be a fair city, and is better situated than any that I have seen in those parts. The houses are built in order, according as the Indians told me, all made of stone with divers stories and flat roofs, as far as I could discern from a mountain, whither I ascended to view the city. The people are somewhat white, they wear apparel, and lie in beds, their weapons are bows, they have emeralds and other jewels, although they esteem none so much as turquoises, wherewith they adorn the walls of the porches of their houses, and their apparel and vessels, and they use them instead of money through all the country. Their apparel is of cotton and of ox-hides, and this is their most commendable and honorable apparel. They use vessels of gold and silver, for they have no other metal; whereof there is greater use and more abundance than in Peru, and they buy the same for turquoises in the province of the Pintados, where there are said to be mines of great abundance. Of other kingdoms I could not obtain so particular instruction. Divers times I was tempted to go thither, because I knew I could but hazard my life, and that I had offered unto God the first day that I began my journey; in the end I began to be afraid, considering in what danger I should put myself, and that if I should die the knowledge of this country should be lost, which in my judgment is the greatest and the best that hitherto has been discovered; and when I told the chief men what a goodly city Cevola seemed to me, they answered me that it was the least of the seven cities, and that Totonteac is the greatest and best of them all, because it has so many houses and people that there is no end of them. Having seen the disposition and situation of the place I thought good to name that country "el nuevo regno de San Francisco," in which place I made a great heap of stones by the help of the Indians, and on the top thereof I set up a small slender cross because I wanted means to make a greater, and said that I set up that cross and heap in the name of the most honorable Lord Don Antonio de Mendoça, Viceroy and Captain-General of Nueva España, for the emperor our lord, in token of possession, according to my instruction; which possession I said that I took in that place of all the seven cities, and of the kingdoms of Totonteac, of Acus, and of Marata. Thus I returned with much more fear than victuals, and went until I found the people which I had left behind me with all the speed that I could make, whom I overtook in two days' travel, and went in their company till I had passed the desert, where I was not made so much of as before; for both men and women made great lamentation for the people which were slain at Cevola, and with fear I hastened from the people of this valley and travelled ten leagues the first day, and so I went daily eight or ten leagues, without staying until I had passed the second desert, and though I was in fear yet I determined to go to the great plain, whereof I said before that I had information, being situated at the foot of the mountains, and in that place I understood that this plain is inhabited for many days' journey toward the east, but I dared not enter into it, considering that if hereafter we should inhabit this other country of the seven cities, and the kingdoms before mentioned, that then I might better discover the same, without putting myself in hazard, and leave it for this time, that I might give relation of the things which I had seen. At the entrance of this plain I saw but seven towns only of a reasonable bigness, which were far off in a low valley, being very green and a most fruitful soil, out of which ran many rivers. I was informed that there was much gold in this valley, and that the inhabitants work it into vessels and thin plates, wherewith they strike and take off their sweat, and that they were people that will not suffer those of the other side of the plain to traffic with them, and they could not tell me the cause of it. Here I set up two crosses and took possession of the plain and valley in like sort and order as I did at other places before mentioned; and from thence I returned on my voyage with as much haste as I could make, until I came to the city of Saint Michael, in the province of Culiacan, thinking there to have found Francis Vazquez de Coronado, Governor of Nueva Galicia, and finding him not there I proceeded on my journey till I came to the city of Compostella, where I found him. I do not write here many other particularities, because they are impertinent to this matter; I only report that which I have seen, and which was told me concerning the countries through which I travelled, and of those which I had information of.

When Blanche had read so far, Uncle Fritz bade her give him the book.

"You see," he said, "all this talk about the seven cities was very exciting to them, because they all had a legend about seven cities which had been founded by seven Portuguese bishops, ages before.

"When the Cabots came back to England from their first voyage, it was reported that they had found 'the seven cities.' And when this lying Father Marco reported seven cities, Mendoça thought he had found the seven cities of the seven bishops.

"Oddly enough, it seems to prove that these pueblo Indians had and have a fancy of building their towns in groups of seven. At least, there are two or three such instances.

"On the strength of this report by the Friar, Coronado started with his party. They had a long march northward parallel with the Gulf of California. They came out near the Gila River, where you will find 'Casa Grande' on the map. This means 'Great House.' It still stands, and they call it Montezuma's house to this day. Then Coronado persevered across the desert and found the 'seven cities.' They were, doubtless, just such pueblos as these you have the pictures of now. He was dreadfully disappointed."

And Uncle Fritz bade Horace Feltham read Coronado's report.

It remains now to certify your honor of the seven cities, and of the kingdoms and provinces whereof the provincial father made report to your lordship; and to be brief, he said the truth in nothing that he reported, but all was quite contrary, saving only the names of the cities, and great houses of stone; for although they are not wrought with turquoises, nor with lime, nor bricks, yet they are very excellent good houses of four or five lofts high, wherein are good lodgings and fair chambers with lathers[1] instead of stairs, and certain cellars under the ground very good and paved, which are made for winter, they are like stones; and the lathers when they are high for their houses are in a manner movable and portable, which are taken away and set down where they please, and they are made of two pieces of wood with their stepps, as ours are. The seven cities are seven small towns, all made with these kind of houses that I speak of, and they stand all within four leagues together, and they are all called the kingdom of Civola,[2] and every one of them have their particular name, and none of them is called Civola, but altogether are called Civola; and this town which I call a city I have named Granada, as well because it is somewhat like it, and also in remembrance of your lordship. In this town where I now remain there may be some two hundred houses, all compassed with walls, and I think that with

1 Old English spelling for ladders. Observe the word "lath" hidden in "lathers."

2 The Civola of Hakluyt is the Cibola and Cevola of the other writers. The change between b and v is not unfrequent.

the rest of the houses which are not walled, there may be altogether five hundred. There is another town near this, which is one of the seven, and is somewhat larger than this, and another as large, and the other four are somewhat less, and I send them all painted to your lordship with the voyage; and the parchment wherein the picture is was found here with other parchments. The people of this town seem to me of a reasonable stature and witty, yet they seem not to be such as they ought, of that judgment and wit to build these houses such as they are. For the most part they are naked, except their private parts which are covered; and they have painted mantles like those which I send to your lordship. They have no cotton wool growing because the country is cold, yet they wear mantles, as your honor may see by the show thereof, and yet it is true that there was found in their houses certain yarn made of cotton wool. They wear their hair on their heads like those of Mexico, and they are well nurtured and conditioned, and they have a good quantity of turquoises, which with the rest of the goods which they had, except their corn, they had conveyed away before I came thither; for I found no women there, nor no youth under fifteen years old, nor no old folks above sixty, saving two or three old folks, who stayed behind to govern all the rest of the youth and men of war. There were found in a certain paper two points of emeralds and certain small stones broken which are in color somewhat like very bad granates, and other stones of crystal, which I gave one of my servants to lay up to send them to your lordship, and he lost them, as he told me. We found here guinea cocks, but few. The Indians tell me in all these seven cities that they do not

eat them, but they keep them only for their feathers.
I do not believe them, for they are excellently good, and
larger than those of Mexico. The season of this country
and the temperature of the air is like that of Mexico,
for sometimes it is hot and it rains, but hitherto I never
saw it rain, but once there fell a little shower with wind,
as they are wont to fall in Spain. The snow and cold
are wont to be great, as the inhabitants of the country
say, and it is very likely to be so, both in respect to the
manner of the country and by the fashion of their
houses, and their fires and other things which this
people have to protect them from the cold. There is
no kind of fruit nor fruit trees. The country is all plain,
and is on no side mountainous, albeit there are some
hills and bad passages. There are small stores of fowl:
the cause is the cold, and because the mountains are
not near. There is no great store of wood, because they
have sufficient wood for their fuel four leagues off in a
wood of small cedars. There is most excellent grass
within a quarter of a league, for our horses, as well to
feed them in pasture, as to mow and make hay, whereof
we stood in great need, because our horses came hither
so weak and feeble. The victuals which the people of
this country have is maize, whereof they have a great
store, and also small white peas and venison, which by
all likelihood they feed upon (though they say no) for
we found many skins of deer, of hares, and of conies.
They eat the best cakes that I ever saw, and everybody
generally eats them. They have the finest order and
way to grind that we ever saw in any place; and one
Indian woman of this country will grind as much as
four women of Mexico. They have most excellent salt
in kernel, which they fetch from a certain lake a day's

journey from here. They have no knowledge of the North Sea, nor of the Western Sea, neither can I tell to which we be nearest. But in reason they should seem to be nearest to the Western Sea, and at the least I think I am an hundred and fifty leagues from thence, and the Northern Sea should be much farther off. Your lordship may see how broad the land is here. Here are many sorts of beasts, bears, tigers, lions, por-. cupines, and certain sheep as big as an horse, with very great horns and little tails. I have seen their horns so big that it is a wonder to see their greatness. Here are also wild goats, whose beards likewise I have seen, and the paws of bears and the skins of wild boars. There is game of deer, ounces, and very large stags, and all men are of opinion that there are some bigger than that beast which your lordship bestowed upon me, which once belonged to John Melaz. They travel eight days' journey into certain plains lying toward the North Sea. In this country there are certain skins well dressed, and they dress them and paint them where they kill their oxen, so they say themselves.

"The salt," said Uncle Fritz, "was from the great Salt Lake, or some place near it. As for the cakes, see what Lieut. Bourke writes to me. He is in our army now, and has lived among the Moquis, who, as he thinks, still inhabit the towns which Coronado called 'Cibola.'"

And Fergus read from Lieut. Bourke's letter : —

"The Moquis still make very good cakes and still use the stone 'metals' for grinding corn and seeds as their ancestors did in 1541. Their meal is reddish and purplish in color, and the bread or cake is baked as a thin sheet, thinner than pie-crust, and afterwards rolled into the shape of a banana. When I visited them with General Crook in 1874, they used, besides corn, grass-seeds, acorns, and the seeds of sunflowers, which they cultivated in large fields."

VII.

THE JESUIT RELATIONS.

WHEN the children met Col. Ingham the next week, Fergus said that as they came out he had been telling the others that he had always wished that people would tell more of the beginnings of America. "To tell the truth," said Fergus, "I had supposed they did not know; but when we made our camp on the Maguadavik River last summer, when I really felt as if we were the first settlers in a wilderness, I wondered very much whether John Smith did just that thing at Jamestown, or whether he began in some other way."

"We may as well confess," said Col. Ingham, "that our people here were very reticent; also, they seem to have had very little paper, very few pens, and almost no ink. My mother used to say that they must have taken solemn oaths that they would record nothing interesting; and when you do find a bright bit of early New England narrative, it is because some faithful 'modern' has gone over a dozen old stories and picked out one plum here and one there, and put them all into one cake for you.

"But there do exist narratives that go into just the sort of detail you ask for, Fergus. Fortunately for us, the Jesuit fathers, who were the special literary men of their time, were obliged to write letters home from the

points where they were at work, and more fortunately
the Society of Jesuits found it advisable to print them.
Many of these narrations are now very rare. But Mr.
Lenox, who founded the Lenox Library in New York,
and other gentlemen of liberality and spirit like his,
have made every effort to collect them, and some of
them have been reprinted."

"Does not Mr. Parkman quote them?"

"Yes, and his skilful use of them and other materials
like them is what makes his books so fascinating for
you boys. Here is a story of a poor fellow who tried
the hospitality of the Six Nations, — the French, you
know, called them 'Iroquois.'"

"Why, we rode out to see them from Syracuse, when
I made my famous visit to Grace."

"The same. See how they would have treated you a
hundred and fifty years ago had you been a French girl.

"Father Isaac Jogues was born of good family in the
city of Orleans, France. He was sent out into New
France in the year 1636, and was attached to the
Mission among the Hurons, where he stayed for six
years. At the end of this time he was sent to Quebec
on some of the business connected with the Mission
there. The following is his own narrative."

FATHER JOGUES'S STORY.

The Superior of the Huron Mission sent for me and
proposed to me a journey to Quebec, — a terrible journey on account of the difficulty of the travelling there
and back, and also because of the ambuscades of Iroquois, who murder many of the Indians friendly to the
French.

This was merely a proposition, not in any way a command, but I accepted eagerly in spite of all the dangers and hazards. We started off then and began our journey and our dangerous adventures at the same time.

The distance was three hundred leagues, and in this distance we had to make forty carriages of our boats and all our baggage around rapids and waterfalls. Although the Indians were very expert in this method of travelling, we experienced several little shipwrecks which were attended with loss of our baggage and danger to our lives. But at last, after thirty-five days' hard travel, we reached Three Rivers, from which place we descended to Quebec. We finished our business at Quebec in a fortnight, and on the first day of August, 1642, we started from Three Rivers on our homeward voyage. We had passed the first day and night and were proceeding quietly on the second morning when some of the men in the first canoe shouted to us that they had seen some footprints on shore. We all landed and examined the tracks they had seen. We could not agree as to what they were. Some said Iroquois, and others said that they were Algonquins, friends of ours. But Eustace Ahatsistari said : —

"Algonquins or Iroquois it matters little ; there are not more of them than there are of us, so let us go on without fear." Eustace was our captain, and all the rest deferred to him both because of his feats of arms and for his prudence and goodness.

So we went onward, up the river; but we had scarcely got on half a league when a volley of arquebuse balls came upon us from an ambuscade on shore. The Hurons, for the most part, were so frightened at the noise that they abandoned their canoes and their arms

and fled into the depths of the woods. Otherwise the
discharge did us small harm, for only one Huron was
wounded, and he but slightly in his hand.

There were four of us Frenchmen, one of whom had
escaped with the Hurons, and eight or ten Christian
Indians, and together we made such head against the
enemy that, although it was thirty to ten or a dozen, the
issue would have been doubtful had not another band
of forty Iroquois, who were hiding on the other side of
the river, opened fire upon us.

Upon this the Hurons lost courage, and those who
could fled, abandoning their comrades to the enemy.
One Frenchman, René Goupil, being left alone, was
surrounded and captured, together with some of the
brave Hurons. I also was taken and so was our brave
Captain Eustace. One other Frenchman who had been
captured, seeing an opportunity, escaped, but suddenly
the thought coming to him that he was abandoning his
Faith and his comrades, he stopped short and determined to come back to us. But as he turned he saw
five of the Iroquois rushing up to him. One of them
aimed his arquebuse at him but missed. The Frenchman's piece did not miss, and the Indian fell back stone-
dead. As soon as he had fired the other four Indians
threw themselves upon him with the madness of lions,
or rather of devils. They beat him with clubs, they bit
him with their teeth, they tore him with their nails and
transfixed him with their swords. As I approached him
to give him some comfort they fell upon me also and
used me badly. In fact, so enraged were they against
the French that they cruelly tortured René Goupil and
me also, biting our fingers with their teeth in a terrible
manner and beating us with sticks.

Finally they all came together again. Those who had been chasing the Hurons returned, and they began all together to rejoice over their prey with loud shouts of joy.

We started, then, to be conducted into a strange country. One old man refused to embark when the Iroquois took to their boats, and the Indians murdered him. There were twenty-two of us in all. For the thirteen days which were taken up in the journey I suffered almost insupportable bodily tortures and mental distresses beyond comparison. Hunger, the glowing heat, the threats and hatred of these leopards, the pain of our wounds,— all these were nothing to the inward grief that I felt at the thought of our Hurons, all firm Christians. I had thought that they would have been the support of this growing Church, and I saw them condemned to death.

A week after we left the banks of the great River St. Lawrence we fell in with two hundred Iroquois who had just returned from an excursion against the French and their Indian allies. As soon as they saw us they thanked the Sun for having put us in their power, and immediately afterward fired a volley from their arquebuses as a salute to the victors. They then sought out a level plain upon the hill and then went to find clubs and thorny sticks. Thus armed they placed themselves in two rows, one hundred on one side and one hundred on the other, and having stripped us of our clothing they forced us to pass through this path of pain and anguish. As we ran by they delivered lusty blows upon our backs with all their strength. They made me run last that I might be the more exposed to their rage. I had hardly run half-way when I fell to the ground from the pain and from the blows. Seeing this the Indians redoubled their efforts. I was unable to force myself to rise, partly through my weakness and partly because I thought I might as well die there. Seeing me fall they threw themselves upon me, and God alone knows how long they beat me. But when they saw that I had not fallen by accident and that I was really too near death to arise, since their anger was not yet appeased, and also because they wished to carry me alive into their own country, they picked me up and carried me, all bleeding, out of the torture, but soon began again to ill-treat me. It would take too long to tell of the sufferings they inflicted upon me. They broke one of my fingers, they crushed the others with their teeth, and also tore my flesh by their nails, with the rage of demons, and when my strength failed me they applied fire to my arms and legs. They treated my companions in like manner. Among the Hurons the brave and valiant christian, Eustace, was treated most cruelly.

These warriors having offered up a sacrifice of our blood pursued their way, and we went ours. On the tenth day after our departure we arrived at a place where we quitted our boats to march on land. This part of the journey was very painful. The Iroquois who had charge of me, having more baggage than he could carry easily, placed a heavy load upon my own back, torn and mangled as it was. For three days we ate nothing but berries which we picked as we went along. The heat of the day, at the hottest part of the summer, and the pain of our wounds weakened us so that we had to march behind the rest. One night when we were a little way from the others I suggested to René Goupil that he should escape. In fact we might have done it, but for my part I would rather have suffered all kinds of torment than have abandoned those whom I might have been able to console. René, seeing that I wished to follow my little flock, would not quit me. "I will die with you," said he, "and I will never abandon you."

One night we arrived at a little river distant about a quarter of a league from the first village of the Iroquois. We found on the banks an assemblage of men and boys armed with sticks with which they beat us with their usual cruelty. I had on my hands but two finger-nails left. These they tore off with their teeth, cutting the flesh to the bone with their own long finger-nails.

After they had satisfied their cruelty they carried us in triumph into the first village, where all the young people were without the gates ranged in rows, armed with sticks, some of them with iron tips which they got from the Dutch. We had to march around among those young people and receive beatings and torturings like those I have described to you. When night had come they brought us to the cabins to be sport for the children. They gave us a little Indian meal boiled in water. They made us lie down, binding us, hand and foot, to four posts stuck in the ground, in the form of a Saint Andrew's Cross. The children, to teach further cruelty to their parents, threw live coals and hot ashes upon our stomachs, taking pleasure in seeing our flesh grill and blacken. O God! what a night! To remain in a very constrained position without the power of moving, to be unable to defend ourselves from the attack of the thousands of vermin which assailed us from every side, to be still suffering from recent wounds, to have nothing on which to sustain life,— in truth, these are grave torments, but God is over all. At sunrise they carried us out again, and for three days and three nights we endured tortures which I have been trying to describe.

We passed in this way through these villages, and in each village we were beaten and tortured terribly. Finally they allowed us to settle down and try to cure our wounds.

. . . . .

When these poor captives had got back a little of their strength, the chiefs of the country began to talk of sending them back to Three Rivers to return them to the French. The business went so far that they considered that it was all arranged; but finally the chiefs found that they could not agree as to the terms, and so the Father and his companions were left as before, in the fear each moment that they would be put to death.

These barbarians have the custom of giving the prisoners, whom they do not wish to put to death, to those families who have lost some of their number in war. These persons take the place of the dead and become members of the family, which alone holds the power of life and death over them. In such cases no one else dares to do anything to them; but when they keep some one as public prisoner, without giving him to any one in particular, the poor man is at all times in danger of instant death. If some wretch kills him, no one cares. He is only enabled to drag on his miserable life through the charity of those who take pity on him. In such a condition was our good Father, and so also was one of his companions. The other Frenchmen had been given to a family in place of an Iroquois warrior who had fallen in battle. . . .

The Father's narrative goes on : —

I left the village in which I was held captive, on Saint Ignatius' day, to go with some Iroquois on an excursion for trading and fishing. After we had finished our business with the Dutch we set to fishing at a place on the river seven or eight leagues below the Dutch village. While we were cleaning the fish we had caught, there came a report that a band of Iroquois had returned from an expedition against the Hurons, of whom they had killed five or six and captured four. Of these four prisoners they had burned two in my village with great cruelties. At this my heart was weighed down with a bitter regret that I had neither been able to see these poor victims nor to console and baptize them. I feared too that something of the sort might happen again, and I therefore went to an old woman who had been very kind to me and said to her : —

" My aunt, I wish to return to our village. I cannot stay here. It is not that I expect to be treated more kindly at the village, where indeed I am daily exposed to every species of torture and am compelled to be witness of most horrible cruelties, but my heart tells me that I should allow no man to suffer death without endeavoring to offer him baptism."

She approved of my words and gave me something to eat on the road. I embarked in the first canoe that was going up the river to our village, accompanied and conducted by five or six Iroquois. When we had reached the Dutch on the river, I learned that our village was much incensed against all the French, and that they only awaited my return in order to burn me alive.

The cause of this was as follows. Some time ago, among all the bands of Iroquois who were continually going upon the war-path against the Algonquins, the Hurons, and the French, there was one band which took the idea of going to spy out the French and their savage allies. Among this band was a Huron who had been captured by the Iroquois and had been adopted into the tribe. This man came to me to ask if I had any letters to send to the French, hoping no doubt to get some information in this way. But as I did not doubt that the French would be upon their guard against him, and moreover as I thought it very necessary that the French should know something of the plans and designs of their enemies, I found means of procuring a bit of paper upon which to write a message. I knew very well the danger to which I exposed myself, and I knew too that if anything should happen to these warriors the blame would fall upon me; that they would hold me responsible and would accuse my letters. I foresaw that I should be put to death, but death seemed to me easy and agreeable when I reflected that it would be used for the well-being and consolation of the French, and the poor Indians who learn from them the word of the Lord. I gave, then, my letter to the young warrior, who never returned. The story that his comrades brought back was that he had carried the letter to the fort of Richelieu, and that as soon as the French had caught sight of them they had fired a cannon at them so that they had fled, scattering in all directions, leaving one of their canoes, together · with their guns and powder and ball and some other baggage.

When these news were brought to the village they cried out that my letters were the cause of this treatment. The report went around and at last came to my ears; they reproached me with their bad luck and spoke of nothing but burning me, and if I had been at the village at the return of the warriors, fire, rage, and cruelty would have cost me my life. Unhappily another band returning from Montreal, where they had been beaten by the French, told of one of their men who had been killed and two who were wounded. Everybody considered me the cause of this ill-luck and was awaiting my return with impatience.

To resume my story. The Captain of the post of Dutch, where we were at this time, knowing pretty well the state of the Indians' mind toward me, and knowing too that the Chevalier de Montmagny had forbidden the Indians of New France to make any attacks upon the Dutch, showed me the means of saving myself. "Here," said he to me, "here is a ship at anchor which is to sail in a few days. Get into it quietly. It is going first to Virginia and then to Bordeaux or La Rochelle."

I thanked him much for the offer, but told him the Indians would surely find out that he had assisted me to escape and might cause his people some trouble.

"No, no," said he, "fear nothing, get on board. The chance is good, you will never find a better one."

I was perplexed at his words, doubting whether it would not redound more to the glory of God if I should expose myself to the danger of fire and to the fury of the Iroquois, with the hope of saving some poor soul. I said then to him that I held the occasion to be of such importance that I could not immediately come to a decision, and I begged of him to give me the night to think it over. He was much astonished, but granted my request, and I promised to tell him on the next morning what resolve I had come to.

I spent the night in meditation and prayer, and came at last to the conclusion that it would be more agreeable to God if I should take this chance which was offered me to escape.

When day was come, therefore, I paid my respects to the Dutch Governor and told him my thoughts and the resolution to which I had come. He called the owners of the vessel and told them his plan, begging them to receive and hide me, and, in a word, to carry me back to Europe. They replied that if I could once set foot on the deck of the vessel I might be sure that I should not leave it until I landed at the wharf at Bordeaux or La Rochelle.

"Very well, then," said the Governor to me, "return with your Indians, and towards evening or at night come quietly to the river. You will find a little boat which I shall have placed there that you may go secretly to the ship."

After giving my humble thanks to these gentlemen I went away from the Hollanders that I might the better conceal my plan. At night I retired with ten or a dozen Iroquois into a barn where we were to pass the night. Before lying down I went out of the place to see how I might most easily escape. The dogs of the Hollanders, who were roaming about, seeing me come out, fell upon me. One of them bit a large piece out of my leg, which gave me such pain that I returned as soon as possible into the barn. The Iroquois immediately shut the door tightly and lay down round about me. There was one of them whose duty it was to take especial care in guarding me, and he lay down in front of the door of the barn.

Seeing myself shut up in this way I feared that I

might never be able to escape. I passed all this night
without sleep, and in the morning I heard the crowing
of the cocks. Soon after, the servant of a Dutch work-
man, who had given us shelter in his barn, entered by
some door, I know not what. I made him a sign softly,
since I did not understand Flemish, to drive away the
dogs. He went out and I after him, taking all my baggage, namely, a breviary and a crucifix. As soon as I got
out of the barn, without making any noise or awakening
my guards, I passed through the gate in the fence surrounding the farm and ran straight to the river in which
the ship was at anchor. In doing this I had great difficulty, on account of my wounded leg, but finally accomplished the distance, and found the boat, as the captain
had told me. But unfortunately the tide had gone down,
and the boat was high and dry on land. I could not
push it into the water on account of its weight, and so I
shouted out to the ship. I do not know whether they
heard me or not; at any rate, nobody appeared.

The sun was by this time rising and would soon ap-
prise the Iroquois of the theft of myself which I had
made. Fearing that they would find me engaged in my
innocent amusement I left off shouting, and, praying God
to increase my strength, I applied myself once more to
the boat. I did so well that I soon got the stern in the
water and after that the rest of it. Having got it afloat,
I jumped into it, and rowed quickly to the ship without
being perceived by any of the Iroquois.

The sailors put me down in the hold to hide me, and
I passed two days in the ship in such an uncomfortable
manner that I feared each minute that I should die of
suffocation. I remembered in this plight the story of
Jonas in the belly of the whale.

On the second night of my captivity the Dutch minister visited me to tell me that the Iroquois were making a great disturbance about my disappearance, and that the Hollanders living around were afraid that they would burn down their houses and kill their beasts. They had good ground for this fear, for the Indians were provided with good arquebuses. I besought him to give me up to them if on account of me all this tumult was arising, and told him that I never had wished to save myself at the risk of others' lives and goods.

Finally I came up from my hiding-place, and though the sailors were much ashamed, saying that they had given their word that I should be saved and that they must hold to it at all costs, I went on shore to the Governor's house, where they concealed me. These goings and comings were achieved in the night so that I was not discovered. The Dutch Captain told me that it was necessary to yield to the storm and wait until the spirits of the Indians were a little calmed. So I am now a voluntary prisoner in the house of the Governor. The ship in which I was to sail has gone without me.

In another letter : —

Finally I am delivered. The Lord has sent one of his angels to take me out of captivity. The Iroquois have finally become pacified by the Dutch Governor, who gave them presents as a ransom to the amount, I believe, of three hundred livres, which I must return to him. When everything was straightened out I was sent to Manhattan, where the Governor of the whole country resides. He received me kindly, gave me a suit of clothes, and sent me across the ocean in a bark. We landed in Falmouth in England, and from thence I crossed over to France.

"Poor man!" said Laura, when the reading was done. "I do not wonder the frontier's people came to hate the Indians."

"It is worth while," said Uncle Fritz, "when you hear people talk of Arcadian homes and the simplicity of nature to know what those words mean."

The Pictorial History is generally lying on the table, or brought out before these American readings are finished; and Tom had the third volume open at the picture of the massacre at Schenectady, where two snow sentinels stood at the gateway of the palisades, and made no opposition to the French and Indians when they rushed in.

"This was long after Father Jogues, I suppose," he said.

"Oh, yes. The massacre did not happen until Leister's time, in the winter of 1689–90; and, by the way, one of the most vivid of the genuine American ballads was printed in Albany then and there about that massacre."

"Where do you find about it, Uncle Fritz?"

"Oh, there is no local history better provided for than that of New York. Look there, on the lower shelf; there are twelve volumes of their documents which you owe to Mr. Bogart's kindness."

The children had learned by this time not to dread a book because it was big and had a dull name, and the various tables soon had different groups dipping through the big volumes Letters of priests; letters of Indians, with their marks in place of signatures; quarrels of governors with their people; the awful tragedy when Leister was executed; Captain Kidd and all his history, — unfolded themselves in the manner in which they were written down at the time; buried for a hundred years and more in archive-rooms, and then brought to light again. The children read a scrap here and a scrap there with fearful violation of chronology, but gaining just the "color" for the history which letters written at the time give, and which nothing else gives. Nothing is more surprising to young readers than to see how very small were the beginnings of an American State. Through the period of the century between Father Jogues and 1736 the whole population of the State of New York was a mere handful, Schenectady a frontier town, and Albany an insignificant fort.

The young people were surprised when the bell rang for tea. Hester confessed, as she walked out with Uncle Fritz, that there had been times when she should not have thought that she could have found half an hour's amusement in reading old documents. "I owe that to you, Uncle Fritz," she said prettily.

"Perhaps I have taught you how to skip," he said. "That is one of the greatest of accomplishments."

Here are two verses of the old ballad : —

> "From forth the woods of Canada
>   The Frenchmen tooke their Way
>   The People of Schenectady
>   To captivate and slay.

> "They march'd for two & twenty Dais
>   All through the deepest Snow;
>   And on a dismal Winter Night
>   They strucke the Cruel Blow."

VIII

NORTHERN DISCOVERIES.

ON New Year's Day, after the children had given their pretty presents to Uncle Fritz, and after he had shown them his New Year's cards and other greetings, he asked if they had brought anything to read.

"We are all alive about the Indians," said Laura. "We have seen Miss La Flesche, who is lovely, and we have heard her talk Indian. She never would have roasted Father Jogues by a slow fire. Is she the same sort as the Iroquois?"

Uncle Fritz sent for the second volume of the Archæologia Americana, and showed them Mr. Gallatin's map of the United States, and the division of it into nine great Indian families. Fergus said the map was copied in a volume of Bancroft's History. The children saw that the Massachusetts Indians are Algonkins, or, as Mr. Gallatin says, Algonkin-Lenape. The Iroquois, who were so cruel to the poor Jesuit Father, are of another race.

"I am glad," said Blanche, "that it was no cousin of my nice Waban who did such awful things."

Blanche lives on Waban Street, though the sign-painters spell it Wabon.

Uncle Fritz said grimly that he was glad Blanche knew he was "nice." The children saw that the Algon-

kin family covered most of the United States north of
the Gulf States and east of the Mississippi, excepting
New York and most of Pennsylvania, where were Iroquois tribes; and that there were Iroquois tribes west
of the Niagara in the peninsula of Canada. They saw
that the Algonkins extended far north, half up the side
of Hudson's Bay.

"But, you know," said Uncle Fritz, "that they are
all great wanderers. You may catch a bit of dialect
thousands of miles off from the tribe where you first
found it. When Mr. Bartlett was on the frontier of
Mexico, he happened to notice a sort of 'click,' like
the Zulu 'click,' in the language of the Apaches, the
roving horsemen of those regions. Mr. Bartlett is a
very accurate linguist, and he remembered that Dr.
Richardson said of the Athapescans on the Arctic
Ocean that they had such a 'click.' He looked in
their vocabularies, and he found they used some of the
same words the Apaches did. These Apaches had
strayed away from them, nobody knows when."

"Apache sounds like Athapescan," said Fergus; and
Uncle Fritz nodded approval of the bold etymology.

"Well, then," said Tom Rising, "I suppose any of
these people painted yellow on the map, these Chip-
peways and the rest, can read your Eliot's Bible, Uncle
Fritz."

"No, my boy, that is asking too much. For the
Massachusetts dialect and Eliot's spelling of it are now
two hundred years old, and probably always our Indians
differed from the Hudson's Bay Indians, for instance,
as much as Italians from Frenchmen. Still Eliot's
grammar and dictionary are useful now to the missionaries among any Algonkin tribes."

The children began comparing words in the vocabulary in Mr. Gallatin's book, and trying to learn them. Here is the Indian for "man," from one language of each of the nine great Eastern races. Mr. Gallatin gives specimens of forty-four languages, which are all grouped under these nine divisions : —

MAN in a language of

Eskimaux	is	TUAK.
Athapescans	is	TENNEE.
Algonkins	is	WOSKETOMP.

And, among Algonkins, the children took the Massachusetts language, so as to know what Blanche's "nice" Waban said.

Iroquois	is	UNGUOH.
Sioux	is	WONGAHAH.
Catawbas	is	YABRECHA.
Cherokees	is	ASKAYA.
Choctaws	is	HOTTOK NOKNI.
Muskhogees	is	ISTAHOUANUAH.

The *Pawnees*, west of these divisions, called " man " TSAEKSH.

" And now," said Uncle Fritz, who had been looking among his Arctic books, " if you want to find about your nice Algonkins of Hudson's Bay and their neighbors, look at my marks in Hearne's Travels here."

" I remember in an old atlas the Arctic Ocean was marked ' Sea seen by Mr. Hearne.' "

" This is that man. On the night between July 17 and July 18, 1771, while your grandfather, Tom, was discussing with other assembly-men here in Boston, how they should circumvent Gov. Hutchinson, Hearne, by the light of a sun which was above the horizon, was making the drawing from which this map which I showed you was made. And I am sorry to say your 'nice' Algonkins, who were with him, were destroying some tents they found of Northern Indians.

"Now you will find some curious things in Hearne's book."

And the children followed Uncle Fritz's book-marks and read these passages : —

When on the northwest side of Seal River I asked Captain Chawchinahaw the distance and probable time it would take before we could reach the main woods, which he assured me would not exceed four or five days' journey. This put both me and my companions in good spirits, and we continued our course between the west by north and northwest, in daily expectation of arriving at those woods, which we were told would furnish us with everything the country affords. These accounts were so far from being true that, after we had walked double the time here mentioned, no signs of woods were to be seen in the direction we were then steering, but we had frequently seen the looming of woods to the southwest.

The cold being now very intense, our small stock of English provisions all expended, and not the least thing to be got on the bleak hills, we had for some time been walking on ; it became necessary to strike more to the westward, which we accordingly did, and the next evening arrived at some small patches of low, scrubby woods, where we saw the tracks of several deer and killed a few partridges. The road we had traversed for many days before was in general so rough and stony that our sledges were daily breaking, and to add to the inconveniency the land was so barren as not to afford us materials for repairing them; but the few woods we now fell in with amply supplied us with necessaries for those repairs, and as we were then enabled each night to pitch proper tents, our lodging was much more comfortable than it had been for many nights before while we were on the barren grounds, where, in general, we thought ourselves well off if we could scrape together as many shrubs as would make a fire. But it was scarcely ever in our power to make any other defence against the weather than by digging a hole in the snow down to the moss, wrapping ourselves up in our clothing and lying down in it, with our sledges set up edgeways to windward. . . . By this time I found that Captain Chawchinahaw had not the prosperity of the undertaking at heart; he often painted the difficulties in the worst colors, took every method to dishearten me and my European companions, and several times hinted his desire of our returning back to the factory. But, finding I was determined to proceed he took such methods as he thought would be most likely to answer his end; one of which was that of not administering toward our support, so that we were a considerable time without any other subsistence but what our two home-guard Indians procured, and the little that I and the two European men could kill, which was very disproportionate to our wants, as we had to provide for several women and children who were with us. Chawchinahaw finding that this kind of treatment was not likely to complete his design, and that we were not to be starved into compliance, at length influenced several of the best Northern Indians to desert in the night, who took with them several bags of my ammunition, some pieces of iron-work,

such as hatchets, ice-chisels, files, etc., as well as several
other useful articles. When I became acquainted with
this piece of villany, I asked Chawchinahaw the reason
of such behavior. To which he answered that he knew
nothing of the affair, but as that was the case it would
not be prudent, he said, for us to proceed any farther,
adding that he and all the rest of his countrymen were
going to strike off another way in order to join the
remainder of their wives and families; and, after giving
us a short account of how to steer our course for the
nearest part of Seal River, which he said would be our
best way homeward, he and his crew delivered me most
of the things they had in charge, packed up their awls,
and set out toward the southwest, making the woods
ring with laughter, and left us to consider our unhappy
situation, near two hundred miles from Prince of Wales's
fort, all heavily laden, and our strength and spirits
greatly reduced by hunger and fatigue. Our situation
at that time, though very alarming, would not permit us
to spend much time in reflection, so we loaded our
sledges to the best advantage, but were obliged to throw
away some bags of shot and ball, and immediately set
out on our return. In the course of the day's walk we
were fortunate enough to kill several partridges, for
which we were all very thankful, as it was the first meat
we had had for several days; indeed, for the five preceding days we had not killed as much as amounted to
half a partridge for each man, and some days had not a
single mouthful. While we were in this distress the
Northern Indians were by no means in want, for as
they always walked foremost they had ten times the
chance to kill partridges, rabbits, or any other thing
which was to be met with than we had. Besides this

advantage they had great stocks of flour, oatmeal, and other English provisions, which they had embezzled out of my stock during the early part of the journey, and as one of my home Indians, called Mackachy, and his wife, who is a Northern Indian woman, always resorted to the Northern Indians' tents, where they got amply supplied with provisions when neither I nor my men had a single mouthful, I have great reason to suspect they had a principal hand in the embezzlement; indeed, both the man and his wife were capable of committing any crime, however diabolical. In our course down Seal River we met a stranger, a Northern Indian, on a hunting excursion, and though he had not met with any success that day yet he kindly invited us to his tent, saying he had plenty of venison at my service, and told the Southern Indians that as there were two or three beaver houses near his tent, he should be glad of their assistance in taking them, for there was only one man with three women at the tent.

Though we were at that time far from being in want of provisions, yet we accepted his offer, and set off with our new guide for his tent, which, by a comparative distance, he told us, was not above five miles from the place where we met him, but we found it to be nearer fifteen, so that it was the middle of the night before we arrived at it. When we drew near the tent the usual signal for the approach of strangers was given by firing a gun or two, which was immediately answered by the man at the tent. On our arrival at the door the good man of the house came out, shook me by the hand, and welcomed us to his tent, but as it was too small to contain us all he ordered his women to assist us in pitching our tent, and in the mean time invited me and as many

of my crew as his little habitation could contain, and
regaled us with the best in the house. The pipe went
round pretty briskly, and the conversation naturally
turned on the treatment we had received from Chawchinahaw and his gang, which was always answered by
our host with "Ah! if I had been there, it should not
have been so!" But, notwithstanding his hospitality
on the present occasion, he would most assuredly have
acted the same part as the others had done, if he had
been of the party. . . .

When the Indians design to impound deer they look
out for one of the paths in which a number of them
have trod, and which is observed to be still frequented
by them. When these paths cross a lake, a wide river,
or a barren plain, they are found to be much the best
for the purpose, and if the path run through a cluster
of woods capable of affording materials for building a
pound, it adds considerably to the commodiousness of
the situation. The pound is built by making a strong
fence with brushy trees, without observing any degree
of regularity, and the work is continued to any extent,
according to the pleasure of the builders. I have seen
some that were not less than a mile round, and am
informed that there are others still more extensive.
The door, or entrance of the pound, is not larger than
a common gate, and the inside is so crowded with small
counter-hedges as very much to resemble a maze, in
every opening of which they set a snare, made with
thongs of parchment deer-skins well twisted together,
which are amazingly strong. One end of the snare is
usually made fast to a growing pole, but if no one of a
sufficient size can be found near the place where the
snare is to be set, a loose pole is substituted in its room,

which is always of such size and length that a deer cannot drag it far before it gets entangled among the other woods, which are all left standing except what is found necessary for making the fence, hedges, etc.

The pound being thus prepared, a row of small brushwood is stuck up in the snow on each side the door or entrance, and these hedge-rows are continued along the open part of the lake, river, or plain, where neither stick nor stump besides is to be seen, which makes them the more distinctly observed. These poles, or brushwood, are generally placed at the distance of fifteen or twenty yards from each other, and ranged in such a manner as to form two sides of a long acute angle, growing gradually wider in proportion to the distance they extend from the entrance of the pound, which sometimes is not less than two or three miles; while the deer's path is exactly along the middle, between the two rows of brushwood. Indians employed on this service always pitch their tent on or near an eminence that affords a commanding prospect of the path leading to the pound, and when they see any deer going that way, men, women, and children walk along the lake or riverside under cover of the woods till they get behind them, then step forth to open view, and proceed towards the pound in the form of a crescent. The poor timorous deer, finding themselves pursued and at the same time taking the two rows of brushy poles to be two ranks of people stationed to prevent their passing on either side, run straight forward in the path till they get into the pound. The Indians then close in and block up the entrance with some bushy trees that have been cut down and lie at hand for that purpose. The deer being thus enclosed the women and children walk round the pound to prevent them from breaking or jumping over the fence, while the men are employed spearing such as are entangled in the snares, and shooting with bows and arrows those which remain loose in the pound. . . .

Agreeably to my instructions, I smoked my calumet of peace with the Copper Indians, who seemed highly pleased on the occasion ; and, from a conversation held on the subject of my journey, I found they were delighted with the hopes of having a European settlement in the neighborhood, and seemed to have no idea that any impediment could prevent such a scheme from being carried into execution. Climates and seasons had no weight with them, nor could they see where the difficulty lay in getting there ; for though they acknowledged that they had never seen the sea at the mouth of the Copper River clear of ice, yet they could see nothing that should hinder a ship from approaching it, and they innocently enough observed that the water was always so smooth between the ice and shore that even small boats might get there with great ease and safety. How a ship was to get between the ice and the shore never once occurred to them.

Whether from hospitality, or from the great advantages which they expected to reap by my discoveries, I know not ; but I must confess that their civility far exceeded what I could expect from so uncivilized a tribe, and I was exceedingly sorry that I had nothing of value to offer them. However, such articles as I had I distributed among them, and they were thankfully received by them. Though they have some European commodities among them, which they purchase from the Northern Indians, the same articles from the hands of an Englishman were more prized. As I was the first whom they had ever seen, and in all probability might be the last, it was curious to see how they flocked about me, and expressed as much desire to examine me from top to toe as a European naturalist would a nondescript animal. They, however, found and pronounced me to be a perfect human being, except in the color of my hair and eyes; the former, they said, was like the stained hair of a buffalo's tail, and the latter, being light, were like those of a gull. The whiteness of my skin also was, in their opinion, no ornament, as they said it resembled meat which had been sodden in water till all the blood was extracted. On the whole, I was viewed as so great a curiosity in this part of the world that during my stay there, whenever I combed my head, some or other of them never failed to ask for the hairs that came off, which they carefully wrapped up, saying, " When I see you again, you shall see your hair." . . .

When a friend for whom they have a particular regard is, as they suppose, dangerously ill, they have recourse to another extraordinary superstition, which is no less than that of pretending to swallow hatchets, ice-chisels, broad bayonets, knives, and the like, out of a superstitious notion that undertaking such desperate feats will have some influence in appeasing death, and procure a respite for their patient. On such extraordinary occasions a conjuring-house is erected, by driving the ends of four long small sticks, or poles, into the ground at right angles, so as to form a square of four, five, six, or seven feet, as may be required. The tops of the poles are tied together, and all is close covered with a tent-cloth or other skin, exactly in the shape of a small square tent, except that there is no vacancy left at the top to admit the light. In the middle of this tent the patient is laid, and is soon followed by the conjuror or conjurors. Sometimes five or six of them give their joint assistance, but before they enter they strip themselves quite naked, and as soon as they get into the house, the door being well closed, they kneel round the sick person and begin to blow at the parts affected, and then in a very short space of time sing and talk as if conversing with familiar spirits, which they say appear to them in the shape of different beasts and birds of prey. When they have had sufficient conference with those necessary agents, or shadows, as they term them, they ask for the hatchet, bayonet, or the like, which is always prepared by another person with a long string fastened to it by the haft, for the convenience of hauling it up again after they have swallowed it, for they very wisely admit this to be a necessary precaution, as hard and compact bodies, such as iron and steel, would be very hard to digest, even by the men who are enabled to swallow them. Besides, as those tools are in themselves very useful, and not always to be procured, it would be very ungenerous in the conjurers to digest them, when it is known that barely swallowing them and hauling them up again is fully sufficient to answer every purpose that is expected from them.

At the time when the forty and odd tents of Indians joined us, one man was so dangerously ill, that it was thought necessary the conjurers should use some of those wonderful experiments for his recovery; one of them therefore immediately consented to swallow a broad bayonet. Accordingly, a conjuring-house was erected in the manner above described, into which the patient was conveyed, and he was soon followed by the conjurer, who, after a long preparatory discourse, and the necessary conference with the familiar spirits, or shadows, as they call them, advanced to the door and asked for the bayonet, which was then ready prepared, by having a string tied to it, and a short piece of wood tied to the other end of the string to prevent him from swallowing it. I could not help observing that the length of the bit of wood was not more than the breadth of the bayonet; however, as it answered the intended purpose, it did equally well as if it had been as long as a handspike. Though I am not so credulous as to believe that the conjurer absolutely swallowed the bayonet, yet I must acknowledge that in the twinkling of an eye he conveyed it to — God knows where; and the small piece of wood, or one exactly like it, was confined close to his teeth. He then paraded back and forth before the conjuring-house for a short time, when he feigned to be greatly distressed in his stomach and bowels; and, after making many wry faces, and groaning most hideously, he put his body into several distorted attitudes very suitable to the occasion. He then returned to the door of the conjuring-house, and after making many strong efforts to vomit, by the help of the string he at length, and after tugging at it for some time, produced the bayonet, which apparently he hauled out of his mouth, to the no small surprise of all present. He then looked round with an air of exultation and strutted into the house, where he renewed his incantations, and continued them without intermission twenty-four hours. Though I was not close to his elbow when he performed the above feat, yet I thought myself near enough to have detected him. Indeed, I must confess that it appeared to me to be a very nice piece of deception, especially as it was performed by a man quite naked.

Not long after this sleight-of-hand work was over some of the Indians asked me what I thought of it, to which I answered that I was too far off to see it so plain as I could wish, which indeed was no more than the strictest truth, because I was not near enough to detect the deception. The sick man, however, soon recovered, and in a few days afterwards we left that place and proceeded to the southwest.[1] . . .

I do not remember to have met with any travellers into high northern latitudes who remarked their having heard the Northern Lights make any noise in the air as they vary their colors or position, which may probably be owing to the want of perfect silence at the time they made their observations. I can positively affirm that in still nights I have frequently heard them make a rustling sound and crackling noise, like the waving of a large flag in a fresh gale of wind. This is not peculiar to the place of which I am now writing, as I have heard the same noise very plain at Churchill River, and in all probability it is only for want of attention that it has not been heard in every part of the northern hemisphere where they have been known to shine with any degree of lustre. . . .

The beaver being so plentiful the attention of my companions was chiefly engaged on them, as they not only furnished delicious food, but their skins proved a valuable acquisition, being a principal article of trade as well as a serviceable one for clothing, etc. The situation of the beaver-houses is various. Where the beavers are numerous they are found to inhabit lakes, ponds, and rivers, as well as those narrow creeks which

[1] Mr. Hearne afterwards gives rather a lame explanation of the least important part of this trick.

onnect the numerous lakes with which this country
bounds, but the two latter are generally chosen by
hem when the depth of water and other circumstances
re suitable, as they have then the advantage of a cur-
ent to convey wood and other necessaries to their
abitations, and because, in general, they are more
ifficult to be taken than those that are built in stand-
1g water.

There is no one particular part of a lake, pond,
iver, or creek, of which the beavers make choice for
uilding their houses on, in preference to another, for
1ey sometimes build on points, sometimes in the hol-
)w of a bay, and often on small islands; they always
hoose, however, those parts that have such a depth of
ater as will resist the frost in winter and prevent it
om freezing to the bottom. The beavers that build
1eir houses in small rivers or creeks, in which the
ater is liable to be drained off when the back supplies
re dried up by the frost, are wonderfully taught by
1stinct to provide against that evil by making a dam
uite across the river, at a convenient distance from
heir houses. This I look upon as the most curious
iece of workmanship that is performed by the beaver;
ot so much for the neatness of the work as for its
trength and real service, and at the same time it dis-
overs such a degree of sagacity and foresight in the
nimal of approaching evils as is little inferior to that
f the human species, and is certainly peculiar to those
nimals.

The beaver-dams differ in shape according to the na-
ure of the place in which they are built. If the
ater in the river or creek have but little motion the
am is almost straight, but when the current is more

rapid it is always made with a considerable curve, convex toward the stream. The materials made use of in those dams are drift-wood, green willows, birch, and poplars, if they can be got, also mud and stones intermixed in such a manner as must evidently contribute to the strength of the dam, but in these dams there is no other order or method observed, except that of the work being carried on with a regular sweep, and all the parts being made of equal strength. In places which have long been frequented by beavers undisturbed, their dams by frequent repairing become a solid bank, capable of resisting a great force both of water and ice, and as the willow, poplar, and birch generally take root and shoot up, they by degrees form a kind of regular-planted hedge, which I have seen in some places so tall that birds have built their nests among the branches.

Though the beaver which build their houses in lakes and other standing waters may enjoy a sufficient quantity of their favorite element without the assistance of a dam, the trouble of getting wood and other necessaries to their habitations without the help of a current must, in some measure, counterbalance the other advantages which are reaped from such a situation, for it must be observed that the beaver which build in rivers and creeks always cut their wood above their houses so that the current, with little trouble, conveys it to the place required.

The beaver-houses are built of the same materials as their dams and are always proportioned in size to the number of inhabitants, which seldom exceed four old and six or eight young ones; though, by chance I have seen above double that number. These houses, though not altogether unworthy of admiration, fall very

short of the general description of them; for, instead
of order or regulation being observed in rearing them,
they are of a much ruder structure than their dams.

Those who have undertaken to describe the inside of
beaver-houses as having several apartments appropriated
to various uses, such as eating, sleeping, store-houses
for provisions, etc., must have been very little acquainted
with the subject, or, which is still worse, guilty of attempting to impose on the credulous by representing the greatest falsehoods as facts. Many years residence among
the Indians, during which I had an opportunity of seeing
hundreds of these houses, has enabled me to affirm that
everything of the kind is entirely void of truth; for,
notwithstanding the sagacity of those animals, it has
never been observed that they aim at any other conveniences in their houses than to have a dry place to lie
on, and there they usually eat their victuals which they
occasionally take out of the water. It frequently happens that some of the large houses are found to have
one or more partitions, if they deserve that appellation,
but that is no more than a part of the main building
left by the sagacity of the beaver to support the roof.
On such occasions it is common for those different
apartments, as some are pleased to call them, to have
no communication with each other except by water; so
that in fact they may be called double or treble houses
rather than different apartments of the same house. I
have seen a large beaver-house built in a small island
that had near a dozen apartments under one roof; and,
two or three of these only excepted, none of them had
any communication with each other but by water. As
there were beaver enough to inhabit each apartment it
is more than probable that each family knew its own,

and always entered at their own door, without having any further connection with their neighbors than a friendly intercourse, and to join their united labors in erecting their separate habitations and building their dams where required. It is difficult to say whether their interest on other occasions was anyways reciprocal.

Travellers who assert that the beaver have two doors to their houses, one on the land side and the other next the water, seem to be less acquainted with those animals than others who assign them an elegant suite of apartments. Such a proceeding would be quite contrary to their manner of life, and at the same time would render their houses of no use, either to protect them from their enemies or guard them against the extreme cold of winter.

The quiquepatches or wolverines are great enemies to the beaver, and if there were a passage into their houses on the land side would not leave one of them alive wherever they came. I cannot refrain from smiling when I read the accounts of different authors who have written on the economy of these animals, as there seems to be a contest between them who shall most exceed in fiction. But the " Compiler of Wonders of Nature and Art " seems, in my opinion, to have succeeded best in this respect, as he has not only collected all the fictions into which other writers on the subject have run, but has so greatly improved on them that little remains to be added to his account of the beaver, beside a vocabulary of their language, a code of their laws, and a sketch of their religion, to make it the most complete natural history of that animal that can possibly be offered to the public. . . . To deny that the beaver

is possessed of a very considerable degree of sagacity
would be as absurd in me as it is in those authors who
think they cannot allow them too much. I shall willingly grant them their full share, but it is impossible
for any one to conceive how, or by what means, a
beaver, whose whole height when standing erect does
not exceed two feet and a half, or three feet at most,
and whose fore-paws are not much larger than a half-
crown piece, can "drive stakes as thick as a man's leg
into the ground, three or four feet deep." Their "wat-
tling those stakes with twigs" is equally absurd, and
their "plastering the inside of their houses with a composition of mud and straw, and swimming with mud and
straw on their tails" are still more incredible. The
form and size of the animal, notwithstanding all its
sagacity, will not admit of its performing such feats,
and it would be as impossible for a beaver to use its
tail as a trowel, except on the surface of the ground on
which it walks, as it would have been for Sir James
Thornhill to have painted the dome of St. Paul's Ca-
thedral without the assistance of a scaffolding. The
joints of their tail will not admit of their turning it over
on their backs on any occasion whatever, as it has a
natural inclination to bend downwards, and it is not
without some considerable exertion that they can keep
it from trailing on the ground. This being the case
they cannot sit erect, like a squirrel, which is their common posture, particularly when eating, or when they are
cleaning themselves as a cat or squirrel does, without
having their tails bent forward between their legs, and
which may not improperly be called their trencher.

So far are the beaver from driving stakes into the
ground when building their houses, that they lay most of

the wood crosswise, and nearly horizontal, and without any other order than that of leaving a hollow or cavity in the middle; when any unnecessary branches project inward they cut them off with their teeth, and throw them in among the rest, to prevent the mud from falling through the roof.   It is a mistaken notion that the wood-work is first completed and then plastered; for the whole of their houses, as well as their dams, are from the foundation one mass of wood and mud, mixed with stones, if they can be procured.   The mud is always taken from the edge of the bank, or the bottom of the creek or pond, near the door of the house; and though their fore-paws are so small, yet it is held close up between them, under their throat, that they carry both mud and stones, while they always drag the wood with their teeth.   All their work is executed in the night, and they are so expeditious in completing it that in the course of one night I have known them to have collected as much mud at their houses as to have amounted to some thousands of their little handfuls, and when any mixture of grass or straw has appeared in it, it has been, most assuredly, mere chance, owing to the nature of 'the ground from which they had taken it. As to their designedly making a composition for that purpose, it is entirely void of truth. . . .   As they are seen to walk over their work and sometimes to give a flap with their tail, particularly when plunging into the water, this has, without doubt, given rise to the vulgar opinion that they use their tails as a trowel, with which they plaster their houses, whereas that flapping of the tail is no more than a custom, which they always preserve, even when they become tame and domestic, and more particularly so when they are startled. . . .

When the beaver which are situated in a small river or creek are to be taken the Indians sometimes find it necessary to stake the river across to prevent them from passing, after which they endeavor to find out all their holes or places of retreat in the banks. This requires much practice and experience to accomplish, and is performed in the following manner: Every man, being furnished with an ice-chisel, lashes it to the end of a small staff about four or five feet long; he then walks along the edge of the banks and keeps knocking his chisels against the ice. Those who are well acquainted with that kind of work well know by the sound of the ice when they are opposite to any of the beaver's holes or vaults. As soon as they suspect any they cut a hole through the ice big enough to admit an old beaver, and in this manner proceed till they have found out all their places of retreat, or at least as many of them as possible. While the principal men are thus employed, some of the understrappers and the women and children are busy in breaking open the house, which at times is no easy task, for I have known these houses to be five and six feet thick, and one in particular was more than eight feet thick on the crown. When the beaver find that their habitations are invaded they fly to the holes in the banks for shelter, and on being perceived by the Indians, which is easily done by attending to the motion of the water, they block up the entrance with stakes of wood, and then haul the beaver out of its hole, either by hand, if they can reach it, or with a large hook made for that purpose, which is fastened to the end of a long stick.

The beaver cannot keep under water long at a time, so that when their houses are broken open, and all their places of retreat discovered, they have but one choice left, as it may be called, either to be taken in their houses or their vaults. In general they prefer the latter; for where one beaver is taken in the house many thousands are taken in their vaults in the banks. . . .

On the eleventh of January, as some of my companions were hunting, they saw the track of a strange snow-shoe, which they followed, and at a considerable distance came to a little hut where they discovered a young woman sitting alone. As they found that she understood their language, they brought her with them to the tents. On examination she proved to be one of the Western Dog-ribbed Indians, who had been taken prisoner by the Athapuscow Indians in the summer of 1770, and in the following summer, when they were near this part, she had eloped from them with an intent to return to her own country; but the distance being so great, and having, after she was taken prisoner, been carried in a canoe the whole way, the turnings and windings of the rivers and lakes were so numerous that she forgot the track, so she built the hut in which we found her to protect her from the weather during the winter, and here she had lived from the first setting in of the fall.

From her account of the moons past since her elopement, it appeared that she had been near seven months without seeing a human face, during all which time she had supported herself very well by snaring partridges, rabbits, and squirrels; she had also killed two or three beaver and some porcupines. The methods practised by this poor creature to procure a livelihood were truly admirable, and are great proofs that necessity is the real mother of invention. When the few deer-sinews that she had an opportunity of taking with her were all expended in making snares and sewing her clothing, she had nothing to supply their place but the sinews of the rabbits' legs and feet; these she twisted together for the purpose with great dexterity and success. The rabbits, etc., which she caught in those snares not only furnished her with a comfortable subsistence, but of the skins she made a suit of neat and warm clothing for the winter. It is scarcely possible to conceive that a person in her forlorn situation could be so composed as to be capable of contriving or executing anything that was not absolutely necessary to her existence; but there were sufficient proofs that she had extended her care much farther, as all her clothing, besides being calculated for real service, showed great taste, and exhibited no little variety of ornament. The materials, though rude, were very curiously wrought, and so judiciously placed as to make the whole of her garb have a very pleasing, though rather romantic appearance.

Her leisure hours from hunting had been employed in twisting the inner rind or bark of willows into small lines, like net-twine, of which she had some hundred fathoms by her; with this she intended to make a fishing-net as soon as the spring advanced. Five or six inches of an iron hoop made into a knife, and the shank of an arrow-head of iron, which served her as an awl, were all the metals this poor woman had with her when she eloped, and with these implements she had made herself complete snow-shoes and several other articles. Her method of making a fire was equally singular and curious, having no other materials for that purpose than two hard, sulphurous stones.

These, by long friction and hard knocking, produced a few sparks, which at length communicated to some touchwood; but as this method was attended with great trouble, and not always with success, she did not suffer her fire to go out all winter.

The singularity of the circumstance, the comeliness of her person, and her accomplishments, occasioned a contest between several of the Indians of my party who should have her for a wife, and the poor girl was actually won and lost at wrestling by near half a score of them the same evening. . . .

From the middle to the latter end of March, and, again, in the beginning of April, though the thaw was not general, yet in the middle of the day it was very considerable. It commonly froze hard in the nights, and the young men took the advantage of the mornings, when the snow was hard crusted over, and ran down a good many moose; for in those situations a man with a good pair of snow-shoes will scarcely make any impression on the snow, while the moose, and even the deer, will break through it at every step up to the belly. Notwithstanding this, however, it is very seldom that the Indians attempt to run deer down. The moose are so tender-footed and so short-winded that a good runner will generally tire them in less than a day, and very frequently in six or eight hours; though I have known some of the Indians continue the chase for two days before they could come up with and kill the game. On those occasions the Indians, in general, only take with them a knife or bayonet, and a little bag containing a set of fire-tackle, and are as lightly clothed as possible; some of them will carry a bow and two or three arrows, but I never knew any of them to take a gun, except such as had been blown or bursted, and the barrels cut quite short, which, when reduced to the least possible size to be capable of doing any service, must be too great a weight for a man to run with in his hand for so many hours together.

When the poor moose are incapable of making farther speed they stand and keep their pursuers at bay with their head and forefeet, in the use of which they are very dexterous, especially the latter, so that the Indians who have neither a bow or arrows, nor a short gun with them, are generally obliged to lash their knives or bayonets to the end of a long stick and stab the moose at a distance. For want of this necessary precaution some of the boys and foolhardy young men who have attempted to rush in upon them have frequently received such unlucky blows from their forefeet as to render their recovery very doubtful. . . .

When two parties of Indians meet, the ceremonies which pass between them are quite different from those made use of in Europe on similar occasions ; for when they advance within twenty or thirty yards of each other they make a full halt, and in general lie or sit down on the ground, and do not speak for some minutes. At length one of them, generally an elderly man, if any be in company, breaks silence by acquainting the other party with every misfortune that has befallen him and his companions from the last time they had seen or heard of each other, and also of all deaths and other calamities that have befallen any other Indians during the same period, at least as many particulars as have come to his knowledge. When the first has finished his oration another aged orator, if there be any, belonging to the other party, relates, in like manner, all the bad news that has come to his knowledge, and both parties never fail to plead poverty and famine on all occasions. If these orations contain any news that in the least affect the other party it is not long before some of them begin to sigh and sob, and soon after break out into a loud cry, which is generally accompanied by most of the grown persons of both sexes, and sometimes it is common to see them all, men, women, and children, in one universal howl. The young girls in particular are often very obliging on those occasions, for I never remember to have seen a crying match but the greatest part of the company assisted, although some of them had no other reason for it but that of seeing their companions do the same. When the first transports of grief subside they advance by degrees, and both parties mix with each other, the men always associating with the men and the women with the women. If they have any tobacco among them, the pipes are passed round pretty freely, and the conversation soon becomes general. As they are on their first meeting acquainted with all the bad news, they have by this time nothing left but good, which in general has so far the predominance over the former that in less than half an hour nothing but smiles and cheerfulness are to be seen on every face, and if they be not really in want small presents of provisions, ammunition, and other articles often take place, sometimes by way of a gift, but more frequently by way of trying whether they cannot get a greater present. They have but few diversions; the chief is shooting at a mark with bow and arrows, and another out-door game, called Holl, which in some measure resembles playing with quoits, only it is done with short clubs, sharp at one end.

They also amuse themselves with dancing, which is always performed in the night. Besides these diversions they have another simple indoor game, which is that of taking a bit of wood, a button, or any other small thing, and after shifting it from hand to hand several times, asking their antagonist, "Which hand is it in?" When playing at this game, which only admits of two persons, each of them have ten, fifteen, or twenty small chips of wood like matches, and when one of the players guesses right he takes one of his antagonist's sticks and lays it to his own, and he that first gets all the sticks from the other in that manner is said to win the game, which is generally for a single load of powder and shot, an arrow, or some other thing of inconsiderable value.

IX

HUMBOLDT'S TRAVELS.

ONE of the boys said that Hearne's Travels seemed to bring them quite within our own time. The stately great quarto is dedicated to the Hudson's Bay Company, and in his holidays last summer Bedford had seen packages addressed to their agents, lying at the station at Montreal.

Tom Rising said that in the preface to Hearne's travels there was a reference to a lively quarrel between him and Mr. Dalrymple.

Col. Ingham said that Mr. Dalrymple was one of the map-makers who stayed at home, and had to plot or put down the observations of the men who travelled. Hearne's latitudes and longitudes did not prove to be quite exact. But, as to the main point, that there was a Northern Ocean somewhere near the parallel of 70°, he settled that matter.

"But now," said he, "you begin to come to the time when geography itself becomes a science. You had better look into some of the magnificent Humboldt books. You all know his name, and what he did is what you would all like to do. Here he was, a young German gentleman, with plenty of money and a taste for natural history. His family was important enough for him to secure good recommendations among diplo-matists and such people. He had the favor of governments, and he had money enough to go where he pleased.

"At that time, almost the first time, the Spanish government relaxed a little the secrecy in which it had tried to keep all the world ignorant of all its immense possessions. They gave Humboldt in 1799 full power to go where he chose in their provinces in America and the East Indies. Humboldt went, and spent nearly five years in America.

"He was in Washington in 1804, and saw President Jefferson, who was himself a bit of a naturalist."

The boys and girls got down different volumes of Humboldt's Travels. Some of them are very elegant, and there is one atlas of prints of curious things he saw in Mexico and South America, in which, to their joy, they found the origins of many pictures still extant in the school geographies.

Laura was looking at his Life. "Why, Uncle Fritz, they were educated by our dear old Campe."

"Who is our dear old Campe?" said Emma. "I never heard of him."

"Campe is — oh, yes, you have, only you forget — he is the man who made the little Robinson Crusoe."

"Oh, he is the stone-axe man?" asked Tom Rising.

Yes, he is the stone-axe man. What the children meant was this, — that he wrote a Robinson Crusoe which some of them had read, in which Robinson Crusoe had a stone axe. In the original Robinson Crusoe, by the Englishman, Defoe, Robinson was supplied with the necessaries of life from the wreck of the ship, just as "Crusoe in New York" was supplied from the old junkshop which had that name. But the French philosopher, Rousseau, said that for a book of education it should show how a man would fare who had actually nothing but his hands.

So this German minister Campe, who had been a chaplain in the army, and had become a teacher of youth, in the hope of thus ameliorating the condition of mankind, wrote his famous Robinson the Younger. I believe he does let Robinson have a jackknife when he is thrown upon the beach, though that violates the principle. When it becomes necessary for Robinson to cut down trees he walks along on the beach, and there he finds a stone sharp on one edge and in the shape of an axe-head. What is more, by great good luck the water has worn through a hole in the stone just where the handle of the axe should be fitted. So Robinson put a handle into the stone and went on his way conquering and to conquer.

This absurdity of the accidental axe-head so impressed the children that they always called the book the stone-axe Robinson. Still it was a book they liked to take down from the Colonel's shelves, and it would be a good book now to put in public libraries. The catalogue title of it in English is "The New Robinson Crusoe." In Germany it is better known, probably, than the original. In the early editions it takes the form of a conversation between a father and his children.

Tom Rising said, "That virtuous boy, who asks the priggish questions, must have been Alexander von Humboldt's brother."

"And the stupid boy," said Bob, "who hardly knows the difference between a needle and a fish-hook, he is Alexander von Humboldt himself. Stupid boys, if they are only stupid enough to be neglected by the schoolmasters, always turn out remarkable men."

The children laughed at Bob's frank confession of his theory of life, but Col. Ingham, who feared that the talk was becoming heretical, bade Fanchon read some of Humboldt's own accounts of his notion in travelling.

HUMBOLDT'S JOURNEY TO THE EQUINOCTIAL REGIONS.

From my earliest youth I felt an ardent desire to travel into distant regions seldom visited by Europeans. This desire is characteristic of a period of our existence when life appears an unlimited horizon, and when we find an irresistible attraction in the impetuous agitations of the mind and the image of positive danger. Though educated in a country which has no direct communication with either the East or the West Indies; living amidst mountains remote from coasts, and celebrated for their numerous mines, I felt an increasing passion for the sea and distant expeditions. Objects with which we are acquainted only by the animated narrations of travellers have a peculiar charm; imagination wanders with delight over that which is vague and undefined, and the pleasures we are deprived of seem to possess a fascinating power, compared with which all we daily feel in the narrow circle of sedentary life appears insipid. The taste for herborization, the study of geology, rapid excursions to Holland, England, and France, with the celebrated Mr. George Forster, who had the happiness to accompany Captain Cook in his second voyage round the globe, contributed to give a determined direction to the plan of travels which I had formed at eighteen years of age. No longer deluded by the agitations of a wandering life, I was anxious to contemplate Nature in all her variety of wild and stupendous scenery; and the hope of collecting some facts useful to the advancement of science incessantly impelled my wishes towards the luxuriant regions of the torrid zone. As personal circumstances then prevented me from executing the projects by which I was so powerfully influenced, I had leisure to prepare myself during six years for the observations I proposed to make on the New Continent, as well as to visit different parts of Europe, and to explore the lofty chain of the Alps, the structure of which I might afterwards compare with that of the Andes of Quito and of Peru. . . .

From the time of leaving Graciosa the horizon continued so hazy that, notwithstanding the considerable height of the mountains of Canary,[1] we did not discover that island till the 18th of June. On the morning of the 19th we discovered the point of Naga, but the peak of Teneriffe was still invisible. The land, obscured by a thick mist, presented forms that were vague and confused. As we approached the road of Santa Cruz we observed that the mist, driven by the winds, drew nearer to us. The sea was strongly agitated, as it most commonly is in these latitudes. We anchored after several soundings, for the mist was so thick that we could scarcely distinguish objects at a few cables' distance, but at the moment we began to salute the place the fog was instantly dispelled. The peak of Teyde appeared in a break above the clouds, and the first rays of the sun, which had not yet risen on us, illumined the summit of the volcano. We hastened to the prow of the vessel to behold the magnificent spec-

---

[1] Isla de la Gran Canaria.

tacle, and at the same instant we saw four English vessels lying to and very near our stern. We had passed without being perceived, and the same mist which had concealed the peak from our view had saved us from the risk of being carried back to Europe.[1]

The Pizarro stood in as close as possible to the fort, to be under its protection. It was on this shore that in the landing attempted by the English two years before our arrival, in July, 1797, Admiral Nelson had his arm carried off by a cannon-ball. . . .

Though the captain had orders to stop at Teneriffe to give us time to scale the summit of the peak, if the snows did not prevent our ascent, we received notice, on account of the blockade of the English ships, not to expect a longer delay than four or five days. We consequently hastened our departure for the port of Orotava, which is situated on the western declivity of the volcano, where we were sure of finding guides. I could find no one at Santa Cruz who had mounted the peak, and I was not surprised at this. The most curious objects become less interesting in proportion as they are near to us; and I have known inhabitants of Schaffaansen, in Switzerland, who had never seen the fall of the Rhine but at a distance. . . .

About three in the morning, by the sombrous light of a few pine-torches, we started on our journey to the summit of the Piton. We scaled the volcano on the northeast side, where the declivities are extremely steep; and after two hours' toil we reached a small plain, which, on account of its elevated position, bears the name of Alta Vista. This is the station of the *neveros*, those natives whose occupation is to collect ice and snow, which

---

1 For this was in time of war.

they sell in the neighboring towns. Their mules, better practised in climbing mountains than those hired by travellers, reach Alta Vista, and the *neveros* are obliged to transport the snow to that place on their backs. We turned to the right to examine the cavern of ice, which is at the elevation of 1,728 toises, consequently below the limit of perpetual snows in this zone. Probably the cold which prevails in this cavern is owing to the same causes which perpetuate the ice in the crevices of Mount Jura and the Apennines. . . . Day was beginning to dawn when we left the ice-cavern. We observed, during the twilight, a phenomenon which is not unusual on high mountains, but which the position of the volcano we were scaling rendered very striking. A layer of white and fleecy clouds concealed from us the sight of the ocean and the lower region of the island. This layer did not appear above eight hundred toises high ; the clouds were so uniformly spread, and kept so perfect a level, that they wore the appearance of a vast plain covered with snow. The colossal pyramid of the peak, the volcanic summits of Lancerota, of Forteventura, and the isle of Palma, were like rocks amidst the sea of vapors, and their black tints were in fine contrast with the whiteness of the clouds.

While we were climbing over the broken lavas of the Malpays, we perceived a very curious optical phenomenon, which lasted eight minutes. We thought we saw on the east side small rockets thrown into the air. Luminous points, about seven or eight degrees above the horizon, appeared first to move in a vertical direction ; but the motion was gradually changed into a horizontal oscillation. Our fellow-travellers, our guides even, were astonished at this phenomenon, without our having made any remark on it to them. We thought, at first sight, that these points which floated in the air indicated some new eruption of the great volcano of Lancerota, for we recollected that Bouguer and La Condamine, in scaling the volcano of Pichincha, were witnesses of the eruption of Cotopaxi. But the illusion soon ceased, and we found that the luminous points were the images of stars magnified by the vapors. . . .

The road, which we were obliged to clear for ourselves, across the Malpays, was extremely fatiguing. The ascent is steep, and the blocks of lava rolled beneath our feet. Unfortunately the listlessness of our guides contributed to increase the difficulty of the ascent. Unlike the guides of the valley of Chamouni, or the nimble-footed Guanches, who could, it is asserted, seize the rabbit or the wild goat in its course, our Canarian guides were models of the phlegmatic. They had wished to persuade us on the preceding evening not to go beyond the station of the rocks. Every ten minutes they sat down to rest themselves, and when unobserved they threw away the specimens we had collected. We discovered at length that none of them had ever visited the summit of the volcano. . . .

We had yet to scale the steepest part of the mountain, the Piton, which forms the summit. The slope of this small cone, covered with volcanic ashes and fragments of pumice-stone, is so steep that it would have been almost impossible to reach the top had we not ascended by the old current of lava, the *débris* of which have resisted the ravages of time. We ascended the Piton by grasping these half-decomposed scoriæ, which often broke in our hands.

Vesuvius, three times lower than the peak of Teneriffe,

is terminated by a cone of ashes almost three times higher, but with a more accessible and easy slope. Of all the volcanos which I have visited, that of Jorullo, in Mexico, is the only one that is more difficult to climb than the peak, because the whole mountain is covered with loose ashes.

When we gained the summit of the Piton, we were surprised to find scarcely room to seat ourselves conveniently. We were stopped by a small circular wall of lava, with a base of pitchstone, which concealed from us the view of the crater. The west wind blew with such violence that we could scarcely stand. It was eight in the morning, and we suffered severely from the cold, though the thermometer kept a little above freezing point. For a long time we had been accustomed to a very high temperature, and the dry wind increased the feeling of cold. . . .

Notwithstanding the heat we felt in our feet on the edge of the crater, the cone of ashes remains covered with snow during several months in winter. The cold and violent wind, which blew from the time of sunrise, induced us to seek shelter at the foot of the Piton. Our hands and faces were nearly frozen, while our boots were burnt by the soil on which we walked. We descended in the space of a few minutes the Sugar-Loaf which we had scaled with so much toil, and this rapidity was in some respects involuntary, for we often rolled down on the ashes. . . .

As we approached the town of Orotava, we met great flocks of canaries. These birds, well known in Europe, were in general uniformly green; some, however, had a yellow tinge on their backs; their note was the same as the tame canary. The yellow canaries are a variety, which has taken birth in Europe, and those we saw in cages at Orotava and Santa Cruz had been bought at Cadiz, and in other parts of Spain. But of all the birds of the Canary Islands, that which has the most heart-soothing song is unknown in Europe. It is the capirote, which no effort has succeeded in taming, so sacred is its soul to liberty. I have stood listening in admiration of his soft and melodious warbling in a garden at Orotava, but I have never seen him sufficiently near to ascertain to what family he belongs. . . .

On the 3d and 4th of July, we crossed that part of the Atlantic where the charts indicate the bank of the maalstrom, and towards night we altered our course to avoid the danger, the existence of which is however doubted. It would have been, perhaps, as prudent to have continued our course. The old charts are filled with rocks, some of which really exist, though most of them are merely the offspring of those optical illusions which are more frequent at sea than in inland places.

From the time we entered the torrid zone we were never weary of admiring at night the beauty of the southern sky, which as we advanced to the south opened new constellations to our view. The pleasure we felt in discovering the Southern Cross was warmly shared by those of our crew who had visited the colonies. In the solitude of the seas we hail a star as a friend, from whom we have been long separated. The Portuguese and the Spaniards are peculiarly susceptible of this feeling; a religious sentiment attaches them to a constellation, the form of which recalls the sign of the faith planted by their ancestors in the deserts of the New

World.   The two stars which mark the summit and the foot of the cross having nearly the same right ascension, it follows that the constellation is almost perpendicular at the moment when it passes the meridian.   This circumstance is known to the people of every nation situated beyond the tropics or in the Southern Hemisphere.   It has been observed at what hour of the night, in different seasons, the cross is erect or inclined.   It is a time-piece which advances very regularly four minutes a day, and no other group of stars affords to the naked eye an observation of time so easily made.   How often have we heard our guides exclaim in the savannahs of Venezuela, or in the deserts extending from Lima to Truxillo, "Midnight is past, the cross begins to bend."   How often these words remind us of that affecting scene, where Paul and Virginia, seated near the source of the river Lataniers, conversed together for the last time, and when the old man, at the sight of the Southern Cross, warns them that it is time to separate. . . .

The banks of the Manzanares are very pleasant, and are shaded by mimosas and other trees of a gigantic growth.   A river, the temperature of which in the season of the floods, descends as low as twenty-two degrees,[1] while the air is at thirty and thirty-three degrees, is an inestimable benefit in a country where the heat is excessive during the whole year, and where it is so agreeable to bathe several times in a day.   The children pass a considerable part of their lives in the water; all the inhabitants, even the women of the most opulent

------

[1] Of Reaumur's thermometer.   Each degree is equal to 2¼ of our thermometers, and the zero is our 32°.

families, know how to swim ; and in a country where man is so near the state of nature, one of the first questions asked on meeting in the morning is, whether the water is cooler than on the preceding evening. One of the modes of bathing is curious. We every evening visited a family in the suburb of the Guayquerias. In a fine moonlight night, chairs were placed in the water ; the men and women were lightly dressed, and the family and strangers assembled in the river, passed some hours in smoking cigars and talking, according to the custom of the country, of the extreme dryness of the season, of the abundant rains in the neighboring districts, and particularly of extravagances of which the ladies of Cumana accuse those of the Caracas and the Havannah. The company were under no apprehension of the crocodiles, which are now extremely scarce, and which approach men without attacking them. We never met with them in the Manzanares, but with a great number of dolphins, which sometimes ascend the river in the night, and frighten the bathers by spouting water.

The pearl-breeding oyster abounds on the shoals which extend from Cape Paria to Cape la Vela. It is warmly alleged by some historians that the natives of America were unacquainted with the luxury of pearls. The first Spaniards who landed in Terra Firma found the savages decked with pearl necklaces and bracelets ; and among the civilized people of Mexico and Peru pearls of a beautiful form were extremely sought after. Benzoni relates the adventure of one Luigi Lampagnano, to whom Charles the Fifth granted the privilege of proceeding with five carvels to the coast of Cumana to fish for pearls. The colonists sent him back with this bold message,—"that the emperor was too liberal of what was not his own, and he had no right to dispose of the oysters which live at the bottom of the sea."

Among the mulattoes whose huts surround the salt lake we found a shoemaker of Castilian descent. He received us with an air of gravity and self-sufficiency which in those countries characterize almost all persons who are conscious of possessing some particular talent. He was employed in stretching the string of his bow and sharpening his arrows, to shoot birds. His trade of shoemaker could not be very lucrative in a country where the greater part of the inhabitants go barefooted, and he only complained that, on account of the dearness of European gunpowder, a man of his quality was reduced to use the same weapons as the Indians He was the sage of the plain; he understood the formation of the salt by the influence of the sun and full moon; the symptoms of earthquakes; the marks by means of which mines of gold and silver are discovered, and the medicinal plants, which, like all the other colonists from Chili to California, he classified into hot and cold. Having collected the tráditions of his country he gave us some curious accounts of the pearls of Cubagua, objects of luxury which he treated with the utmost contempt. To show us how familiar to him were the sacred writings, he took a pride in reminding us that Job preferred wisdom to the pearls of the Indies. After a long discourse on the emptiness of human grandeur, he drew from a leathern pouch a few very small opaque pearls, which he forced us to accept, enjoining upon us at the same time to notice on our tablets that a poor shoemaker of Araya, but a white man, and of noble Castilian race, had been enabled to give us something which, on the other side of the sea, was sought for as very precious.

I here acquit myself of the promise I made to this worthy man, who refused to accept of the slightest recompense.

When a traveller, newly arrived from Europe, penetrates for the first time into the forests of South America, he beholds nature under an unexpected aspect. He feels at every step that he is not on the confines, but in the centre of the torrid zone; not in one of the West India Islands, but on a vast continent where everything is gigantic, — mountains, rivers, and the mass of vegetation. If he feels deeply the beauty of picturesque scenery, he can scarcely distinguish what most excites his admiration, the deep silence of these solitudes, the individual beauty and contrast of forms, or that vigor and freshness of vegetable life which characterize the climate of the tropics. We walked for some hours under the shade of arcades which scarcely admit a glimpse of the sky; the latter appeared to me of an indigo-blue, the deeper in shade because the green of the equinoctial plants is generally of a stronger hue, with somewhat of a brownish tint. In this place we were struck, for the first time, with the sight of those nests in the shape of bottles or small bags which are suspended from the branches of the lowest trees, and which attest the wonderful industry of the orioles, which mingle their warblings with the hoarse cries of the parrots and the maccaws. These last, so well known for their vivid colors, fly only in pairs, while the real parrots wander about in flocks of several hundreds. A man must have lived in those regions, particularly in the hot valleys of the Andes, to conceive how these birds sometimes drown with their voices the noise of the torrents which dash down from rock to rock. . . .

The road skirted with bamboos led us to the small village of San Fernando, situated in a warm place, surrounded by very steep rocks. This was the first mission we saw in America. The missionary was a Capuchin, a native of Aragon, far advanced in years, but strong and healthy. His extreme corpulency, his hilarity, the interest he took in battles and sieges, ill accorded with the ideas we form in northern countries of the melancholy reveries and the contemplative life of the missionaries. Though extremely busy about a cow which was to be killed next day, the old monk received us with kindness and permitted us to hang up our hammocks in a gallery of his house. Seated, without doing anything the greater part of the day, in an arm-chair of redwood, he complained bitterly of what he called the indolence and ignorance of his countrymen. Our missionary, however, seemed well satisfied with his situation; he treated the Indians with mildness, he beheld his mission prosper, and he praised with enthusiasm the waters, the bananas. and the dairy produce of the district. The sight of our instruments, our books, and our dried plants drew from him a sarcastic smile, and he acknowledged, with a *naïveté* peculiar to the inhabitants of those countries that, of all the enjoyments of life, not excepting sleep, none were comparable to the pleasure of eating good beef; thus does sensuality obtain an ascendency where there is no occupation for the mind.

The days we passed at the Capuchin convent in the mountains of Caripe glided swiftly away, though our manner of living was simple and uniform. From sunrise to nightfall we traversed the forests and neighboring mountains to collect plants. When the winter rains prevented us from undertaking distant expeditions we visited the huts of the Indians or those assemblies in which the alcaldes every evening arrange the labors of the succeeding day. We returned to the monastery only when the sound of the bell called us to the refectory to share the repast of the missionaries. Sometimes, early in the morning, we followed them to the church, to attend the *doctrina*, — that is to say, the religious instruction of the Indians. It was rather a difficult task to explain dogmas to these neophytes, especially those who had but a very imperfect knowledge of the Spanish language. On the other hand, the monks are yet almost totally ignorant of the language of the Chaymas ; and the resembling sounds confuse the poor Indians, and suggest to them the most whimsical ideas. I saw a missionary laboring earnestly to prove that *inferno*, hell, and *invierno*, winter, were not one and the same thing. The Chaymas are acquainted with no other winter than the season of rains, and consequently they imagined the " hell of the whites " to be a place where the wicked are exposed to frequent showers. The missionary harangued to no purpose ; it was impossible to efface the first impression produced by the analogy between the two consonants. He could not separate in the mind of the neophyte the ideas of *rain* and *hell*. The same men who manifest quickness of intellect, and who are tolerably well acquainted with the Spanish, were unable to connect their ideas, when, in our excursions around the convent, we put questions to them through the intervention of the monks. They were made to affirm or deny whatever the monks pleased ; and that wily civility, to which the least cultivated Indian is no stranger, induced them sometimes to give to their answers the turn that seemed to be suggested by our questions. Travellers cannot be enough on their guard against this officious assent when they seek to confirm their own opinions by the testimony of the natives. To put an Indian alcalde to the proof, I asked him one day whether he did not think the little river of Caripe, which issues from the cavern of the Guacharo, returned into it on the opposite side by some unknown entrance after having ascended the slope of the mountain. The Indian seemed greatly to reflect on the subject, and then answered, by way of supporting my hypothesis, "How else, if it were not so, would there always be water in the bed of the river, at the mouth of the cavern?"

We remained a month longer at Cumana, employing ourselves in the necessary preparations for our proposed visit to the Orinoco and the Rio Negro. We had to choose such instruments as could be most easily transported in narrow boats, and to engage guides for an inland journey of ten months, across a country without communication with the coasts. The astronomical determination of places being the most important object of this undertaking, I felt desirous not to miss the observation of an eclipse of the sun which was to be visible at the end of October; and in consequence I preferred remaining till that period at Cumana, where the sky is generally clear and serene. It was now too late to reach the banks of the Orinoco before October, and the high valleys of Caracas promised less favorable opportunities, on account of the vapors which accumulate round the neighboring mountains. I was, however, near being compelled by a deplorable occurrence to renounce, or at least to delay for a long time, my journey to the Orinoco. On the 27th of October, the day before the eclipse, we went as usual to take the air on the shore of the gulf. It was eight in the evening, and the breeze was not yet stirring. The sky was cloudy, and during a dead calm it was excessively hot.

We crossed the beach which separates the suburb of the Guayqueria Indians from the embarcadero. I heard some one walking behind us, and on turning I saw a tall man of the color of the Zambos, naked to the waist. He held almost over my head a great stick of palm-tree wood, enlarged to the end like a club. I avoided the stroke by leaping towards the left; but M. Bonpland, who walked on my right, was less fortunate. He did not see the Zambo so soon as I did, and received a stroke above the temple, which levelled him with the ground. We were alone, without arms, half a league from any habitation, on a vast plain bounded by the sea. The Zambo, instead of attacking me, moved off slowly to pick up M. Bonpland's hat, which, having somewhat deadened the violence of the blow, had fallen off and lay at some distance. Alarmed at seeing my companion on the ground, and for some moments senseless, I thought of him only. I helped him to raise himself, and pain and anger doubled his strength. We ran towards the Zambo, who, either from cowardice, common enough in people of this caste, or because he perceived at a distance some men on the beach, did not wait for us, but ran off in the direction of the Tunal, a little thicket of cactus. He chanced to fall in running, and M. Bonpland, who reached him first, seized him round the body. The Zambo drew a large knife; and in this unequal struggle we should infallibly have been wounded if some Biscayan merchants, who were taking the air on the beach, had not come to our assistance. The Zambo, seeing himself surrounded, thought no longer of defence.

He again ran away, and we pursued him through the thorny cactuses.   At length, tired out, he took shelter in a cow-house, whence he suffered himself to be quietly led to prison.   M. Bonpland was seized with fever during the night ; but, being endowed with great energy and fortitude, and possessing that cheerful disposition which is one of the most precious gifts of nature, he continued his labors the next day.   The inhabitants of Cumana showed us the kindest interest.   It was ascertained that the Zambo was a native of one of the Indian villages which surround the great lake of Maracaibo. He had served on board a privateer belonging to the Island of St. Domingo, and in consequence of a quarrel with the captain he had been left on the coast of Cumana, when the ship quitted the port.   Having seen the signal which we had fixed up for the purpose of observing the height of the tides, he had watched the moment when he could attack us on the beach.   But why, after knocking one of us down, was he satisfied with simply stealing a hat?   In an examination he underwent his answers were so confused and stupid that it was impossible to clear up our doubts.   Sometimes he maintained that his intention was not to rob us ; but that, irritated by the bad treatment he had suffered on board the privateer of St. Domingo, he could not resist the desire of attacking us when he heard us speak French.   Justice is so tardy in this country that prisoners, of whom the jail is full, may remain seven or eight years without being brought to trial ; we learned, therefore, with some satisfaction, that a few days after our departure from Cumana the Zambo had succeeded in breaking out of the castle.

We quitted the shores of Cumana as if it had been

our home. This was the first land we had trodden in a zone towards which my thoughts had been directed from earliest youth. There is a powerful charm in the impression produced by the scenery and climate of these regions, and after an abode of a few months we seemed to have lived there during a long succession of years.

AROMATIC SHRUBS.

We spent a long time in examining the fine resinous and fragrant plants of the Pejual. Wandering in this thick wood we suddenly found ourselves enveloped in a thick mist; the compass alone could guide us; but in advancing northward we were in danger at every step of finding ourselves on the bank of that enormous wall of rocks, which descends perpendicularly to the depth of six thousand feet towards the sea. We were obliged to halt. Surrounded by clouds sweeping the ground, we began to doubt whether we should reach the eastern peak before night. Happily the negroes who carried our water and provisions rejoined us, and we resolved to take some refreshment. Our repast did not last long. Possibly the Capuchin brother had not thought of the great number of persons who accompanied us, or perhaps the slaves had made free with our provisions on the way; be that as it may, we found nothing but olives and scarcely any bread. Horace, in his retreat at Tibur, never boasted of a repast more light and frugal; but olives, which might have offered a satisfactory meal to a poet, devoted to study, and leading a sedentary life, appeared an aliment by no means substantial for travellers climbing mountains. We had watched the greater part of the night, and we walked for nine hours without finding a single opening. Our guides were discouraged ; they wished to go back, and we had great difficulty in preventing them. We sent off half our servants with orders to hasten the next morning to meet us, not with olives, but with salt beef.

COW TREE.

In returning from Porto Cabello to Aragua, we stopped at the farm of Barbula, near which a new road to Valencia is in the course of construction. We had heard several weeks before of a tree, the sap of which is a nourishing milk. It is called the cow-tree, and we were assured that the negroes of the farm, who drink plentifully of this vegetable milk, consider it a wholesome aliment. It was offered to us in a calabash. We drank considerable quantities of it in the evening before we went to bed, and very early in the morning, without feeling the least injurious effect. Among the great number of curious phenomena which I have observed in the course of my travels, I confess there are few that have made so powerful an impression on me as the aspect of the cow-tree. It is at the rising of the sun that this vegetable fountain is most abundant. The negroes and natives are seen hastening from all quarters, furnished with large bowls to receive the milk, which grows yellow and thickens at the surface ; some empty their bowls under the tree itself, others carry the juice home to their children.

HOWLING MONKEYS.

Before I trace the scenery of the llanos I will briefly describe the road we took from Nueva Valencia, to the little village of Ortiz, at the entrance of the steppes. We left the valley of Aragua on the 6th of March before sunrise. We passed over a plain richly cultivated, keeping along the southwest side, by the lake of Valencia, and crossing the ground left uncovered by the waters of the lake. We were never weary of admiring the fertility of the soil, covered with cala-bashes, water-melons, and plantains. The rising of the sun was announced by the distant noise of the howling monkeys. Approaching a group of trees which rise in the midst of the plain, between those parts which were anciently the islets of Don Pedro and La Negra, we saw numerous bands of Araguatos moving as in procession, and very slowly, from one tree to another. A male was followed by a great number of females, several of the latter carrying their young on their shoulders. The howling monkeys, which live in society in different parts of America, everywhere resemble each other in their manners, though the species are not always the same. Wherever the branches of the neighboring trees do not touch each other, the male who leads the party suspends himself by the callous part of his tail, and, letting fall the rest of his body, swings himself till he reaches the neighboring branch. The whole file performs the same movements in the same spot. It is almost superfluous to add how dubious is the assertion of Ulloa, and so many otherwise well-informed travellers, according to whom the monkeys with a prehensile tail form a sort of chain, in order to reach the opposite side of a river. We had opportunities during five years of observing thousands of these animals, and for this very reason we place no confidence in statements possibly invented by Europeans themselves, though repeated by the Indians of the missions, as if they had been transmitted to them by their fathers.   Man, the most remote from civilization, enjoys the astonishment he excites in relating the marvels of his country.   He says he has seen what he imagines may have been seen by another.   Every savage is a hunter, and the stories of hunters borrow from imagination in proportion as the animals of which they boast the artifices are endowed with a high degree of intelligence.

FINDING WATER.

After having passed two weary nights on horseback, and having sought in vain by day for some shelter from the heat of the sun, we arrived before night at the little Hato del Caymen,[1] called also La Guadaloupe.   It was a solitary house in the steppes, surrounded by a few small huts covered with reeds and skins.   The cattle, oxen, horses, and mules are not penned, but wander freely over an extent of several square leagues.   There is nowhere any enclosure ; men, naked to the waist and armed with a lance, ride over the savannahs to inspect the animals, bringing back those that wander too far from the pastures of the farm, and branding all that do not bear the mark of their proprietor.   These mulattoes, who are known by the name of *peones llaneros*, are partly freedmen and partly slaves.   Their food is meat dried in the air and a little salted, and of this even their horses sometimes partake.   Being always in the saddle, they fancy they cannot make the slightest exertion on foot.   We found an old negro slave, who managed the farm in the absence of his master.   He told us of herds of several thousand cows that were grazing on the

---

1 " Farm of the Alligator."

steppes, yet we asked in vain for a bowl of milk. We were offered in a calabash some yellow, muddy, and fetid water drawn from a neighboring pool. The indolence of the inhabitants of the llanos is such that they do not dig wells though they know that almost everywhere, at ten feet deep, fine springs are found in a stratum of red sandstone. After suffering one half the year from the effects of inundations, they quietly resign themselves during the other half to the most distressing deprivation of water. The old negro advised us to cover the cup with a linen cloth and drink as through a filter, that we might not be incommoded by the smell, and might swallow less of the yellowish mud deposited in the water. We did not then think that we should afterwards be forced during whole months to have recourse to this expedient. The waters of the Orinoco are always loaded with earthy particles ; they are even putrid, where dead bodies of alligators are found in the creeks, lying on beds of sand, or half-buried in the mud.

No sooner were our instruments safely placed than our mules were set at liberty to go, as they say here, "to search for water." There are little pools round the farm which the animals find, guided by their instinct, by the view of some scattered tufts of mauritia, and by the sense of humid coolness caused by little currents of air amid an atmosphere which to us appears calm and tranquil. When the pools of water are far distant, and the people of the farm are too lazy to lead the cattle to these natural watering places, they confine them during five or six hours in a very hot stable before they let them loose. Excess of thirst then augments their sagacity, sharpening as it were their senses and their instinct. No sooner is the stable opened than the horses and mules rush into the savannahs. With upraised tails and heads thrown back they run against the wind, stopping from time to time as if exploring space ; they follow less the impressions of sight than of smell, and at length announce, by prolonged neighings, that there is water in the direction of their course.

ELECTRICAL EELS.

Having obtained very uncertain results from an electric eel which had been brought to us alive, but much enfeebled, we repaired to the Caño de Bera, to make our experiments in the open air, and at the edge of the water. The Indians told us that they would "fish with horses" (embarbascar con caballos).[1] We found it difficult to form an idea of this extraordinary manner of fishing, but we soon saw our guides return from the savannah, which they had been scouring for wild horses and mules. They brought about thirty with them, which they forced to enter the pool. The extraordinary noise caused by the horses' hoofs makes the fish issue from the mud, and excites them to the attack. These yellowish and livid eels, resembling aquatic serpents, swim on the surface of the water, and crowd under the bellies of the horses. A contest between animals of so different an organization presents a very striking spectacle. The Indians, provided with harpoons and long, slender reeds, surround the pool closely, and some climb up the trees, the branches of which extend over the water. By their wild cries and the length of their reeds they prevent the horses from running away and reaching the bank of the pool. The eels,

---

[1] Excite the fish with horses.

stunned by the noise, defend themselves by the repeated discharge of their electric batteries. For a long interval they seem likely to prove victorious. Several horses sink beneath the violence of the invisible strokes which they receive from all sides, in organs the most essential to life, and, stunned by the force and frequency of the shocks, they disappear under the water. In less than five minutes two of our horses were drowned. The eel, being five feet long, and pressing itself against the belly of the horses, makes a discharge along the whole extent of its electric organ. It is natural that the effect felt by the horses should be more powerful than that produced upon man by the touch of the same fish at only one of his extremities. The horses are probably not killed, but only stunned. They are drowned from the impossibility of rising amid the prolonged struggle between the other horses and the eels.

We had little doubt that the fishing would end by killing successively all the animals engaged, but by degrees the impetuosity of this unequal combat diminished and the wearied gymnoti dispersed. They require a long rest and abundant nourishment to repair the galvanic force which they have lost. In a few minutes we had five large eels, most of which were but slightly wounded.

CROCODILES.

The Indians told us that at San Fernando scarcely a year passes without two or three grown-up persons, particularly women who fetch water from the river, being drowned by the crocodiles. They related to us the history of a young girl of Uritucu, who, by singular intrepidity and presence of mind, saved herself from the jaws of a crocodile. When she felt herself seized she sought the eyes of the animal and plunged her fingers into them with such violence that the pain forced the crocodile to let her go, after having bitten off the lower part of her left arm. The girl, notwithstanding the enormous quantity of blood she lost, reached the shore, swimming with the hand that still remained to her. In those desert countries, where man is ever wrestling with nature, discourse daily turns on the best means that may be employed to escape from a tiger, a boa, or a crocodile; every one prepares himself in some sort for the dangers that may await him. "I knew," said the young girl of Uritucu coolly, "that the cayman lets go his hold if you push your fingers into his eyes." Long after my return to Europe I learned that in the interior of Africa the negroes know and practise the same means of defence. Who does not recollect, with lively interest, Isaac, the guide of the unfortunate Mungo Park, who was seized twice by a crocodile, and twice escaped from the jaws of the monster, having succeeded in thrusting his fingers into the creature's eyes while under water.

JAGUARS.

Near the Joval nature assumes an awful and extremely wild aspect. We there saw the largest jaguar we had ever met with. The natives themselves were astonished at its prodigious length, which surpassed that of any Bengal tiger I had ever seen in the museums of Europe. The animal lay stretched beneath the shade of a large zamang.[1] It had just killed a chiguire, but had not yet touched its prey, on which it

[1] A species of mimosa.

kept one of its paws. The vultures were assembled in great numbers to devour the remains of the jaguar's repast. They presented the most curious spectacle; by a singular mixture of boldness and timidity they advanced within the distance of two feet from the animal, but at the least movement he made they drew back. In order to observe more nearly the manners of these creatures we went into the little skiff that accompanied our canoe. Tigers very rarely attack boats by swimming to them, and never but when their ferocity is heightened by a long privation of food. The noise of our oars led the animal to rise slowly and hide itself behind the bushes that bordered the shore. The vultures tried to profit by this moment of absence to devour the chiguire, but the tiger leaped into the midst of them, and in a fit of rage, expressed by his gait and the movement of his tail, carried off his prey to the forest.

We passed the night in the open air, in a plantation, the proprietor of which employed himself in hunting tigers. He wore scarcely any clothing, and was of a dark brown complexion like a Zambo. This did not prevent his classing himself amongst the whites. He called his wife and daughter Doña Isabella and Doña Manuela. Without having ever quitted the banks of the Apure, he took a lively interest in the news of Madrid, enquiring eagerly respecting "those never-ending wars and everything down yonder" (todas las cosas de alla). He knew, he said, that the king was soon to come and visit "the grandees of the country of Caracas," but he added with some pleasantry, "as the people of the court can eat only wheaten bread, they will never pass beyond the town of Victoria, and we shall not see them here." I had brought with me a chiguire, which I had intended

to have roasted, but our host assured us that such " Indian game " was not food fit for " nos otros caballeros
blancos " (white gentlemen like ourselves and him).
Accordingly he offered us some venison which he had
killed the day before with an arrow, for he had neither
powder nor fire-arms. We supposed that a small wood
of plantain-trees concealed from us the hut of the farm ;
but this man, so proud of his nobility and the color of
his skin, had not taken the trouble of constructing even
a hut of palm-leaves. He invited us to have our hammocks hung near his own, between two trees ; and he
assured us, with an air of complacency, that if we came
up the river in the rainy season we should find him beneath a roof. We soon had reason to complain of a
system of philosophy which is indulgent to indolence,
and renders a man indifferent to the conveniences of
life. A furious wind arose after midnight, lightnings
flashed over the horizon, thunder rolled, and we were
wet to the skin. During this storm a whimsical incident
served to amuse us for a moment. Doña Isabella's cat
had perched upon the tamarind-tree, at the foot of which
we lay. It fell into the hammock of one of our companions, who, being hurt by the claws of the cat, and
suddenly aroused from a profound sleep, imagined he
was attacked by some wild beast of the forest. We ran
to him on hearing his cries, and had some trouble to
convince him of his error. While it rained in torrents
on our hammocks and on our instruments which we had
brought ashore, Don Ignatio congratulated us on our
good fortune in not sleeping on the shore, but finding
ourselves in his domain, among whites and persons of
respectability. Wet as we were, we could not easily
persuade ourselves of the advantages of our situation,

and we listened with some impatience to the long narrative our host gave us of his pretended expedition to the Rio Meta, of the valor he had displayed in a sanguinary combat with the Guahibo Indians, and "the services that he had rendered to God and the king, in carrying away Indian children from their parents to distribute them in the missions." We were struck with the singularity of finding in that vast solitude a man believing himself to be of European race, and knowing no other shelter than the shade of a tree, and yet having all the vain pretensions, hereditary prejudices, and errors of long-standing civilization !

A COMFORTABLE NIGHT.

On the 1st of April, at sunrise, we quitted Señor Don Ignatio and Señora Doña Isabella, his wife. . . . Beyond the Vuelta del Cochino Roto, in a spot where the river has scooped itself a new bed, we passed the night on a bare and very extensive beach. The forest being impenetrable we had the greatest difficulty in finding dry wood to light fires, near which the Indians believe themselves in safety from the nocturnal attacks of the tiger. The night was calm and serene, and there was a beautiful moonlight. The crocodiles, stretched along the shore, placed themselves in such a manner as to be able to see the light. We thought we saw that its blaze attracted them, as it attracts crayfish, and other inhabitants of the water. The Indians showed us the tracks of three tigers in the sand, two of which were very young. A female had no doubt conducted her little ones to drink at the river. Finding no tree on the strand, we stuck our oars in the ground, and to these we fastened our hammocks. Everything passed tranquilly till eleven at night, and then a noise so terrific arose in the neighboring forest that it was almost impossible to close our eyes. Amid the cries of so many wild beasts howling at once, the Indians discriminated such only as were at intervals heard separately. These were the soft little cries of the sapajous, the moans of the alouate apes, the howlings of the jaguar and couguar, the peccary, and the sloth, and the cries of the curassao, the parraka, and other gallinaceous birds. When the jaguars approached the skirt of the forest our dog, which till then had never ceased barking, began to howl and seek for shelter beneath our hammocks. Sometimes, after a long silence, the cry of the tiger came from the tops of the trees, and then it was followed by the sharp and long whistling of the monkeys, which appeared to flee from the danger which threatened them. We heard the same noises repeated during the course of whole months, whenever the forest approached the bed of the river. The security evinced by the Indians inspires confidence in the minds of travellers, who readily persuade themselves that the tigers do not attack a man lying in his hammock.

When the natives are interrogated on the causes of the tremendous noise made by the beasts of the forest at certain hours of the night, the answer is, " They are keeping the feast of the full moon." I believe this agitation is most frequently the effect of some conflict that has arisen in the depths of the forest. The jaguars, for instance, pursue the peccaries and the tapirs, which, having no defence but in their numbers, flee in close troops, and break down the bushes they find in their way. Terrified at this struggle, the timid and mistrustful monkeys answer, from the tops of the trees, the cries of the large animals. They awaken the birds that live in society, and by degrees the whole assembly is in commotion. It is not always in a fine moonlight, but more particularly at the time of a storm and violent showers that this tumult takes place among the wild beasts. "May Heaven grant them a quiet night and repose, and us also!" said the monk who accompanied us to the Rio Negro, when, sinking with fatigue, he assisted in arranging our accommodations for the night.

A PLEASANT WALK.

We stopped at noon in a desert spot called Algodonal. I left my companions while they drew the boat ashore and were occupied in preparing our dinner. I went along the shore to get a near view of a group of crocodiles sleeping in the sun, and lying in such a manner as to have their tails, which were furnished with broad plates, resting on one another. This excursion had nearly proved fatal to me. I had kept my eyes constantly fixed towards the river; but, whilst picking up some spangles of mica agglomerated together in the sand, I discovered the recent footsteps of a tiger, easily distinguishable from their form and size. The animal had gone towards the forest, and turning my eyes on that side I found myself within eighty paces of a jaguar that was lying under the thick foliage of a ceiba. No tiger ever appeared to me so large. There are accidents in life against which we may seek in vain to fortify our reason. I was extremely alarmed, yet sufficiently master of myself and of my motions to enable me to follow the advice which the Indians had so often given us as to how we ought to act in such cases. I continued to walk on without running, avoided moving my arms, and I thought I observed that the jaguar's attention was fixed on a herd of capybaras which was crossing the river. I then began to return, making a large circuit towards the edge of the water. As the distance increased I thought I might accelerate my pace. How often was I tempted to look back in order to assure myself that I was not pursued! Happily I yielded very tardily to this desire. The jaguar had remained motionless. These enormous cats with spotted robes are so well fed in countries abounding in capybaras, peccaries, and deer that they rarely attack men. I arrived at the boat out of breath, and related my adventure to the Indians. They appeared very little interested by my story; yet, after having loaded our guns, they accompanied us to the ceiba beneath which the jaguar had lain. He was there no longer, and it would have been imprudent to have pursued him into the forest, where we must have dispersed, or advanced in single file, amidst the intertwining lianas.

ONE-EYED MEN.

Beyond the Great Cataracts of the Orinoco an unknown land begins. It is partly mountainous, receiving at once the confluents of the Amazon and the Orinoco. We found but three Christian establishments above the Great Cataracts, along the shore of the Orinoco, in an extent of more than a hundred leagues; and these three establishments contained scarcely six or eight white persons, that is to say, persons of European race. We cannot be surprised that such a desert region should have been at all times the land of fable and fairy visions. There, according to the statements of certain missionaries, are found races of men, some of whom have eyes in the centre of the forehead, while others have dogs' heads, and mouths below the stomachs. There they pretend to have found all that the ancients relate of the Garamantes, of the Arimaspes, and of the Hyperboreans. It would be an error to suppose that these simple and often rustic missionaries had themselves invented all these exaggerated fictions ; they derived them in great part from the recitals of the Indians. A fondness for narration prevails in the missions, as it does at sea, in the East, and in every place where the mind seeks amusement. A missionary, from his vocation, is not inclined to scepticism ; he imprints on his memory what the natives have so often repeated to him, and when returned to Europe and restored to the civilized world he finds a pleasure in creating astonishment by a recital of facts which he thinks he has collected, and by animated description of remote things. These stories, which the Spanish colonists call "tales of travellers and of monks," increase in improbability in proportion as you increase your distance from the forests of the Orinoco, and approach the coasts inhabited by the whites. When at Cumana, Nueva Barcelona, and other seaports which have frequent communication with the missions, if you betray any sign of incredulity, you are reduced to silence by these few words : "The fathers have seen it, but far above the Great Cataracts."

PLAGUE OF FLIES.

Persons who have not navigated the great rivers of equinoctial America, for instance, the Orinoco and the Magdalena, can scarcely conceive how, at every instant, without intermission, you may be tormented by insects flying in the air, and how the multitude of these little animals may render vast regions almost uninhabitable. Whatever fortitude be exercised to endure pain without complaint, whatever interest may be felt in the objects of scientific research, it is impossible not to be constantly disturbed by the mosquitos, zancudos, jejens, and tempraneros, that cover the face and hands, pierce the clothes with their long, needle-formed suckers, and getting into the mouth and nostrils occasion coughing and sneezing whenever any attempt is made to speak in the open air. In the missions of Orinoco, in the villages on the banks of the river, surrounded by immense forests, the *plaga de las moscas*, or the plague of the mosquitos, affords an inexhaustible subject of conversation. When two persons meet in the morning the first questions they address to each other are: " How did you find the zancudos during the night? How are we to-day for the mosquitos?" . . . " How comfortable must people be in the moon!" said a Salive Indian to Father Gumilla. "She looks so beautiful and so clear that she must be free from mosquitos." . . .

INTERLOCKED RIVERS.

During the night we had left the waters of the Orinoco, and at sunrise found ourselves as if transported to a new country, on the banks of a river the name of which we had scarcely ever heard pronounced, and which was to conduct us by the portage of Pimichin to the Rio Negro, on the frontiers of Brazil. " You will go up," said the president of the missions, who resides at San Fernando, "first the Atabapo, then the Temi, and finally the Tuamini. When the force of the current of ' black waters ' hinders you from advancing you will be conducted out of the bed of the river through forests which you will find inundated. Two monks only are settled in those desert places between the Orinoco and the Rio Negro, but at Javita you will be furnished with the means of having your canoe drawn overland in the course of four days to Caño Pimichin. If it be not broken to pieces you will descend the Rio Negro without any obstacle, as far as the little fort of San Carlos ; you will go up the Cassiguiare, and then return to San Fernando in a month, descending the upper Orinoco from east to west." Such was the plan traced for our passage, and we carried it into effect without danger, though not without some suffering, in the space of thirty-three days.

X.

A YOUNG MAN'S VOYAGE.

"UNCLE FRITZ," said Horace, "why did you say, when we were talking of Humboldt, that those were the days of boys?"

"Oh, my boy, I am very sorry I said so, if it seemed as if those were more the days of boys than these are. There were never times when young men, well trained, came to the front more readily than they do now. What I meant to say was, that in just that period of the Napoleon wars, old things had been so thoroughly broken up that boys had chances they had not fifty years before. Those boys have since become old men. They have written their lives and adventures, and so there is a literature of that time about the adventures of youngsters, which we do not have of earlier times, and cannot, as yet, have of later.

"Will you go into Lady Oliver's sitting-room, take the steps, and look along the books at C till you find two little volumes of Cleveland's Travels?"

Horace found the book in a moment. It is a miscellaneous collection in that room, and they catalogue themselves by the convenient way, for such a collection, of standing in alphabetical order of the authors.

"Now, here," continued Uncle Fritz, "is a charming little book of adventures, written at the end of life by a gentleman who was sent out from Salem very young, in command of a vessel which was to go to Mocha for coffee. But they stopped at Havre, in France, first. There the vessel was recalled, and poor Cleveland found himself in a strange port without an adventure.

"What does he do but make one. He bought a little Dover packet-boat of thirty-eight tons. Packet-boats between Dover and Calais were not worth much when France was at war with England. He had fifteen hundred dollars with which to buy a cargo. Two friends contributed each a thousand, on condition that all three should share equally when the voyage was over. This little vessel he meant to take to the Island of Bourbon, knowing well what that market required. See what happened to him."

A VOYAGE WITH FOUR SAILORS.

The difficulty of procuring men seemed to increase with each additional day's detention. Those whom I engaged one day would desert the next, alarmed by some exaggerated story of our first attempt. In the course of three weeks I shipped no less than four different men as mates, and as many different crews, and each in turn abandoned me. At length I procured an active and capable young seaman from a Nantucket ship, one whom the captain recommended, as mate, and another man and a boy in addition to George, who had held true to his engagement. I was desirous of procuring one more, but my attempt to do so was unsuccessful, and, fearing that by any delay for this purpose I might lose those already on board, I sailed immediately.

Our expedition had become a subject of general conversation in the town, and the difficulty of getting away the Indiaman (as she was called) was known to every one. The day, therefore, that we sailed the pier-head was again thronged with people, who cheered us as we passed by, wishing us "un bon voyage," but no small portion of them considered us as bound to certain destruction. It was now the 21st day of December, a season of the year when the loss of a few hours only of the easterly wind then blowing might be attended with disagreeable, if not disastrous consequences. We therefore set all our sail to improve it, and, while making rapid progress towards the channel, were brought to by a British frigate, commanded by Sir R. Strachan. The boarding officer was very civil. He declared our enterprise to be a very daring one, caused us as little detention as possible, and, returning to his ship, immediately made the signal that we might proceed.

It was soon very evident that no person on board, excepting the mate and myself, was capable of performing the very common and indispensable business of steering; and though there was no doubt our men would soon learn, yet, in the mean time, we had the prospect before us of a tedious, though not very laborious course of duty. As the wind continued to be favorable, our passage down the Channel was easy and expeditious, and the day after leaving Havre we passed by and in sight of the Island of Ushant. We were now in a position to feel the full effect of the westerly gales, which are so prevalent at this season of the year; and in order to have plenty of sea-room in case of encountering one, I directed a course to be steered which should carry us wide of Cape Ortegal. . . .

A sufficient time had now elapsed since leaving Havre (it being the third day) to give me a very tolerable knowledge of my crew, whose characters, peculiarities, and accomplishments were such that a sketch of them may not be without interest to the reader. My mate, Reuben Barnes, was a young man of nineteen or twenty, who, having been engaged in the whale-fishery, had profited by that excellent school to acquire not only the knowledge of the seaman's profession, but also enough of the mechanic arts to fish a spar with dexterity, to caulk a seam, or to make a bucket or a barrel. The intelligence, activity, watchfulness, and adroitness of this young man relieved me from much anxiety and care, and in his conduct with me he evinced all the steadiness and fidelity which the recommendation he brought, as well as the place of his birth, had led me to expect.

Decidedly the most important personage of my foremast hands was the black man, George, who had dared to embark on our second voyage, after having shared in the disasters of the first. In his capacity and dialect, George was the veriest negro that can be imagined. For honesty, fidelity, and courage he may have been equalled, but can never have been surpassed. He stood about six feet and three inches, was rather slender, very awkward, and of a much more sable hue than common, but with an expression of countenance mild and pleasing. With simplicity of character approximating to folly, he united a degree of self-conceit which led him to believe that he could do whatever could be done by another, and, in some cases, to suppose he could make great improvements, — an instance of which occurred before we had been out a week. In his previous voyages George had been cook, and had therefore nothing to do with the compass ; but now, having to take his regular turn at steering, he was greatly puzzled with its unsteadiness. He could steer in the night with tolerable accuracy, by giving him a star by which to steer, but the compass appeared to him to be calculated only to embarrass. With a view of remedying this difficulty George had taken off the cover to the till of his chest, on which, having marked the points of the compass, and pierced a hole in the centre for the pivot, he brought it aft, and with great appearance of complacency and expectation of applause, placed it on deck before the helmsman, with the proper point directed forward to correspond with the course, and then exclaimed: " Dair, massa, dat compass be teady. George teer by him well as anybody."

But this simplicity and conceit was more than redeemed by his tried fidelity and heroic courage, of which the following is a remarkable instance : George had been a slave to some planter in Savannah ; and one day, being in the woods with his master, they encountered an Indian, who was hunting. Some dispute arising, the Indian, having the advantage of being armed, threatened to shoot them. In consequence of this threat they seized him and took away his gun, but after a little while, and with urgent entreaties and fair promises from him, they were induced to return it, first taking the precaution to dip it into water to prevent an immediate use of it. This served again to rouse the anger of the Indian, who immediately took the readiest means for drying it. In the mean time George and his master had entered a canoe, and, pursuing their way in a narrow river or creek, had got a long distance from the spot where they had left the Indian, when, on looking back, they perceived him running after them on the bank. On arriving abreast of them he immediately took aim, which George perceiving threw himself as a shield between his master and the ball, and was so severely wounded that his life was for many weeks despaired of.

After a confinement of six months he entirely recovered, and, as a reward, his master gave him his liberty.

At the time he engaged with me he had been a sailor about two years, and had been so invariably cheated out of his wages that he had no other means of clothing himself than the advance I paid him. Such treatment had been productive of a tinge of misanthropy, and it was not until after long acquaintance that he gave me his entire confidence. As this acquaintance continued for many years (even as long as he lived), and as he was a sharer of my various adventures, I shall have frequent occasion to mention his name in connection with my own while narrating them.

My other man had been a Prussian grenadier. He had served in the army of the Duke of Brunswick at the time of his invading Holland to restore the authority of the Stadtholder, and in other campaigns; but having a dislike to the profession, he had deserted, and had been about eighteen months a sailor in English vessels. During this time he had not acquired such a knowledge of steering that we could leave him at the helm without watching him, and however brave he may have been in the ranks, he was the veriest coward imaginable when called to the performance of duties aloft. In addition to this incapacity he possessed a most ungovernable temper; and, being a powerful man, we had considerable difficulty in keeping him at all times in a state of subordination, — a difficulty which was in some degree augmented by his very imperfect knowledge of our language and the consequent embarrassment he found in making himself understood.

The last as well as the least of our members was a little French boy of fourteen years, who possessed all the vivacity peculiar to his countrymen, and who, having been some time on board the Carmagnole and other privateers, had acquired many of the tricks of a finished man-of-war's man. Some months' residence in an English prison had given him the command of a few English words, but they were not of a selection that indicated much care in the teacher.

It was not uncommon for George, the Prussian grenadier, and the French boy to get into a warm debate on the relative merits of their respective countries, for they were all men of great vivacity and patriotism; and sometimes (probably from not understanding each other) they would become so angry as to render it necessary for the mate to interfere to restore tranquillity. At such moments I used to think that if Hogarth could have been an observer his genius would have done justice to the group. It may fairly be presumed, however, that such a ship's company, for an India voyage, was never before seen, and, moreover, that we " ne'er shall look upon its like again."

For several days after passing the Isle of Ushant, the wind was light from northwest and west-northwest, accompanied with a heavy swell from that quarter, and though our progress was in consequence slow, it was proportionally comfortable. Before we had reached the latitude of Cape Finisterre the light wind, before which we had been sailing with all our canvas spread, died away, and left us some hours becalmed. During this time one of our pigs had got overboard and was swimming away from the vessel. George, being an excellent swimmer, did not hesitate to go after him; but when he had caught him, at the distance from us of about twenty fathoms, a light puff of wind, termed by seamen a cat's-paw, took the sails aback, and suddenly increased our distance from George, who perceiving it and becoming alarmed let go the pig and swam for the vessel, crying out lustily, as he approached, " I dead, I dead !" As he had not been long in the water, nor used such exertion as to cause extraordinary exhaustion, I was apprehensive that he might be attacked by a shark. We threw towards him a spar and set immediately about clearing away the boat, but before we could be ready to launch it George had seized the spar, and, by its aid, had succeeded in getting alongside. When taken on board he did not hesitate to express his belief that our going from him was intentional, and that, had the breeze continued, we should have left him for the purpose of saving his wages. Nor was it until after long experience, and repeatedly receiving his wages when due, that he would acknowledge that he had judged me erroneously.

The day succeeding this adventure we had another, which nearly brought our voyage to a close. Early in the morning we fell in with the British frigate, Stag. The wind was so light and its influence on the manœuvres of the ship so counteracted by a deep and hollow swell that, getting sternway, her counter came in contact with our broadside with a tremendous force, which threatened immediate destruction, and which must have been the result but for the order instantly given and obeyed to " fill away." This saved us from a second shock, and we were happy to perceive we had received no other damage than that of breaking the rail. The officer of the frigate very politely offered to send their carpenter on board to repair this, but I declined, from my desire of not losing a moment's time in advancing towards those latitudes where gales of wind were of less frequent occurrence. When we were released from this visit the mate immediately set about exercising his ingenuity as carpenter ; and, with great application, he completed the repairs, in a work-manlike manner, on the third day after meeting the accident.

We had now advanced far into the second week of our departure. The wind, though light, was fair, and the prospect was favorable for the continuance of good weather. These encouraging circumstances led me to hope that we should reach the tropical latitudes without encountering a gale, and also without meeting what was more to be dreaded, any one of those Spanish or French privateers, which had frequented the track we were passing, and whose conduct, in many instances, to defenceless merchant vessels had nearly equalled that of the ancient buccaneers.

We had passed by many vessels, but had carefully avoided speaking with any one. At length, on a very fine morning, as the sun rose, and when we were about fifty leagues west of Cadiz, we perceived a small sail in the northwest. At ten o'clock she was equally plain to be seen, and by noon we were satisfied she was in chase of, and was gaining on us. We kept steadily on our course, hoping that an increase of wind would give us an advantage, or that some other object might divert their attention. But our hopes were fallacious. The wind rather decreased, and when this was the case we observed she appeared to approach us faster. By two o'clock we perceived she had lateen sails, and hence had no doubt of her being a privateer. Soon after she began to fire at us, but the balls fell much short. As the wind continued very light it was soon apparent that we could not escape, as we perceived that her progress was accelerated by means of a multitude of sweeps. To run any longer would only have been incurring the risk of irritating the captain of the buccaneer; we therefore rounded to and prepared to be plundered.

As they came up with us, about five o'clock, they gave such a shout of " Bonne prise ! bonne prise !" as would be expected from banditti subject to no control; but I felt considerable relief in the persuasion that, as their flag indicated, they were French, and not Spanish. After the shouting had ceased I was ordered, in very coarse terms, to hoist out my boat and come on board with my papers. I replied that I had not men sufficient to put out the boat. The order was reiterated, accompanied with a threat of firing into us. I then sent my men below and waited the result, which was that they got out their own boat. The officer who came on board I suppose to have been the captain himself, from the circumstance of his being a very intelligent man, and from my presence not being required on board the privateer. A cursory examination of our papers convinced him of our neutral character, and the exhibition of a passport, with a seal and signature of one high in authority in the French government, while it astonished, seemed also to satisfy him that the less trouble and detention he gave us the better, as he immediately ordered his ruffians to desist from clearing away for opening the hatches, which they had already begun, and to go on board their boat, where, after wishing me a good voyage and regretting the detention he had caused, he joined them, and they returned to their privateer and sailed in pursuit of other adventures.

The result of this rencontre was better than I had anticipated, aware, as I was, of the general insubordination on board of vessels of this description. I had feared that, even if the chief had been disposed to prevent his men from plundering, it would not have been in his power, and I was much relieved by finding myself mistaken.

Pursuing a course for the Cape de Verde Islands, we came in sight of them the thirtieth day from leaving Havre. It was my intention to stop at Port Praya to obtain a supply of fruit and vegetables, but I was prevented by a gale of wind, in which we lay to twelve hours, and had a fair opportunity of testing the good properties of the vessel for this important purpose. This was the only gale of any severity that we experienced during the passage; and, as evidence that it was of no inconsiderable violence, a ship came into the Cape of Good Hope, three days after our arrival there, which had lost her mizzenmast in the same gale.

It is well known to all who have crossed the ocean, and may easily be imagined by those who have not, that a passage at sea presents to the observer little else, from day to day, than the same unbounded and (in tropical climes) unvaried horizon; the same abyss of waters, agitated more or less as it is acted upon by the wind; the same routine of duties to be performed on board, which, in the trade winds, have seldom even the ordinary excitement caused by reducing and making sail; and when this monotonous round is interrupted by speaking a vessel, by catching a porpoise, or by seeing a whale, the incident is seized with avidity as an important item to be inserted in the ship's log-book, or journal of the day's transaction.

As our experience was of this kind I have only to notice that we crossed the equator in the longitude of 25°, and that we met with no occurrence, worthy of note, from the time of our leaving the Cape de Verde Islands to our arrival at the Cape of Good Hope, excepting that one night, when going before the wind with a strong breeze, the Prussian soldier brought over the main boom with such violence as to part the sheet and rouse all hands from their slumbers. As there was a considerable sea, it was not without great difficulty and risk that the boom was again secured.

On passing the equator we discovered that one of our casks of water had nearly leaked out ; and, having failed to fill up the empty ones, it was doubtful if we had sufficient to carry us to the Isle of France. This consideration, and the desire of obtaining refreshments and a short respite from the fatigue and anxiety of such a passage, determined me to stop at the Cape, as I believed, also, that our cargo might be sold advantageously there.

Shaping our course accordingly, we came in sight of the Table Mount on the 21st March, 1798, just three months from the time of our leaving Havre. We were so near in before dark as to perceive that we were signalled at the lion's head, but were not able to reach the anchorage until between nine and ten o'clock in the evening. We had scarcely dropped our anchor when we were boarded by a man-of-war's boat ; the officer of which, finding we were from France, immediately hurried me ashore, in my sea-garb, to see the Admiral (Sir Hugh C. Christian), who, surrounded by a group of naval officers, appeared very earnest for such European news as I could give them. After passing nearly an hour with the Admiral, who treated me with great civility, and answering the many questions which were asked by the company, the officer who took me from my vessel was desired to convey me on board again ; an hour having been previously nan.ed by the Admiral at which I was to meet him, the next morning, at the government house.

The arrival of such a vessel from Europe naturally excited the curiosity of the inhabitants of the Cape, and the next morning being calm, we had numerous visitors

on board, who could not disguise their astonishment at
the size of the vessel, the boyish appearance of the master
and mate, the queer and unique characters of the two
men and boy who constituted the crew, and the length of
the passage we had accomplished.

Various were the conjectures of the good people of the
Cape as to the real object of our enterprise. While some
among them viewed it in its true light, that of a commercial speculation, others believed that under this mask we
were employed by the French government for the conveyance of their despatches, and some even went so far as
to declare a belief that we were French spies, and, as
such, deserving of immediate arrest and confinement.
Indeed, our enterprise formed the principal theme of conversation at the Cape during the week subsequent to our
arrival.

At the hour appointed I presented myself at the government house, and was introduced to the Governor, Lord
Macartney, in whose company I found, also, the Admiral.
There was so much urbanity and affability in the reception
I met with from the Governor as well as the Admiral that
it inspired me with confidence and prevented my feeling
any embarrassment. The Governor very politely handed
me a chair; and, seated between these two distinguished
men, I was prepared to answer, to the best of my knowledge, such questions as they should ask me, and to give
them all the information respecting European affairs that
my residence in that country and my recent departure
enabled me to do. It was just at this period that the
flotilla was assembling in the ports of the Channel for the
invasion of England, and on this subject in particular they
were very earnest to obtain information, seeming to be
not without apprehension that an invasion was really

intended. While I related to them what had come under my own observation with regard to the preparation and what I had heard from others, I expressed to them the belief, founded on the desperate nature of the undertaking, that nothing more was intended by it than to keep England in a state of alarm, and to cause a corresponding increase of expenses.

Having interrogated me to their satisfaction on the political affairs of France, they adverted to the more humble business of the object of my enterprise, which the Admiral did not hesitate to declare he believed to be for the conveyance of despatches for the French government; and, in this belief, informed me that he should take measures to prevent my going to the Isle of France. At the same time, and as an additional evidence of this persuasion, he had ordered that a search should be made on board my vessel for the supposed despatches, and that all the letters and papers found on board should be brought to him. Consequently, my journal, book of accounts, and private letters and papers were submitted to his inspection, and the letters I had for French gentlemen in the Mauritius were all broken open.

On the conclusion of my visit to the Governor, who gave me permission to dispose of my cargo here if I desired, I went to the house of an old acquaintance, where I had lodged in a former voyage, and in what he considered more propitious times. Both he and his family seemed glad to see me, and invited me to take up lodgings there again; but the safety of my vessel required my presence on board not less in port than at sea, and I therefore declined.

The day following my letters and papers were returned to me by the secretary of the Admiral, and I was surprised

by a proposition from him for the purchase of my vessel.
I delayed giving an answer until the next day, and in the
mean time my inquiries led me to believe that my cargo
would sell advantageously, but there was nothing but
specie which would answer my purpose to take away for
it, and this was prohibited. With a provision for the
removal of this difficulty, and a good price for my vessel,
I was prepared to negotiate with the secretary. Meeting
him, therefore, at the time appointed, and both being
what in trade is called off-hand men, we soon closed the
bargain by his engaging to pay me, on delivery of the
Caroline and stores, five thousand Spanish dollars, and to
obtain for me permission to export ten thousand. This
so far exceeded the cost of the vessel, and was even so
much more than I had expected to receive at the Isle of
France, that I considered myself already well indemnified
for all my trouble and anxiety.

As the Admiral was pressing to have the vessel dis-
charged, it was my intention to land the cargo, next day,
on my own account; but in the mean time, I contracted
with the merchant, at whose house I now resided, for the
whole of it, at a moderate advance on the invoice; it
being agreed that he was to pay the duties, the expense
of landing, etc. My spirits were now much elevated with
my success, and with the prospect of soon being rid of
the Caroline and of the care inseparable from having such
a vessel, so circumstanced.

But I was allowed but a short period to my exultation;
new and alarming difficulties awaited me, of which I had
no suspicion, and which were more harassing than the
dangers of the winds and the waves. It appeared that
the duties on entries at the custom house were a percent-
age on the invoice, and that it was a very common prac-

tice with the merchants to make short entries. The purchaser was aware that, to stand on equal footing with other merchants, he must do as they did; but he seems not to have reflected that, being known to be more hostile to the English government than any other individual at the Cape, he would be rigidly watched, and, if detected, would have less indulgence than any other. The consequence was a detection of the short entry and seizure of vessel and cargo. The merchant went immediately, in a supplicating mood, to the collector, in the hope of arranging the affair before it should become generally known; but it was all in vain.

The only alternative which seemed now to be left me was to appeal to the highest authority, and I determined to write to Lord Macartney and prove to him that, by my contract for the sale of the cargo, the duties were not to be paid by me, and that consequently I should have derived no benefit had the attempt for evading them succeeded; but that, on the other hand, if the vessel and cargo were to be confiscated I should be the sufferer, as it was doubtful if the merchant could make good the loss. I hoped that he might thus be induced to advise a less severe course than the collector intended to pursue. But how to write a suitable letter embarrassed me. I had no friend with whom to advise. I was entirely ignorant of the manner of addressing a nobleman, and at the same time was aware of the necessity of doing it with propriety. In this dilemma I remembered to have seen, in an old magazine on board, some letters addressed to noblemen. These I sought as models, and they were a useful guide to me. After I had completed my letter in my best hand, and enclosed it in a neat envelope, I showed it to the Admiral's secretary, who appeared to be friendly to me.

He approved of it, and advised my taking it myself to his lordship immediately.

As the schoolboy approaches his master after having played truant, so did I approach Lord Macartney on this occasion. I delivered my letter to him ; and, after hastily reading it, he sternly said, " he could not interfere in the business; there were the laws, and if they had been infringed the parties concerned must abide the consequence," but added, " he would speak to the collector on the subject." This addition, delivered in rather a milder tone, led me to encourage the hope that the affair would not end so disastrously as if left entirely to the discretion of the collector. Nor were my hopes unfounded, as the next day the vessel and that part of the cargo yet remaining on board were restored to me, while the portion in the possession of the collector was to be adjudged in the fiscal court, where it was eventually condemned, to the amount of about two thousand dollars.[1] The success of my letter was a theme of public conversation in the town, and was the means of procuring me the acquaintance of several individuals of the first respectability.

The delay caused by this controversy with the collector was unfavorable to the views of the Admiral, who began to evince symptoms of impatience, and would probably ' have taken out the cargo with his own men if we had not set about it with earnestness as soon as the vessel was released from seizure. Having, the day following, completed the unlading, I delivered the vessel to the officer who was authorized to take possession. In two days after she was expedited with a lieutenant and competent number of men (I believe for India) ; and, in a subsequent

---

1 As a favor to the merchant, I consented to share the loss with him.

voyage, I learned that she had never been heard of afterwards.

"Now," said Uncle Fritz, "that man went to sea at
eighteen, at twenty-one he commanded a vessel. See
what your friend Richard H. Dana — yes, Two-Years-
before-the-Mast Dana — says of such commanders. Here
is a scrap from his review of Cleveland's book.

"'We do not hesitate to say that an intelligent, firm
young man, who, at the age of eighteen or twenty, after
some years spent in receiving an education on shore,
enters for the first time the nautical service, makes a long
voyage before the mast, keeps his watch and carries on
duty a year or so in each of the inferior grades of office,
by the help of his books and a close practical observation
and diligent attention while master, and the acquired
habit of commanding others and relying upon himself,
will work a ship better at thirty than one of the same age
would do who was set adrift at twelve, and has stayed in
the forecastle splicing ropes and hauling out ear-rings
until he was six-and-twenty.'"

"That advice," said Tom Rising, "does not seem to
favor Bob's escape from his tyrants by the sheets of his
bedroom, and going a-whaling before he knows a vulgar
fraction from a noun predicate."

Uncle Fritz laughed. "If you want to know how these
youngsters crossed oceans in boats with such assistants,
read what Captain Cleveland wrote at sixty-seven years of
age.

"'To the present sixty-eighth year of my life I have
never taken a drop of spirituous liquor of any kind ; never
a glass of wine, of porter, ale, or beer, or any beverage
stronger than tea or coffee ; and, moreover, I have never

used tobacco in any way whatever, and this not only without injury but, on the contrary, to the preservation of my
health. Headache is known to me by name only, and,
excepting those fevers which were produced by great
anxiety and excitement, my life has been free from sickness.' Now go on with your story." So Tom went on.

It is probable that the officer in charge, having been
accustomed only to large and square-rigged vessels, was
not aware of the delicacy of management which one so
small and differently rigged required, and to this her loss
may be attributed.

The various drawbacks on my cargo, arising from seizure,
some damage, and some abatement, reduced the net proceeds to about the original cost. This, with the amount
of the vessel, I collected in Spanish dollars, making
together, after my various disbursements, the sum of
eleven thousand dollars, which I kept in readiness to embark in the first vessel that should enter the bay on her
way to India or China.

"But," said Uncle Fritz, "you must not suppose that
these gentlemen found it all sunshine in such enterprise.
Look further and you will find my mark at an adventure
Cleveland had in Valparaiso. That will show you what is
meant in our history by 'Spanish claims,' or claims on
the Spanish government. It will show you, also, how
prompt and how brave these adventurers had to be."

On entering the Bay of Valparaiso we were boarded by
a naval officer from a guardacosta, then lying in port. He
desired us not to cast anchor till the captain had presented himself to the Governor and obtained his per-

mission. Consequently, while Mr. Shaler accompanied this officer to the Governor, we lay off and on in the bay. More than an hour had elapsed before his return with a permission to anchor, and to remain till a reply could be received from the Captain-General at Santiago to our request for leave to supply our wants, for which a despatch was to be forwarded immediately.

We were surprised to find no less than four American vessels lying here, viz.: the ship Hazard of Providence, on a voyage similar to our own, detained on suspicion of being English, from the circumstance of being armed; the ship Miantonomo and schooner Oneco of Norwich, Conn., each with valuable cargoes of seal-skins taken at the Island of Masafuera, both detained, and finally confiscated on a charge of having supplied English privateers, then on the coast, with provisions which they had obtained at Talcahuaua; and the ship Tryal, of Nantucket, a whaler, also detained for alleged illicit trade. If we were surprised to meet so many of our countrymen here, we were equally mortified, and in some degree alarmed for our own safety, to find them a ˙ under seizure. Yet, while we violated no law, and required no other than the privileges secured to us by treaty, we could not believe that we should be molested.

On the third day after the Governor's messenger had been despatched a reply was received from the Captain-General, the purport of which was that our passage had been so good that we could not be in want of provisions if we had provided such quantity in Europe as we ought to have done. But if it were otherwise, and our wants were as urgent as represented, the mode by which we proposed paying for them, by a bill on Paris, was inadmissible; and, therefore, that it was his Excellency's order that we should leave the port at the expiration of twenty-four hours after this notification. On remonstrating with the Governor, and pointing out to him the inhumanity of driving us to sea, while in possession of so small a supply of the first necessaries of life, he very reluctantly consented to our remaining another post, and even promised to make a more favorable report on the urgency of our necessities than he had done. But, as the order was reiterated, we doubted his having performed his promise, and therefore determined to write directly to the Captain-General. In conformity with this decision Mr. Shaler addressed a letter to the Captain-General, in the Spanish language, expressing his surprise at the order for his departure, without affording him the supplies which were indispensable, and for which provision had been made by treaty. " Presuming that his Excellency's intentions had been misconceived by the Governor, he had ventured to disobey the order, and to remain in port till the reception of his Excellency's reply." A prompt and very polite answer to the letter was received, granting us permission to supply ourselves with everything we desired ; and, what was very extraordinary, giving us further permission, which had not been asked, of selling so much of the cargo as would be sufficient to pay for the supplies. After which he desired we would leave the port immediately, and added that if we entered any other port on the coast we should be treated as contrabandists.

The latter paragraph of his Excellency's letter evidently conveyed a doubt in his mind whether our destination and the object of our voyage was what we had stated it to be. But, having subjected ourselves to the mortification of having the correctness of our statement doubted, there seemed to be no other remedy than patience and forbearance. At any rate, our embarrassments were more entirely relieved than we had anticipated. We procured our provisions and paid for them in manufactures, and were engaged in settling our accounts preparatory to our departure on the morrow, having already exceeded a month since our arrival.

But we were unconscious of what a day would bring forth, and entirely unprepared for a train of unfortunate events, in which every American in port was more or less involved. It appeared that a part of the cargo of the ship Hazard consisted of muskets. These were demanded by the Governor, on pretext of being contraband of war, and were very properly refused by Captain Rowan, who stated to the Governor that they were taken on board at a neutral port, that they were not destined to any port of the enemies of Spain, and that they did not come under the sixteenth article of the treaty.

During our stay here we had ascertained that the actual Governor of the place was with his family on a visit to the capital, and that the person with whom we had been treating, and who represented here the Majesty of Spain, Don Antonio Francisco Garcia Carrasco, was an officer of inferior grade, acting as governor during the absence of his superior. Don Antonio was about sixty years of age, of pleasing manners, of prepossessing countenance, and apparently of amiable disposition, but of no decision of character; of contracted mind, puffed up with vanity, and confounded at the audacity that should dare to refuse compliance with an order given in the name of his king; indeed, in his person, character, and capacities, there was a striking resemblance to the portrait drawn by Cervantes of the celebrated Governor of Barrataria.

The pride of the Governor was evidently wounded by the refusal of Rowan to obey his demand of the muskets, and his subsequent measures to obtain them were calculated to exhibit his folly, and to increase his mortification and hostile feelings. To suppose, with his feeble means, that he could coerce a compliance with his demand, was to suppose the American to be as great a poltroon as himself. As far, however, as the attempt could prove it, he certainly did expect to do so.

The troops of the garrison, about thirty in number, with drums beating and colors displayed, were seen marching from the castle to the sea-shore, in the afternoon of the day on which the muskets had been refused. Rowan, who was on the alert, saw them embark in a large launch, accompanied by the Governor, and prepared himself for resistance. The launch, which with rowers and soldiers was excessively crowded, approached the Hazard with the royal colors flying. When within hail of the ship the Governor stood up, and demanded if he might come on board. Rowan replied that he should be happy to be honored with his company, but that he would not permit any one of his soldiers to come on board. The launch approached nearer to the ship, to enable the parties to converse with more ease. The Governor again formally demanded the surrender of the arms, and was again refused. He remonstrated, and urged the consequences of resisting the authority of the King's representative. But it was all unavailing, and perceiving that neither threats nor persuasion had the desired effect, that armed sentries were stationed at the gangways of the ship, and the proper precautions taken against a *coup de main*, he returned to the shore with his soldiers, deeply mortified, excessively irritated, and vowing vengeance.

But it is not unusual that what is done in the moment of great excitement is not of the most judicious character, and that by suffering ourselves to be controlled by our passions, we commit acts which increase the absurdity of a ridiculous position, and augment our embarrassments. This was precisely the case with the Governor, in this instance. Without adverting to consequences, but influenced by the violence of his passion, he, immediately on landing, ordered every American who could be found on shore to be arrested and shut up in the castle. Shaler, Rouissillon, and myself, being of this number, were accordingly arrested, and, with four others of our countrymen, were marched to prison in charge of a file of soldiers, who by their conversation during the time, evinced that their feelings were in unison with those of the Governor.

At the same time with the order for our arrest, and as if to consummate his folly, the Governor made another attempt to intimidate, by ordering the captain of a large Spanish ship, which mounted eighteen heavy guns betwixt decks, to bring his broadside to bear on the Hazard, and order her colors to be hauled down in token of submission, on penalty of being sunk. After what had occurred, to make such a threat, without daring to take the responsibility of executing it, served only to increase the awkwardness of the Governor's position. While all, both on shore and on board the shipping, were watching with intense interest the result of this threat, a man was observed on board the Hazard engaged in nailing the colors to the mast. A more significant reply could not possibly be made. The Governor was foiled, and a calm succeeded the storm, during the time required to despatch a courier to the Captain-General, and to receive his instructions in the case.

Our arrest prevented our sailing, as we intended to do, the same evening. Having passed a most uncomfortable night, without beds, in the castle, where we were annoyed by myriads of fleas, and having been without food of any kind since noon of the preceding day, we wrote to the Governor in the morning, requesting to be provided with food and beds. Our letter was returned unopened ; but about noon, by a verbal message from the Governor, we were informed that liberty was given us to go on board our respective ships. We were doubtful of the propriety of availing ourselves of this liberty, so ungraciously proffered, till an apology should be made to us for the aggression. It was finally settled that Shaler, being the most important person, as master of the vessel, should remain in prison. We therefore sent to him a bed and provisions. This was a determination for which the Governor was entirely unprepared, and which seemed to confound him. With characteristic imbecility, he went to the castle, and greeting Mr. Shaler with apparent cordiality, begged him to go on board his vessel, and proceed to sea. This Shaler offered to do, on condition of receiving a written apology for imprisoning us. He declined giving it. Permission was then asked to send an express with a letter to the Captain-General. This he peremptorily and angrily refused, and then suddenly started off to superintend the preparations which he was making to compel a surrender of the Hazard, the orders for which he expected to receive the next day.

Although the ostensible reason for refusing a compliance with the Governor's orders to go to sea was to obtain satisfaction, yet the real cause of our delay was the hope and belief of being able to render essential service in aiding to extricate Rowan from his difficulties. It was evident that the Governor desired only the sanction of the Captain-General to attempt coercion ; and, in expectation of receiving it, he was making the requisite preparations.

The soldiers of the garrison, and the populace, were busily engaged, under the direction of the Governor, in placing cannon in every direction to bear on the ship. The inhabitants of the houses in the vicinity left them, and retired to the hills. The activity and bustle of business had given place to the preparation and excitement of war, and the confusion and apprehension could hardly have been exceeded if the town had been on the point of being taken by assault.

While Mr. Rouissillon and myself were walking through one of the streets we encountered the Governor, who saluted us, and asked me if I was not next in command on board to Mr. Shaler. Answering in the affirmative, he ordered me to go on board, and proceed to sea. On my rejoining that I could not go without my captain, he threatened to seize the vessel, and without waiting for a reply, left us abruptly, and apparently in an angry mood. In the course of the following day, being the fourth from the beginning of hostilities, the express arrived from Santiago, bringing a letter to Captain Rowan from the Captain-General. It contained such promise of redress, if he would comply with the requisitions of government by delivering up the arms, that he was induced to yield. The arms were accordingly delivered to the order of the Governor, and his receipt taken for them. The portentous cloud, which had been lowering over the affairs of our countrymen in this place, appeared to be now dissipated. The colors of defiance, which had been waving on the ships and at the castle from the beginning of the dispute, were hauled down; the cannon which had been transported to the beach were returned to their ancient position; the sentries were no longer seen at the gangways of the Hazard; the old women and children returned to their habitations; and everything indicated peace and repose.

This repose, however, was only the treacherous calm that precedes the hurricane. The Governor could not brook the indignity he had suffered. The vengeance he had vowed, and which he had not the courage to take openly, he determined to execute treacherously; and his measures, which were taken with great secrecy, and with the stimulus of plunder, were executed with such success as must have satisfied his highest ambition, and served as a balm to his wounded feelings.

On the evening of the day when the muskets were surrendered, Mr. Rouissillon and myself made a visit to the Governor, and found him to be as affable and pleasant as was naturally to be expected on attaining the object of which he had so long been in pursuit. He hoped we should proceed to sea the next day, and inquired why Rowan did not come on shore; adding, to our surprise, that if he did not come voluntarily he should use coercion. We assured him of our belief that his not having been on shore that day was accidental, and not from any apprehension of molestation, begged him not to think of coercion, and offered our guarantee that he should present himself at the castle in the morning. On leaving the Governor we went on board the Hazard and reported to Rowan our conversation with the Governor. He had no hesitation in determining to act in accordance with his desire by visiting him as early as it was permitted strangers to be on shore.

BOARDING THE HAZARD.

Fearing, in this instance, a' too ready compliance, in which case the opportunity for revenge would escape him,

the Governor must have had everything planned and prepared in the evening, probably while we were with him, to
execute his cowardly design in the morning, before it was
permitted to Rowan to come on shore. The launches,
which were used to transport wheat from the shore to the
large ship before mentioned, passed and repassed near the
Hazard while thus engaged; consequently, they would
excite no suspicion when approaching the ship. An enter-
prize involving so little risk, and which promised so golden
a harvest of plunder, had not to wait for the requisite number of men. About two hundred ruffians, armed with pistols, swords, and knives, embarked in the launches used
for carrying wheat, and boarded the Hazard on each
side, while her men were entirely off their guard, unsus-
picious of any cause of hostility. To save their lives, such
of the crew as were able made a hasty retreat to the hold.
But there were two poor fellows lying sick in their hammocks, and these were both dangerously wounded. Rowan
was screened from the vengeance of the banditti by the
interference of an officer, taken immediately on shore, and
sent to the castle.

The scene of plunder and confusion which ensued beg-
gars all description. Perceiving that the mischief was
likely to be more extensive than he had imagined, the
Governor went on board with a party of soldiers to arrest
its progress. But he soon discovered that it is easier to
set a mob in motion than to control it afterwards. With
his utmost efforts, aided by the soldiers, and by the com-
mandant of the custom-house guards and his satellites, he
was incapable of resisting the progress of the plunderers,
until, being satiated, they retreated with their booty to the
shore as opportunity offered. When there were but few
remaining he succeeded in driving them away, and placed
the ship in charge of the mates.

After such an achievement, such a gathering of laurels, there was some hazard to a foreigner in calling on the Governor, even though it were to compliment him. But, being determined that the Captain-General should have our version of the transaction, I called on him at noon for leave to send an express to the capital to complain of the outrage, and to demand that redress there which we asked in vain here. In an angry tone, and instead of replying to my request, he inquired if we were desirous of provoking him to serve us in the manner he had done the ship. I replied that I hoped there was no danger of our causing him any provocation, but should it be our misfortune to do so to the extent intimated, there could exist no cause for such violent measures as had been used towards the ship, as no resistance would be made. I then remarked on the advantage that would result to the government in keeping away the rabble, and thus securing the whole property. I stated, also, that there were many valuable instruments, charts, and books on board which would be useful to the Spanish marine, but which might be destroyed if, as he suggested, " he served us in the manner he had done the ship "; and I repeated a hope that he would not do so. Seeing that I was not to be intimidated, and was, moreover, determined not to go to sea without communicating with the Captain-General, he at length reluctantly consented to our sending an express. . . .

LETTERS.

The letter written by Mr. Shaler in Spanish, and complaining of the outrageous conduct of the Governor to the

unoffending citizens of a friendly power, was sent by a
· courier. It produced an interchange of several letters, the
purport of which was, on one side, to deny the right of
any foreign vessel to traverse these seas, which, his Excellency said, like the territory, belonged exclusively to his
Catholic Majesty; on the other, to refute the absurd doc-
trine of any nation's possessing an exclusive right to any
particular sea, and giving chapter and verse in the treaty,
not only for our right to sail where we please, but to enter
their ports and demand succor. His Excellency closed
the correspondence by expressing a hope that if we did
not admit their exclusive right to these seas, we would, at
least, allow them to be masters in their own ports. . . .

WAIT ON THE GOVERNOR.

Having assisted in bringing Rowan's affairs into such
a train as promised a speedy and satisfactory adjustment,
there existed no farther inducement to remain longer in
port. Accordingly, having settled our various accounts of
disbursements, Mr. Shaler, accompanied by Mr. Rouissillon, waited on the Governor to notify him of his intention
to proceed to sea next morning, and to take leave. He
received them with great cordiality, expressed much regret
at what had occurred, promised to remedy the mischief as
far as he was able, offered us every facility in his power to
insure our departure at the time appointed, and, though
it would not have been surprising if he had wished us to
the devil, on the contrary, wished us a good voyage.

There was a number of our unfortunate countrymen in
port, principally the crews of the condemned vessels, who
had lost their little all, and whose situation excited com-
miseration. We knew that if they could get to Masafuera

with the provisions they could obtain here, they would, by
pursuing their vocation, soon bring up arrears. We determined, therefore, to go so far out of our way as to give
them all passages thither. They all very gratefully accepted our invitation. Being ready on the 21st of April,
and on the point of leaving the port, a message was
brought from the Governor, requesting to see Mr. Shaler.
He went immediately to him, and found, to his astonishment, that he wanted him to defer his departure a few
days. It appeared that some suspicious or malicious person had suggested to this silly governor that our object in
taking so many men on board was to capture the large
ship, then on the point of sailing for Lima. To guard
against this, he begged Mr. Shaler to defer sailing till
forty-eight hours after that ship had sailed, and, moreover,
hoped we would not revenge ourselves on any unarmed
Spanish vessel we might chance to meet. . . .

QUICKSILVER.

The time we had agreed to wait had not quite expired
when we were all taken aback again. It appeared that
one of our sailors, an Irishman, who had deserted, had
given information that we had many kegs of dollars on
board, stowed under the ballast. As he had pointed out
precisely where they were, an armed force came on board
by order of the Governor, and, proceeding directly to the
place indicated by the sailor, found, instead of kegs of
dollars, kegs of quicksilver, of which they took away four,
giving a receipt for them.

We flattered ourselves that this aggression would be the
means of opening the way for our going to the capital.
Renewing, therefore, our correspondence with the Cap-

tain-General, to complain of this outrage, and remarking
on our entire want of confidence in the capacity or honesty of the Governor and his advisers, we reiterated our
request for leave to repair to Santiago for the more speedy
adjustment of our grievance. In reply, his Excellency
remarked on the loss of time which our coming to Santiago would cause, and observed that the difficulty could
be easily adjusted at Valparaiso by answering satisfactorily
the following questions, viz.: Why was the quicksilver
hidden under the ballast? To whom does it belong?
To what port destined? These interrogatories, being
solemnly propounded by the Governor to Mr. Shaler, a
notary public being present, he replied to the first that it
was not hidden ; to the second, that it belonged to the
owners of the vessel and cargo ; to the third, that its destination was round the world ; and to this deposition he
took an oath on an odd volume of Shakespeare, presented
him by the Governor for that purpose.

The result of this investigation was immediately despatched to the Captain-General, and an answer returned
by his Excellency with the least possible delay, the purport of which was that the four kegs of quicksilver should
be restored to us on board, and that we should then leave
the port without further delay. . . . During this controversy, the men whom we intended taking to Masafuera
had dispersed in various directions, so that having on
board only our original small complement of men, the
authorities had no cause to apprehend any acts of piracy
from us.

TAKING LEAVE.

The functions of Don Antonio as Governor *ad interim*
having ceased on the arrival of his senior from Santiago,

when we were on the point of sailing, we made him a visit as soon after his arrival as etiquette would permit. He gave us a most cordial, frank, and friendly reception, and expressed much regret at having been absent on our arrival; as, he said, not only would the trouble we had experienced have been avoided, but he would have obtained permission for us to visit Santiago. The order for our departure, however, being now given by the Captain-General, was irrevocable, and he therefore hoped there would be no further delay. On taking leave he inundated us with civilities and good wishes, promising, moreover, to use his best endeavors to bring the affair of our unfortunate countryman, Rowan, to a speedy and satisfactory conclusion. These civilities, professions, and promises passed with us for no more than they were worth, after the observations our opportunities had afforded us of judging of the character and motives of action of the authorities here.

It was now the 6th of May, being two and a half months from the date of our arrival, — a long time, considering that we were allowed only twenty-four hours by the Captain-General to remain in port; and for the third time had settled our accounts, and made all ready for our departure. No further obstacle to our sailing occurring, and having taken leave of our acquaintance and countrymen, we left Valparaiso to the great satisfaction of the Governor and authorities, no less than of ourselves.

"Another such book," said Uncle Fritz, "is Captain Bennett Forbes's account of his reminiscences. But as you are all Boston bred, I suppose you have all seen that."

And it proved that they had.

XI.

THE NORTHWEST.

"UNCLE FRITZ, you spoke of Jefferson as a geographer or naturalist."

" Oh, yes," said Uncle Fritz, "when he was in France he was a great deal with the philosophical set, who all thought that if people knew the length of a degree of the meridian, and could rightly analyze water, all would be well."

" They should learn Dr. Watts," said Esther.

" Dr. Watts!   Frenchmen learn Dr. Watts? "

" Why, Dr. Watts implies that knowing is not quite enough.   Don't you remember?

> ' Who know what 's right, not only so,
> But also *practise* what they know.' "

And Esther gave a very funny emphasis and accent to " practise," just as she said Mr. Ockley, thè Sunday-school teacher at North Holderness, did.

Uncle Fritz, not displeased with the comment, went on to say that some of Jefferson's worst follies and some of his most sensible enterprises were dictated by his wish to be called a philosopher. " Of the whole set of the philosophers whom he used to meet in the society of Paris, about the time when the French Revolution was brewing, he only came to an important post of power.

"One of his theories was peaceful war. He thought that the United States could starve Europe into submission, if he cut off all trade. But alas! It was the United States which starved, and Europe did not know that anything was happening.

"Then he had a plan for keeping his navy on land, and carrying it about in carts wherever the enemy might attack. But this never worked well.

"But he wrote an interesting book on the resources of Virginia, — he was president of the Philosophical Society, and when you go and visit Mary Lesley, at Philadelphia, she will take you to the library, and show you no end of curious things in the archives, which have to do with him.

"I have a copy of a letter which he wrote to our old friend, Phil. Nolan, when he was hunting wild horses in Texas. His namesake, Mr. Joseph Jefferson, was kind enough to hunt that up for me in the State Department at Washington.

"Philip Nolan was the first person to bring back to the United States any accurate knowledge of the wonderful resources of Texas. The Spaniards caught him there, violated their own safeguard, and killed him in 1801. That is probably the reason why we have no answer to Mr. Jefferson's letter to him.

"Then, when Jefferson was well established in the presidency, he determined to find what there was between the Mississippi and the Pacific. Nobody who had left any reliable account had ever gone across in the regions north of Mexico.

"If you will look in the Popular History again," said Uncle Fritz, "where you were looking when we had the Coronado reading, you will find how four poor fellows of

Narvaez's expedition straggled across from the gulf, slaves most of the time to Indians, in the years following 1528. But after them there was no authentic account of any passage.

"It is odd enough," continued Uncle Fritz, " that every cyclopædia, till within a few years, says that Carver, who went from here to Lake Superior in 1768, went to the Pacific. You will find that in the earlier editions of Appleton. So the old French cyclopædias say that Chateaubriand, in 1792, went to the Pacific. In truth, he never went beyond the Red River of Louisiana. Lewis and Clarke were the first men to cross the Rocky Mountains and back, from the Mississippi to the Pacific.

"You see that as long ago as 1792, in that very fur-trade of which Captain Cleveland gives you some account, Robert Gray, from Salem, here in the ship Columbia, discovered the Columbia River. He sailed up, gave his vessel's name to it, and on that discovery, in a considerable measure, rested, at one time, our claim to Oregon. Jefferson selected two captains from the army, Meriwether Lewis and George Clarke, and bade them organize an expedition to find this same Columbia River and descend to the sea. This they did in the years 1804, 1805, and 1806. You see, there were as yet no steamboats. They had to row, sail, and tow, on their way up the Missouri, till they came to the mountains. Slow work it was, to be sure. Then they bought horses from the Indians and crossed the passes, — in the same regions where the Northern Pacific Railroad is to be pressed through, — and to them are due the names of Lewis's River and Clarke's River, the two branches which unite in the Columbia River.

"When they came back, they had not been heard from for more than two years.

"This was the beginning of a series of government explorations which have lasted till our time. There is a good abridgment of Lewis and Clarke's narrative in Harper's Family Library. But, to say truth, it is dull. They had not the art of telling their story well, though they had so much to tell. Of all the books made out of the journals of those explorations, Irving's " Astoria " and " Captain Bonneville " are the most entertaining. Later down Francis Parkman's book, when he spent a summer with the Sioux, is charming. Fremont is very entertaining. There are several of his reports.

"Yes, Tom, he is the Fremont who was almost chosen President; he was general in the War of the Rebellion, and is now Governor of Arizona.

"Suppose we try the Great Northwest. That is a country which, before Fulton invented the steamboat, seemed so useless that we almost lost it at the treaty of Ghent by the mere indifference of our own negotiators.

"It was our dear old John Quincy Adams who hung on. He hated the English so that he would not let them have even a wilderness if he could help it."

Then Uncle Fred asked Clement to bring him the third volume of Adams's Memoirs,[1] and he showed Clem. some of his marks at passages in the negotiation of the treaty of 1814 with England.

"Mr. Gallatin told them that if they considered the remainder of the article, the forty-ninth parallel of latitude, an equivalent, he wished them to understand that we attached no importance to it at all. It would, indeed, be a convenience to have the boundary settled; but the lands there were of so little value, and the period when they might be

---

[1] Memoirs of John Quincy Adams.

settled so remote, that we were perfectly willing that the boundary there should remain as it is now, and without any further arrangement."

"Why, Uncle Fritz, it was the State of Minnesota which Gallatin says was of so little value," said Bedford, who was on the floor, with Colton's Atlas open.

"To be sure it was, my boy. But please think what the State of Minnesota would be without steamboats and without railroads. And even in 1814, even Mr. Gallatin did not dream of what steamboats were to do.

"But the steamboat was already pushing its nose into every river of the West. And nine years after that remark of Mr. Gallatin, Col. Long was sent up there to see where the new boundary — which is our present boundary of 49° north latitude — would run. The old boundary of the first treaty had proved quite impossible, because the Mississippi did not rise where they thought it did."

"And with Col. Long," said Col. Ingham, "your readings connect with Uncle Fritz. For this same Col. Long afterwards was interested in railroads, and invented a locomotive which should burn hard coal, — anthracite. When I was a boy, Mr. Hale bought one of these engines for the Boston and Worcester Railroad. Those were days, Bedford, when a good-natured boy had more rights than he has now, and rules and regulations were not so many. I used to be a good deal at the railroad station in Washington Street, and more than once have I coaxed a good-natured engine-driver to give me a ride on 'Col. Long,' as we always called his engine. What her real name was I have forgotten.

"But Laura did not come here to hear stories about locomotives; she is all ready to read."

And Laura read from the narrative of an expedition to
the source of St. Peter's River.

PLAN OF THE PARTY.

The success which attended the expedition to the
Rocky Mountains, and the important information which it
imparted concerning the nature of the valley drained by
the Missouri and its tributaries, of which nothing was
known but what had been observed by Lewis and Clarke,
induced the Government of the United States to continue
its endeavors to explore the unknown wilds within its
limits. The first object which appeared to it deserving of
investigation was the district of country bounded by the
Missouri, the Mississippi, and the northern boundary of
the United States.

Accordingly it was determined in the spring of 1823,
by the executive, that an expedition be immediately fitted
out for exploring the river St. Peter's and the country
situated on our northern boundary between the Red River
of Hudson's Bay and Lake Superior.

The command of the expedition was intrusted to Major
S. H. Long, and he received orders from the War Department, dated April 25, 1823, from which the following is
taken : —

"The route of the expedition will be as follows : com-
mencing at Philadelphia, thence proceeding to Wheeling
in Virginia, thence to Chicago via Fort Wayne, thence to
Fort Armstrong or Dubuque's Lead Mines, thence up the
Mississippi to Fort Anthony, thence to the source of the
St. Peter's River, thence to the point of intersection
between Red River and the forty-ninth degree of north
latitude, thence along the northern boundary of the United

States to Lake Superior, and thence homeward by the lakes.

"The object of the expedition is to make a general Survey of the country on the route pointed out, together with a topographical description of the same, to ascertain the latitude and longitude of all the remarkable points, to examine and describe its productions, animal, vegetable, and mineral, and to inquire into the character, customs, etc., of the Indian tribes inhabiting the same." . . .

The party travelled in light carriages from Philadelphia to Wheeling, where they disposed of them and purchased horses in exchange. The usual route through Lancaster, Columbia, York, and Gettysburg, was travelled. Here they left the Pittsburg turnpike road and reached Hagerstown in Maryland by a cross road; from Hagerstown they continued along the Maryland turnpike road to Cumberland, where it unites with the national road, upon which they travelled to Wheeling. . . .

The country about the Muskingum appears to have been at a former period the seat of a very extensive aboriginal population. Everywhere do we observe in this valley remains of works which attest at the same time the number, the genius, and the perseverance of those departed nations. Their works have survived the lapse of ages, but the spirit which prompted them has disappeared. We wander over the face of the country; wherever we go we mark the monuments which they have erected; we would interrogate them as to the authors of these mighty works, but no voice replies to ours save that of the echo. The mind seeks in vain for some clew to assist it in unravelling the mystery. Was their industry stimulated by the desire of protecting themselves against the inroads of invaders, or were they themselves the trespassers? did they migrate to this spot, and if so, whence came they? who were they? where went they? and wherefore came they here? Their works have been torn open; they have been searched into, but all in vain. The mound is now levelled with the sod of the valley; the accumulated earth, which was perhaps collected from a distance into one immense mass to erect a monument, deemed indestructible, over the remains of some western Pharaoh, is now scattered over the ground so that its concealed treasure may be brought to light. Every bone is accurately examined, every piece of metal or fragment of broken pottery is curiously studied; still no light has as yet been thrown upon the name and date of the once populous nation which formerly flourished on the banks of the numerous tributary streams of the Ohio.

Such were the reflections suggested to us by our visit to the numerous mounds and Indian works which abound in this part of the country, the first of which we observed in the small village of Irville, situated eleven miles west of Zanesville. It has been opened, and as usual it has yielded bones. This mound was about fifteen 'feet in diameter and four and a half in height; it appears to have had an elliptic basis. Our guide told us that he was present at the opening of it, and that there were a number of human bones, and among others a tolerably entire skeleton which laid with its head to the northwest; the arms were thrown back over the head. Besides the bones there were numerous spear and arrow points, and of the latter we picked up one on the spot. There was also a plate of copper of the length of the hand, and from five to six inches in width; it was rolled up at the sides and had two holes near the centre; its weight we were told might have been about a quarter of a pound, but was probably heavier ; for it must have been very thin, if, with those dimensions, it weighed so little. What could have been the use of it, except as an ornament, was not determined ; indeed, the inhabitants of that part of the country are so much accustomed to dig up the bones and remains of the aborigines that they are very careless about observing or recording the objects found, and the circumstances under which they were discovered. We are told that pieces of copper, and even of brass, had been frequently collected. The copper may be easily accounted for without a reference to a higher degree of civilization or to an intercourse with nations more advanced in the arts. The existence of native copper strewed upon the surface of the ground in many places will easily account for the circumstance of its being used by the natives as an ornament, in the same manner that the Copper Indians of the north have been known, from the earliest days of their discovery by the whites, to adorn their persons with it ; but we cannot account for the discovery of ornaments of brass unless we admit an intercourse with nations that had advanced in civilization.

The existence, therefore, of fragments of this alloy in mounds appears to us doubtful ; for, if true, the Indians who constructed them must have been much more refined than we can suppose they were, or they must have had intercourse with civilized nations. The erection of these mounds, which appear to be in a great measure contemporary, was certainly much anterior to the discovery of this continent in the fifteenth century ; and therefore it is not from Europeans that these pieces of brass were obtained, if, again we repeat it, they have been found interred in these works.

Besides this mound there are many others in the immediate vicinity of Irville, some of which have very great dimensions. We observed one near the road, which had been but recently excavated at its summit; it was perhaps thirty-five or forty feet high. These mounds were for the most part overgrown with bushes; we could discover no order or plan in their relative positions, and from the scattered and irregular manner in which they lie, it does not appear that they were intended to be connected with any work of defence; it is more probable that they were erected as mausoleums over the remains of the dead, and that the difference in their size was intended to convey an idea of the difference in the relative importance of those whose bones they covered. We were informed that this valley and the neighboring hills abound in excavations resembling wells. We met with none of these; they are said to be very numerous, and are generally attributed to the first French adventurers, who, being constantly intent upon the search of the precious metals, commenced digging wherever they observed a favorable indication. Not having seen any of these, we could not pretend to express an opinion upon their origin, but from the number in which they are represented to be, as well as from their dimensions, they appear to us far exceeding the abilities of those to whom they are attributed, and to have required a much more numerous and permanent population than these adventurers are known to have brought over with them; we would, therefore, prefer the opinion which ascribes them to the nations that erected the mounds, and who may have sunk these wells, either for purposes of self-defence according to the usual mode of Indian warfare, or as habitations, in the manner known to be practised by some tribes, or, finally, for some other cause as yet undiscovered. Their great depth, which is said at this time to

exceed twenty feet, may be considered as an objection to
the opinion which we have advanced. The supposition
of Mr. Atwater that these wells, which he states to be at
least a thousand in number, were opened for the mere
purpose of extracting rock-crystal and horn-stone, appears
to us too refined. Whatever may have been the advances
in civilization of these nations, we have no reason to believe that they had carried them so far as to be induced
to undertake immense mining operations for the mere
purpose of obtaining these articles.

"All this," said Uncle Fred, "is about Ohio, you see.
"Now if you will turn over to my mark you will find
something further off."

AN INDIAN TRIBE.

While travelling over the prairie which borders upon
that part of St. Peter that connects Lac-qui-parle with Big
Stone Lake, our attention was aroused by the sight of what
appeared to be buffaloes chased across the prairie. They,
however, soon proved to be Indians. Their number, at first
limited to two, gradually increased to near one hundred.
They were seen rising from every part of the prairie, and
after those in the advance had reconnoitered us and made
signals that we were friends by discharging their guns, they
all came running toward us, and in a few minutes we
found ourselves surrounded by a numerous band. They
had at first been apprehensive that we might be enemies,
and this was the cause of the different manœuvres which
they made previous to discharging their guns. The effect
of these guns fired upon the prairie in every direction, and
by each as soon as he had required the requisite degree of

certainty that the strangers were friends, was really very beautiful.

As they approached we had an opportunity of observing that these Indians were good-looking and straight; none were large, nor were remarkable for the symmetry of their forms. They were for the most part destitute of clothing, except the breech-cloth which they wore. Some of them, and particularly the young men, were dressed with care and ostentation. They wore looking-glasses suspended to their garments. Others had papers of pins, purchased from the traders, as ornaments. We observed that one who appeared to be a man of some note among them had a live sparrow-hawk upon his head by way of distinction; this man wore, also, a buffalo-robe, on which eight bear-tracks were painted. Some of them were mounted on horseback, and were constantly drumming with their heels upon the sides of their horses, being destitute of whip and spur. Many of them came and shook hands with us, while the rest were riding all round us in different directions. They belonged, as we were told, to one of the tribes of the Dakotas. Their chief being absent, the principal man among them told us that they had thirty lodges of their people at the lower end of the lake, and invited us to visit them, which invitation we accepted. These Indians demonstrated the greatest friendship and affection at seeing us. The village to which they directed us consisted of thirty skin-lodges, situated on a fine meadow on the bank of the lake.

Their permanent residence, or at least that which they have occupied for the last five years, is on a rocky island in the lake, nearly opposite to, and within a quarter of a mile of their present encampment. Upon the island they cultivate their cornfields, secure against the aggressions of their enemies. They had been lately engaged in hunting buffalo, apparently with much success.

The principal man led us to his lodge, wherein a number of the influential men were admitted, the women being excluded. But we observed that they, with all the children, went about the lodge, peeping through the crevices, and not unfrequently raising the skins, to observe our motions. They soon brought in a couple of large wooden dishes filled with pounded buffalo meat boiled, and covered with the marrow of the same animal; of this we partook with great delight. It was the first time that several of the party had tasted fresh buffalo meat; and it was the first meal made by any of us upon fresh meat since we had left Fort Anthony.

During the entertainment Major Long made known to them the objects of the expedition, at which they appeared very much gratified. As we rose to depart we were informed that another feast was preparing for us in one of the adjoining tents, of which we were invited to partake. We were too familiar with Indian manners not to know that the excuse of having just eaten a very hearty meal would not be considered as sufficient among them ; and so we readily resigned ourselves to the necessity of again testifying our friendly disposition by doing honor to their meal. It consisted of a white root, similar in appearance to a small turnip; it is called by the French *pomme blanche*. It was boiled down into a sort of mush, and was very much relished by most of the party ; had it been seasoned with salt or sugar, it might have been delicious. This was held, even by the guides, to be a great treat. As we were rising from this meal we were informed that a third was preparing for us. We begged to decline it, having a considerable distance to travel that afternoon ; but

we were informed that this would be a great disappointment to him who had prepared the feast, as, in order to
outdo all the others, he had killed a dog, which is considered not only as the greatest delicacy, but also as a
sacred animal, of which they eat only on great occasions.
In order to meet his wishes we deferred our journey for an
hour, but the repast not being then prepared we were
compelled to leave the village, to the great and manifest
mortification of our third host, and to the no small disappointment of most of our party, who were desirous of
tasting of the sacred animal.   In order to make a return
for the civilities which we had received at the hands of the
Indians, we informed them that if they would despatch a
messenger with us we would send them from a neighboring trader's house some tobacco, all ours having been lost
on the river. They gladly accepted the proposal, and sent
two lads with us for it.   We met on the bluff which com-
mands the superintendent's house an Indian who claims
the command of the Mahkpatoons.   We had declined his
invitation to stay at his lodge in the afternoon, being desirous of reaching Mr. Moore's house as early as possible,
but we promised to return about sunset, and he accordingly made all due preparations to receive us.   The chief
and his principal men were in waiting.   We entered the
skin-lodge, and were seated on fine buffalo-robes spread
all around ; on the fire, which was in the centre of the
lodge, two large iron kettles, filled with choicest pieces of
buffalo, were placed.   When the chief took his seat he
had near him a large pouch or bag, decorated with but
little taste, although he seemed to have gathered up all
that he could collect in the way of ornament.   Among
other things we observed an old and dirty comb.   He
had, since our first visit, bedaubed 'his face with white

clay. After the usual preliminaries of shaking of hands, smoking the pipe of peace, etc., we proceeded to the feast, which was found excellent. The buffalo meat had been selected with care, the fat and the lean judiciously portioned out, the whole boiled to a proper degree; and in fine, though our appetites were not stimulated to a long fast, this repast was one of the best of which we had ever partaken. Our hosts were gratified and flattered at the quantity which we ate; the residue of the. feast was sent to our soldiers. In this, and every other instance where we have been invited to a feast by the Indians, we observed that they never eat with their guests.

Tatanka Wechachita is the nephew of a man of considerable distinction among these Dakotas. Since the death of his uncle he has attempted to be considered as his successor; but the former was never duly acknowledged as chief, this title residing in Nunpakea, a man of considerable bravery, who, by the influence of his family and his talents, acquired that dignity in preference to his first cousins on the death of their father.

Our host boasted of many flags and medals which his uncle had obtained from our government, and which were then in his possession; these and the influence of his great magician may probably secure to him the dignity to which he aspires if he has talent enough to uphold it. After the feast was over our host rose, shook hands with all the gentlemen of our party, then resumed his seat and delivered a speech which at the time appeared to us very pertinent and interesting. It was delivered with apparent feeling, but not without some hesitation. Having expressed to Renville our satisfaction at the speech, he immediately observed that it expressed too much adulation and too much whining; had Tatanka Wechachita been the chief that he professed himself to be, his tone would have been more imposing, and his style more dignified and decisive.

"Brothers, the subject upon which I am to address you is grievous to me ; and this grief is the motive which has thus far prevented me from speaking to you. Since the lamented death of my revered uncle, who died last year, I have been called upon to succeed him, but as I am not endued with experience to know how to direct myself, I shall follow the advice which I have received from him, and therefore I rejoice at seeing you, and I am gratified at your visit.

"I regret that my followers are now all absent. This is our hunting season. In the autumn we collect in our villages to meet the traders. Had you seen us thus collected, you would have found me at the head of a large and powerful band of men. At present I am alone ; still I am pleased to see you.

"Brothers, there are two roads which we Dakotas usually travel ; my uncle trod both these paths. The first led him to the British, far towards the rising sun. From them he received both kindness and honor ; they made him many presents, among which were flags and medals. The other road led him to the Americans at St. Louis ; this road he subsequently travelled. From them he, in like manner, received flags and medals. These he has bequeathed all to me.

"I should have unfurled my flags at your approach, but I am unacquainted with the customs of your nation, and I am new in the duties of my rank. I am ignorant how to act ; but I am desirous of following the advice of my dying uncle, who bade me remain at peace with the Americans, and always consider them as my friends ; and as such I hold you.

"My friends, I am poor and very destitute; not so was my uncle. But I have as yet followed neither of the roads which he travelled. Since I have been called upon to rule over my people I have dwelt among them, and have not been able to visit St. Louis in order to obtain presents of powder and tobacco.

"I have already told you that my followers are absent; they are hunting at the north; I have left with them my flags. I know not whither you are going, but I presume you may meet them. They will exhibit to you my flags, and you will know them, for they are those of your nation. I shall send them word of your intention to travel that way, and bid them if they see you to treat you with becoming respect, assist you, supply you with provisions, and with whatever else you may require.

"My friends, I am poor, and could not do much; but I have prepared this little feast. You have partaken of it, and it has gratified me. I am young, and inexperienced in speaking, but I have done my best. Again I thank you for your flattering visit."

While riding quietly across the prairie, with the eye intent upon the beautiful prospect of the buffaloes that were grazing, our attention was suddenly aroused by the discharge of a gun in the vicinity of the river (Red River), which flowed about half a mile west of the course that we were then travelling. While we were reckoning up our party to know if any had straggled to a distance, we saw two Indians running across the prairie; their number increased very soon to twelve or fifteen, who hastened towards us, but as soon as they came near our party, stopped and examined us with minuteness, after which they presented their hands to us; we gave them ours. It was immediately observed that they were in a complete state of preparation for war, being perfectly naked with the exception of the breech-cloth. They had even laid their blankets by. All of them were armed with guns, apparently in very good order, or with bows and arrows, and some with both. Their appearance, though at first friendly, soon became insulting. Their party had, in the mean while, increased to thirty or forty, so that they outnumbered ours. We found that they belonged to the Wahkpakota or Leaf Indians, whose character, even among their own countrymen, is very bad. We availed ourselves of Mr. Snelling's knowledge of the language to communicate to them, in the course of conversation, our objects and intentions, as well as the friendly reception which we had met with on the part of Wanotan and the other Indians whom we had seen. In a tone rather imperative than courteous, they expressed their wish that we should go to their camp and speak to their old chief. This we declined doing, informing them that some of our party had separated from us, and that we had a long journey to travel.

They pointed to the sun, which was then low in the horizon, and added that we had no time to proceed further, and that we had better encamp with them that night.

While this conversation was going on Mr. Say remarked that, either through design or accident, the Indians had intermixed themselves so with our party that every one of our number was placed between two or more of theirs. Mr. Snelling overheard them talking of our horses, admiring them, and examining the points of each ; one of their band had even ventured so far as to ask him which horse was considered the best of the party.

Finding that all further conversation was a waste of

time, and having given them as much tobacco as our small stock allowed us to spare, Major Long mounted his horse and gave his men orders to march. The Indians attempted no opposition at the time, but after we had travelled about a quarter of a mile, they following in our rear, a gun was fired at some distance on the prairie to the right of our line, and a number of mounted Indians were seen in that direction coming towards us. Those who had followed us then made a signal to them that we were white men, and ran up to desire that, as their chief was then coming up, we would stop and shake hands with him. The party halted until the mounted Indians had come up and greeted us in the usual manner. Observing that their chief was not among them, Major Long again set his men in motion, but before we had proceeded far several of them ran up to the head of the line, fired their guns across our path, reloaded them immediately, and formed a crescent in front of the leader to prevent him from proceeding. At that time the number of Indians must have been about seventy or eighty, while ours amounted only to twenty-five. Their intentions could not be misunderstood. It was probable they did not care to harm our persons, but they were anxious to pilfer our baggage, and especially to secure our horses ; and as we were resolved not to part with them without a struggle, it was evident that the first gun fired would be the signal for an attack which must end in the total destruction of our party ; for the number of the Indians, and their mode of dispersing upon the prairie, and continually changing their situation during a skirmish, would have given them a very great advantage over us, as, in order to protect our horses and baggage, we would have remained in a body, and exposed to their arrows and balls. But even in such a case they must have lost some of their number, and this consideration, all-powerful with Indians, probably induced them to defer their attack until night, when their advantages would be still greater ; and hence their anxiety that we should encamp in the vicinity. Had Major Long been entirely free to act as he pleased he would have avoided all further conversation, and have proceeded the whole night without stopping at all that evening ; but this he could not do so long as some of the gentlemen were separated from us, for in such a case they would easily have been cut off by the Indians. It was to give them a chance to overtake us that he had continued the conference so long, and that he finally decided upon encamping at a point of wood then in sight, but further than that which had been proposed by the Indians.

With this view the Major ordered his men to march, when one of the Indians advanced up to the head of the line, stopped the horse of the leader, and cocked his gun. The soldier who was there, and whose name was George Bunker, immediately imitated this action, determined to be prepared for a shot as soon as his antagonist. At this moment Major Long marched up to the head of the line and led off his party. There can be no doubt that the resolution thus manifested had a great influence in preventing the Indians from making an immediate attack. The party being again safely united, Major Long considering that if an attack was intended it would be made a short time before daylight, determined to allow the horses to rest until midnight, when the moon, rising, would make it safe and pleasant to travel. Accordingly at that hour we resumed our line of march. Our preparations were made with the greatest expedition and silence, so as not to be observed by the Indians at a distance, and to avoid disturbing the old Indian sleeping, or affecting to sleep, under one of our carts. In the latter purpose, however, we failed ; the old man awoke, and seeing what we were about, he left us immediately, notwithstanding the attempt made to amuse him with conversation until we should be ready to start ; but we could not detain him ; we saw him walk over the prairie, and by the light of the moon traced his figure until he approached near to the river, when he disappeared in the woods. This was the last Dakota whom we saw. . . .

Had not our attention been seriously occupied by the hostile disposition manifested by these Indians we should have taken much interest in witnessing one of their great diversions.

Some time before we met them we observed a fine buffalo bull, who seemed to challenge a combat with our party ; he travelled for about two miles abreast of us, and almost within gun-shot ; his eyes were intently bent upon us. Though occasionally driven off by our dog, he would constantly return, and continue in a parallel line, as though he were watching our motions. This fearless character, so unlike that of buffaloes in general, excited our surprise and admiration ; and accordingly we determined to spare him and see how long he would continue to travel with us. But the noble animal offered too strong a temptation to the Indians. Seeing him stop at the same place where we halted, a few of them, especially the youngest of the party, ran up to him, and in a few moments several balls and perhaps a dozen arrows had reduced the animal to his last gasp. They then approached on all sides, and while he was engaged in keeping off those on his left the youths on his right would come so near him as to draw his attention to them ; the animal appeared galled, his rage was extreme, but his weakness was equally so. At length some of them came very near to him and caught hold of his tail : at this moment he was observed to be tottering ; they all drew off, the animal fell, and after two or three convulsive throes he expired. A shout from the Indians announced the death of their victim. This seemed to be a schooling for the youngest of their party, a few of whom were mere boys.

XII.

SIBERIA AND KAMTSCHATKA.

THEY were talking abont the Nihilists, and being exiled to Siberia. Some of the children had been at the theatre two years ago, and had seen the Exiles of Siberia, with white paper snow, and real oxen to draw the sledge.

Bertha asked, with a shudder, whether anybody ever came back to tell the story.

"Why, Bertha, Uncle Fritz himself built a telegraph across the Lake of Baikal."

Then they all looked at Uncle Fritz. But he would not go into any detail of his Siberian adventures. It is a subject on which he is always shy. But the boys got out "The Ingham Papers," and began looking for "Nofpo Ston" on the map.

"If you will go to the fountain of all knowledge," said Will Withers, "that is, to Robinson Crusoe, you will have a good travelling knowledge of Siberia."

"Siberia!" cried Alice. "It is not a year since you all said that Robinson Crusoe lived in the Oronooko.[1] I was disgraced. I thought he lived in Juan Fernandez before. And now I am told that he raised his melons under the shade of an avalanche, and that the savages were clothed

[1] See Stories of the Sea, p. 107.

in bear-skins, and skated across to his island. I am in despair."

"My dear Alice," said Will, who is very fond of her, "if he had never come back from the 'great river Oronooko,' we should never have known anything about him."

"All the same," the girl persisted, "he came home to England. The fact of his coming home does not prove that the book told about Siberia. Now see here, — here is dear Uncle Fred's table copy."

As has been said already, Robinson Crusoe is one of seven books always at Uncle Fritz's side. Sure enough, there was not a word about Siberia on the titlepage.

' But Will was not to be defeated. "Why do you read me the titlepage to the first volume?" he said. Then he turned to the title of the second volume, "The Further Adventures of Robinson Crusoe."

"You see he went to Nanquin, where your famous Capt. Cleveland could not go. A Chinese exclusiveness had not been settled on then. He went to the great city of Peking, and here he sold opium, among other things."

"Just as he had sold slaves before," said Alice, and she pretended to shudder. "A famous hero, indeed!"

"My dear Alice, it was the error of his time. That is what you must always say." And the boy rapidly turned the pages. "See! 'Robinson joins a caravan proceeding to Moscow,' and here, 'I could not but discover an infinite satisfaction that I was so soon arrived in a Christian country.'"

"But here," persisted Alice, "they are burning an idol."

"I cannot help that," said poor Will, who was no match for her in changing his ground and hopping from point to point. "All the same, it was Siberia"; and as he turned

he read in triumph, " I came to Tobolski, the capital city
of Siberia, where I continued some time."

" I should think he would," said Uncle Fred. " There
is a very decent hotel there now. I stayed there a good
while. I saw the annual gathering of the convicts before
they were scattered to the villages. Tobolsk is the place
where they meet."

" Uncle Fred, you should write your travels in Siberia.
If no one has been there since poor Robinson Crusoe, and
nobody but Will Withers knows that, you should make a
book."

The old gentleman smiled grimly. But he said that
plenty of people had gone to Kamtschatka and to Siberia
also. And he sent Alice for Peter Dobell's travels.
" That's a very good book, and you may read me to
sleep by hunting up my marks in it. I read that book as
I was floating down the Obi River on a timber raft."

" I had a great deal rather read your book, Uncle
Fritz," said the girl, with admiration.

" For that, my dear child, you must wait till it is
written." So Alice began : —

A POORGA.

We were happy on the 9th to inhale the fresh air, and
leave our smoky habitation at Timlatee to pursue our
journey, which now lay over a mountainous country, along
the sea-coast, and almost wholly bare of timber. The
morning was clear and cold, but the wind blew rather
fresh from the sea, and the white clouds hurried rapidly
over the blue expanse. About ten o'clock the Toyune of
Govenskoy came to me and said, " We must not stop at
twelve to-day, as usual, to take our luncheon, as I perceive

we are going to have one of those cold poorgas, which on
these plains are very violent; and we may be frozen to
death, should we not chance to meet with the Reindeer
Karaikees. For a long distance," added he, " there is no
house, or hut, or any sort of shelter : therefore order your
people to push on, and keep close together; for if the
Karaikees are here, they will be on the middle of the
moor, but yet a considerable distance from us."

Knowing how well the natives of that country understand the weather, although I could see nothing that
indicated a storm, I gave orders as he directed, and he
led the way with his own dogs. These, he said, were
his hunting dogs, and could be relied on. We went on
quite well, and briskly, until a little before twelve o'clock,
when, all of a sudden, the wind began to blow with great
violence, and, drifting the snow in quantities, thickened
the atmosphere so that we could not see a yard before us.
For the first part of our progress the sky above our heads
was clear; but this, after a while, became covered with
black clouds, and a kind of sharp sleet descended, which
was borne on the wind so violently that we could no
longer keep our faces to windward, and were obliged to
stop. As we had lost our way from the commencement,
the Toyune came to me to hold a consultation as to what
was to be done. I told him he was an inhabitant of the
country, and must be the better judge, and I should leave
it to him to decide. He said, " As it is impossible to
make a fire, if we remain here and the poorga continues
all night, we shall all be frozen to death. We had, therefore, better keep moving; but don't you give a dram to
any one till I tell you ; for watky is not good at such a
time. I have great confidence in my dogs, and if there is
a reindeer on the plain they will find him."

After this speech he pushed on his dogs to take what road they liked, first giving orders to the party to watch each other strictly and not to separate on any account. To our surprise the dogs, instead of taking what we imagined to be the road, turned off from the sea and brought the wind nearly on our backs. Although this alarmed many, who thought they were going wrong, they found it much more comfortable than to go against the sharp sleet which tore the skin from their faces. We continued travelling in this manner for upwards of two hours. The poorga raged with redoubled fury; the clouds of sleet rolled like a dark smoke over the moor, and we were all so benumbed with cold that our teeth chattered in our heads. The sleet, driven with such violence, had got into our clothes, and penetrated even under our parkas, and into our baggage, wherever there was the smallest crevice.

At length the Toyune's dogs began to snuff the air, bark loudly, and set out at full speed. It was like a shock of electricity. The rest of the dogs followed this example, and strained every nerve to keep pace with them. Our hearts now beat high, for we were sure the dogs smelt the reindeer, and this emotion had already infused a warmth through our veins, as we anticipated the happiness of finding shelter from a dreadful storm that threatened us with death. In about ten minutes more we had the ineffable pleasure of finding ourselves near a large Karaikee jourta, where we saw a fine fire blazing. The Karaikees had all run out with their clubs and spears to defend their reindeer from the dogs, which our drivers, benumbed as they were, could hardly keep from running on the herd that surrounded the jourta. The Karaikees, who were to lee-ward of us, had heard the dogs for some time, and, anticipating our arrival, had already killed a fine fat buck, and the women were skinning him when we arrived.

Our host was a fine hospitable old man, who possessed a herd of nearly three hundred sleek reindeer, and he seemed overjoyed to have us for guests. He made me sit down on some nice warm bear-skins spread near the fire, which was in the centre of the jourta. Behind me was a place apart, well hung and lined with deer-skins, for me to sleep on.

My interpreter, who was of Karaikee origin, found out at last that the host was a relation of his. This circumstance occasioned much joy, and was the cause of the death of another fine buck to regale his relation. The Toyune of Evashka being in possession of an order from government to collect the tax and tribute from the Reindeer Karaikees in that quarter, he made the interpreter explain his powers to the other Toyune, and ask him if he was prepared to pay them. He replied that he would pay the tribute with great cheerfulness, but he could not pay the tax in money, because he had none, nor did he know how to get it. "I wish," said he to me, "as you are going to St. Petersburg you would tell the Emperor that the Reindeer Karaikees, though a wild people, are good loyal subjects, and are always ready to pay the tribute in furs, although they cannot pay him money. Our habits of life," continued he, "are such that we never buy or sell anything for money; how then can he. expect us to find it? When I want tobacco, knives, kettles, needles, or watky, I buy them with fox, sable, and deer skins, and I know nothing farther of trade; besides, I have heard that amongst you who trade for money the effect often spoils the heart and creates bad blood between man and man. I am glad, therefore, there is so little money

amongst our Karaikees, who are warm-tempered." After
having made this speech, which was delivered in a serious
tone, he ordered a bundle of fox and sable skins to be
brought, and, throwing them at the feet of the Toyune,
"There," said he, "is our tribute. Let the interpreter
write me a paper and do you sign it to say you have
received it."

This request being complied with, and the afternoon
being very fine and serene, we deemed it best to resist the
kind invitation of the chief to pass the night with him,
and proceeded on our journey. After leaving Tolbachik,
the roads were good, and we soon arrived at Oushkee.
Here the inhabitants were few, and those few miserable.
I therefore distributed some presents amongst them which
I had brought for that purpose. My distribution was
nearly finished when I observed a lad whose features I
recognized, and I immediately asked him where he belonged. He said, "I am from the Tigil coast, and have
been sent here to assist travellers, and I helped to row
you down the river last summer. As I have been always
very busy I have been but once at the chase; but I killed
a sable, and I kept it on purpose to repay your kindness
for the knife and flints you gave me." Seeing that this
poor fellow was misery personified, not a shirt on his back,
and the skin dress he had on all in tatters, I refused to
accept his offer. He burst into tears and was about to
leave the room when I made him return, and took his
sable from him in return for what I had ordered to be
given him, at which he seemed quite happy.

"Look further on," said Uncle Fritz. "Find that which
I have marked 'A Gentle Hint.' It tells how they cut
short visits when the stores run low."

And Hugh read first : —

A GENTLE HINT.

The Kamtchadales are not only grateful for favors, but they think it absolutely necessary to make some return for a present, and are highly offended if it is refused. One of my Chinese servants, who was a very good-hearted fellow, was so affected at the circumstance I have told and the miserable appearance of the boy, that he went and brought one of his blue Nankin shirts' and made him a present of it.

All the Kamtchadales I met with were Christians of the Greek persuasion, and appeared attentive to their devotions. Their hospitality is excessive, and it is carried to an extreme amongst themselves that becomes ridiculous. They pay one another visits which last for a month or six weeks, until the generous host, finding his stock of provisions exhausted, is forced to give a hint to his guest to take his departure. This is managed by presenting to him at dinner a dish called *tolkootha,* a kind of olio, or hodge-podge, composed of a number of meats, fish, and vegetables, all mixed together, and very difficult to prepare. It is the *dernier ressort* of the master of the house, and the moment this dish is served up the guests take the hint and leave him the following day without feeling in the least dissatisfied.

The first thing a traveller must do, on arriving at a Kamtchadale house, is to treat the family with tea, of which they are excessively fond. I once saw a Kamtchadale drink eleven half-pint bowls of tea at a sitting, and he declared he could have completed the dozen had there been water enough in the kettle. They speak very slowly,

with rather an effeminate voice, making use of the simplest
language, but almost always with good sense. When they
do not wish to come to the point directly they convey
their meaning by some curious allegory, having relation to
bears, dogs, fishing, and hunting.

PRINCE ZACHAR.

A circumstance occurred whilst we were at Govenskoy
that inspired me with respect for the greatness of soul, the
courage, and the *sang-froid* exhibited by my friend, the
Prince Zachar, and revealed to me at once the cause of
the great influence he possessed over the Karaikees of the
coast. My Klutchee Kyoorchiks begged of me to give
them some watky to buy reindeer, silk, parkas, and boots,
and one of the prince's men, who had drunk too much of
it, became quite furious. With a large knife in his hand
he sought the prince, crying out that he was an unjust
man, and he would stab him. The other Karaikees tried
in vain to stop him until he had got quite near to the
prince's dwelling, when he called with all his force, "Come
out, Zachar, if you dare! I am prepared to kill you!"
Zachar, who was quietly drinking tea with me, heard all of
a sudden this extraordinary summons, which the interpreter
immediately explained to me. The prince put down his
cup of tea and, rising slowly from his seat, went out of the
jourta. I followed him closely, with a pair of loaded
pistols, which I always kept ready in case of necessity.
When he perceived that I followed him he desired the
interpreter would tell me not to interfere, as he would very
soon settle the affair himself. During this time the drunk-
en Karaikee foamed with rage and was trying to extricate
himself from the crowd that surrounded him. Zachar,

who had already thrown off his parka, now unbuttoned his shirt, exposed his breast, and ordering the crowd to stand aside, advanced boldly up to the Karaikee, and then, with a terrible voice and an undaunted countenance, he said to him, " Here is the breast of your prince ; strike at it if you dare ! " The Karaikee seemed thunderstruck ; he raised his hand, but was afraid to strike, and the knife fell to the ground. " Coward," said Zachar, " you have saved your life, for if you had aimed a blow at me I would have thrown you down at the same instant, and your own knife should have drawn your heart's blood." He then ordered his men to confine him till he should be sober, and returned with me to finish his tea.

THE REINDEER.

The reindeer may fairly be called the ox of these countries, and not the horse, as some people have called him. He does not possess either the noble temper or the docility of the latter animal. When the snow is deep and the roads are difficult, if the reindeer be pressed to exert himself, he becomes restive and stubborn, and neither beating nor coaxing will move him. He will lie down and remain in one spot for several hours, until hunger presses him forward ; and if, at the second attempt, he is again embarrassed, he will lie down and perish in the snow for want of food.

A Karaikee related to me the story of a keeper whose herd was dispersed in that way, but who, by very great exertions, after four or five days, collected them together again. However, he found he had wandered far beyond his usual haunts, and lost his way, so that he remained and roamed about with his herd nearly two years before he had the good fortune to meet with any of the Reindeer Karaikees.

We had now arrived at the last Karaikee ostrog on that coast, and it became necessary to direct our course to Kammina, across the moors, for two hundred and fifty versts, where there was scarcely a forest, much less a hut, to afford us shelter from the weather, should it prove bad again.

Here I separated from my friends, the Toyune of Evashka and the Prince Zachar, with real regret, for they had behaved to me with the kindness of brothers. On parting Zachar observed to me, "You are too late in the season; but you must do the best you can. I therefore advise you, even though the distance will be greater, to follow, as much as possible, the course of the creeks and rivers. There you will find shelter should a poorga commence; but on the moors, at this late period, it is very dangerous."

SLEEPING IN SNOW.

Early on the morning of the 19th we started again. It began to snow not long after our departure, and before midday the wind had increased to a storm, and my guide said we should have a regular poorga. We therefore directed our course for a small creek or branch that unites Veyvinskoia to Kammina River. We were not long before we got there, and followed its winding course, whilst its high banks defended us from the rigors of the snow-storm. After travelling in this way about an hour, we stopped to prepare our dinner, but found the wind and snow beat over the banks with such violence that we could not keep our fire burning five minutes at a time. After many attempts we persisted no longer, and contented ourselves with eating some cold boiled venison that had fortunately been prepared the day before; and very happy were we that my Chinese cook had been so provident. By the time we had finished our cold repast, we found it impossible to proceed any farther, and, drawing our sledges close under the windward bank of the creek, with the dogs in front, we passed the night on this dreary spot. A dismal night it was, for the snow and sleet beat in whirlwinds over the bank with unceasing violence; and it was impossible to hold one's face towards the wind for an instant. Although I slept in a kibitka that I tried to close up as tightly as possible, the snow beat into the crevices; and when I first awoke I found myself completely covered, and with difficulty extricated myself. The dogs, sledges, and men were so entirely concealed that I could only discern the marks where they lay; and I beat about and trampled amongst them some time before I could rouse them.

As the latter part of the night was warmer, and the snow fell in immense quantities, or rather drifted over us, we slept very warmly and comfortably. On the 20th, the wind having abated, and the weather proving mild, we determined to set off again, first spending an hour or two in shaking the snow off our clothes, baggage, and sledges, where it was found in abundance. It was absolutely necessary to depart, for not a stick of wood, nor even a twig, could we find to make a fire; and we travelled on until near eleven o'clock in the day before we arrived where there was wood enough to boil the tea-kettle. With what pleasure and satisfaction did we swallow a warm and cheering cup of tea, that delicious beverage, far exceeding every other when one is cold and weary! Ardent spirits will warm you more quickly, but their effects are not so lasting, and occasion a stupor that makes you feel afterwards quite drowsy.

SLEIGHING IN MAY.

We got off early on the 8th, and, although the surface of the snow was still soft, I found we got forward much better than on the day before. Travellers in this country during the spring should always take advantage of the night; indeed, the sun in the day being excessively hot, shining upon you for fourteen hours, and thawing a deep snow, is sufficient to prove the advantage of travelling by night. A tedious spring day, in a high northern latitude, with a hot sun reflected from the glassy surface of an immense snow-covered plain, entirely destitute of trees, not only inflames the eyes, but creates a lassitude of the body and mind. We had now a plain to cross of about a hundred versts in length, and about twenty versts in breadth, bounded on either side by steep mountains. Here the snow, which we frequently fathomed, was often four, and never less than three orshins deep, a measurement equal to from seven to nine English feet. We got away early on the 12th of May, and took care to move briskly, the surface being frozen, and still strong enough to bear the deer. The guide directed his course towards the centre of the plain, from an idea that when the snow became soft, we should find it not so deep there as close under the mountains. However, it proved the contrary; and we were not a little alarmed at the fearful distance that lay between us and the only places where we could procure food for our deer, now scarcely able to crawl, either by driving or coaxing.

Although I beat the road myself for them, on snow-

shoes, they plunged in so deeply as to be obliged to stop
and lie down every ten or twelve yards, panting for breath.
My Karaikee interpreter, with one of the Tongusees, drew
the sledge after them ; and about one o'clock in the day
we were all so worn down we were obliged to rest ourselves.   To add to our disappointment the nearest mountain appeared yet a considerable distance off.   After a
while the driver said we must continue our journey, and
force the deer on in the best way we could, for if they remained twenty or thirty hours more without food, they
would be too weak to proceed at all, and must perish in
the snow.   Indeed, I was well aware of the danger, and
was prepared to walk as long as I had a sinew to support
my tired limbs.

Having been every day since I left Towisk on snow-
shoes, I became a practised pedestrian in this way ; nor
found myself inferior to the natives of the country.   In
fact, without snow-shoes, I should have been like a man
in the middle of the ocean, who knew not how to swim,
and was without even a chip to save him from drowning.
It was impossible to drive through such snows, when a
deer with the greatest difficulty carried a small portion of
baggage, and when that oftentimes was obliged to be taken
from his back to enable him to extricate himself.   I had
taken care also to teach my servants to walk in snow-shoes
whilst in Kamtchatka.

Between six and seven in the evening I thought I perceived the last row of trees which intercepted our view of
the mountains ; and we pushed eagerly on to pass it.   Our
disappointment was excessive when we could plainly distinguish two more intersections ; but again, not seeing
anything beyond them, we consoled ourselves with the
idea that those were certainly the last.   Arriving at them,

we were chagrined to find the largest stream we had yet encountered. This, however, after being completely soaked through, and our strength almost exhausted, we contrived to pass. When on the other side, there were yet some versts between us and the foot of the mountain, which the Karaikee declared he was too weak to accomplish. The Tongusee likewise complained, but said we were now so near that, if I could give him a little food of any sort to recruit his strength, we might remain on the spot where we were until the baggage-deer came up with us, while he would take his own to the mountains to pasture. I now recollected that my cook formerly kept in my sledge one of the small vessels with the deer's feet he had boiled down. On examination I found it, together with a little salt, and we were all not a little rejoiced thereat, being at a great distance from my baggage, and having taken nothing but water all the day. As we had no bread, and but a small portion of jelly for each person, we were obliged to make up the deficiency by drinking two or three large draughts of water.

Scanty as was our repast, we were all much refreshed. I had often supped more plentifully, but certainly never with a better appetite. Immediately after, the Tongusee, whom I armed with a Spanish knife and a spear to protect him against the bears, left us, whilst the Karaikee and myself collected wood, made a large fire, and placing a quantity of bushes before it on the snow, wrapped ourselves up in our parkas and went to sleep.

Between three and four in the morning of the 13th, I was awaked by the arrival of my servants and the baggage-deer. They had followed the track we had made, without which, they said, the deer would never have been able to accomplish the distance. We now got a good breakfast, and

then started again under the hottest sun I had yet experienced. Both deer and men suffered so much from the
heat they could scarcely crawl, and it was eleven o'clock
before we arrived at the mountain. Our deer were obliged
to go to the summit before moss could be procured.

After getting over the first mountain, on looking round
to examine our party, we found these two fellows had
absconded with two of the reindeer that were not laden.
This was a most unpleasant circumstance, as I was told
that they knew the road better than any of the rest. The
road proved like that before described, except that the
snow was not quite so deep. Descending the mountain,
we came to an open stream, narrow, deep, and rapid, and
were obliged to make a bridge to take over the sledges,
the deer going about a verst higher up, where there was a
spot fordable. One of them had the slender remains of
my stock of biscuit and my skin coverings on his back,
which he contrived to shake from him into the stream;
and, before we could recover them, the biscuits were all
completely soaked and spoiled. Pitching our tent on a
rising ground on the opposite side, I dried a dozen of
them that were not broken in the sun; the rest we consumed at once, as we perceived they would not keep in
that state.

A MOUNTAIN HOME.

It was my intention, on going to rest, to have awakened
about ten o'clock at night in order to set out early; but
the severe fatigue we had undergone the day before made
me sleep soundly until after midnight. On awaking I
called aloud for some time before any one came. At length
one of my Chinese servants entered my tent, and told me
the Tongusees were nowhere to be found! I now roused

my guide and the Karaikee, when, to our grief and astonishment, we perceived these unfeeling rascals had gone off in the night, not leaving us even a single deer for food, and returning by the road they came. We were now five in number, namely, the Cossack, a Karaikee, two Chinese servants, and myself, left, with all our baggage, on one of the highest mountains in Siberia, in a wild, uninhabited country! We had already been twelve days from Towisk, and had therefore every reason to believe we were not more than three or four days' march from some Tongusee tabboon; but, as we were all totally ignorant of the road, it was difficult to decide which way to direct our course. The Cossack, who did not deserve the name, was a perfect woman in character, more alarmed than anybody else, frightening the young Karaikee and my servants, and proposing a hundred different schemes. I would not listen to any of them, until I had weighed the matter maturely, and examined well the country about us. The first thing, however, was to see what stock of provisions we had. I found it to consist of a few pounds of reindeer meat almost spoiled, two or three pounds of rice, a small quantity of Manilla sweet chocolate, our biscuits reduced in number to twelve, about the size of a dollar each, two or three small lumps of sugar remaining, and a very small quantity indeed of salt and pepper, but fortunately a little box full of good tea. After this review of our provisions, I felt assured that, with rigid economy, we could keep our bodies and souls together for at least twelve or fifteen days. In the mean time it was highly probable I should be able to shoot something to assist in preventing us from starving. I had a map of Kamtchatka that included the shores of the Ochotsk Sea, on the Siberian side, as far as Zamsk, and, assisted by a pocket-compass, showed me on which side the sea lay. But the Cossack declared he had seen it the day before from the mountain on the opposite side of the rivulet. I therefore determined we should go together to a high peak only a few versts distant, to assure ourselves whether it was or was not the sea that he had seen.

When about to depart we looked in vain for our snow-shoes, of which it appeared those fellows had robbed us to prevent our overtaking them suddenly. About six o'clock on the morning of the 17th we left the encampment, and, although we kept in the tracks of the reindeer, we sunk above our knees at every step and suffered the severest fatigue before attaining the height from whence we expected to behold the sea. At the first view the expanse appeared to me no more than an immense extent of low ground covered with fog. The Cossack persisted to the contrary and showed me a valley on the opposite side where we could distinguish the trees and which appeared so very different from that before us that I was induced to give in to his opinion of its being the ocean. Not feeling perfectly satisfied, however, on the subject I told him we must visit, on the following morning, the ridge of mountains that surrounded us in the form of a crescent, about thirty versts in extent. This, I added, might be easily accomplished by making ourselves snow-shoes with the boards of our sledges. He seemed lost, and wavering every minute, sometimes proposing one thing and sometimes another, and at length asked that he and the Karaikee might go in search of reindeer men, while we remained on the mountain to await their return. I was obliged to put a stop to any further proposals of that kind by telling him that I was perfectly aware of his cowardice and deceit, and that, as I was ignorant of the character of the Karaikee, I should watch them both narrowly. "You see," said I, "how I am armed, and I shall put the first man to death who attempts anything improper or disobeys my orders." This threat had the desired effect; he became instantly more obedient. On my return to the tent I armed my Chinese servants, privately desiring them to keep a strict watch on the other two, as I had reason to believe they wished to rob us of our provisions and make their escape. At night, before I went to sleep, I collected all the provisions together, also my little axe, knife, guns, and pistols, and slept near them. The Karaikee and Cossack I placed in the middle of the tent, and my Chinese servants at each side of them.

I should have premised that previously to going to rest I visited another height, about two versts off, on the same side as that where our tent stood. Though I could not discover the sea I had the good fortune to find my snow-shoes amongst the bushes, the Tongusees having hidden them purposely.

On the 18th of May, at three o'clock in the morning, we set out on our excursion after I had armed myself with two guns, in full hopes that, as we had seen some tracks in coming up the mountain, we should have the good fortune to meet with a bear. With much labor and fatigue we contrived to climb the summit of the highest mountain of the opposite ridge. We had now an extensive view of the country around us and were most wofully disappointed in beholding the sea that we thought we had seen the day before transmuted into trees, hills, and plains! We now found ourselves immediately opposite our tent, having a steep descent to make, a rivulet of considerable size to cross in the valley, and the high mountain to ascend on which it stood. As the snow was

soft and my snow-shoes large I drew them both together,
and, sitting down on them, held my two guns with my left
arm, the butts resting on the snow-shoes, and with a short
stick in my right hand to guide myself I went down with
the rapidity of lightning. The Cossack followed safely in
my path.

LOST IN A WILDERNESS.

Our companions were greatly dejected on hearing that
all appearance had vanished of the sea, which the Cossack was so confident of having seen. The Karaikee said
he had been considering the distance we had made, and
thought it was too great to attempt to return, and he was
willing now to obey my orders and accompany me
through whatever road I chose to take. I explained to
them the necessity of firmness and an unaltered resolution, telling them that they must put their trust in God,
while exerting every nerve and all their fortitude of mind
to keep themselves from sinking under the incessant
fatigue we must inevitably experience, for that we had but
a scanty allowance of food, and must push on in full
hopes of being able to procure more by the road, though
we could form no judgment as to when the period of our
troubles and labors would arrive.

I made the Cossack and the Chinese join their hands
to ours, and, turning to the East, cross themselves as I
did to confirm their promise, assuring them that I would
eat, drink, sleep, and work the same as the rest, nor require
of them one single act that I was not ready and willing
to assist in performing myself. We left on this spot everything superfluous in the way of clothes, etc., making the
sledges as light as possible. The Cossack and myself led
the way. I soon perceived that we should have some

difficulty in accomplishing the business, but the danger was not so great as we imagined. Having only a scanty portion of food we drank tea twice every twenty-four hours, and in the morning we took thin rice-water, with a small lump of chocolate each, to make it palatable. We perceived that, laborious as was our march, this nourishment was enough to keep us alive until it should please Heaven to direct us where we might procure, with our guns, the means of living well. I was pleased at finding my companions more cheerful and seemingly determined to exert all their fortitude, courage, and perseverance so necessary to conquer difficulties and insure our safety. We were an unfortunate little band, thrown upon a wide wilderness, but relying on heaven and our good stars, entirely ignorant of the country, and having nothing but a pocket-compass to direct us towards the ocean, as to which, whether it was one hundred or twenty versts distant, we could not possibly tell. . . .

On the 31st we threw everything away except what was absolutely necessary. Just as we were about to depart, on the evening of this day, two wild geese flew over us. I fired at them and thought I had missed, but my Chinese boy declared he heard the shot strike and had seen them alight, about two hundred yards off, on a spot which he pointed out. The Cossack and myself repaired thither with all possible speed. One of the geese fled at our approach, and the other that was wounded remained in the middle of a large bog, where, if shot, I was fearful we should find great trouble in getting it. After shooting it I entered the bog, but found the surface of a tough sod that sank down, bringing the mud and water to my middle without breaking. I had used the precaution to take a large stick in my hand, or I should not have been able to

extricate myself. The sod at length broke and let me
down to my arm-pits, and I was obliged to tell the Cossack, who was a much lighter man, to try what he could
do. He succeeded remarkably well until he got nearly
back with the goose, when he sunk suddenly up to his
neck, and began to roar and bawl in a most hideous manner, being so alarmed at the same time that he could
hardly make use of the stick. I had the utmost difficulty
to get near him with the other stick, which he laid hold
of, and I pulled him out, almost suffocated with mud.
Dangerous as was the situation of my companion, his
ridiculous figure made me burst into a fit of laughter, and
the Chinese joined me heartily ; this caused him to scream
the more loudly, in order to impress me with the fuller
idea of his perilous situation. When extricated from the
bog he crossed himself a dozen times and then laughed as
heartily as myself. Indeed, the goose was such a prize as
gave us spirits to laugh. . . .

In the evening I went to the summit of the mountain
again, imagining that as the sun descended I might discover better what was on the opposite side of some extensive low grounds that lay before us. Whilst there, and
holding my compass to take the direction for our route of
the following day, I thought I plainly saw, at a great distance to the northward and eastward, three or four men,
and as many reindeer or horses. I immediately called
out to the two Chinese to light a large fire, and making
the Cossack and Karaikee come up to me endeavored to
point out to them the objects that had just met my eyes.
Although I felt confident I saw men and animals moving,
I could not with all my care direct their sight so as to distinguish them, and they persisted in saying they could see
nothing. This made me quite unhappy. . . .

Scarcely had we made our fire when the grass all around us was in a blaze, obliging us to move to another spot; and the fire raged with such violence it was in vain to attempt extinguishing it. At length the woods — the whole country around — were on fire. We were not sorry for an accident that might, perhaps, if any of the natives were near, bring them to the spot. It also helped to destroy some large swarms of mosquitoes that plagued us not a little on our arrival. Indeed, we suffered almost as much from these insects as from fatigue and hunger. Those flying leeches of Siberia never quitted us day or night, unless when on the mountains, or when the wind blew hard enough to sweep them away. We got off early on the 4th, and had a most fatiguing time till twelve o'clock, when the sun became so oppressive it was impossible to proceed any farther without refreshment. The skin being chafed from our shoulders, and our feet sore, added to the difficulty of wading the deep marshes that occurred at every instant; we were all completely exhausted. My two Chinese, for the first time, lay down and began to cry! I consoled them with the assurance that we must either discern the sea, or arrive at some place where we should find plenty of food, in the course of a day or two; and that it was a folly to give up when we were now at the moment of getting over our difficulties. Taking out the rest of the small biscuits that I had carefully preserved, I divided them equally between the Cossack, the Karaikee, and themselves, and having boiled our kettle, and drunk heartily of tea, the whole party was soon put into good spirits again. As I kept no part of this slender provision for myself, it was some time before I could prevail upon the two Chinese to eat their biscuit without sharing it with me. However, I would not take it from them; for, although I was tired, I did not feel my strength exhausted as they did.

While my companions slept I drew on my boots, that scarcely deserved the name, and made an excursion with my gun to see if I could find any game, and also to examine the route necessary to be pursued in the afternoon. It grieved me considerably to perceive that the impediments we had met in the morning increased so much as to render it necessary to proceed due south. I was almost .in despair, when I beheld six large sea-gulls flying in that direction, and which at length seemed to alight near a forest some distance off, which place, however, I thought we should be able to reach, by exerting ourselves, before seven or eight in the evening. I returned immediately to my companions, who were not a little delighted by this joyful news, the Karaikee assuring me there must be a large river or lake near, as the kind of gulls I had seen strongly indicated this.

We now found the way moss-covered, dry, and even, and between six and seven in the evening arrived at the forest. To our great astonishment we beheld what we supposed a narrow lake of great length, forming a crescent, the opposite banks being also covered with fine timber. Here we determined to pass the night, and pitched our tent behind a small copse, that concealed it from the lake, in order to prevent its frightening away any water-fowl that might visit it. This being accomplished, leaving the Chinese and Cossack to boil the tea-kettle, the Karaikee and myself went to examine the lake. On approaching the banks I discovered two small ducks quite near the shore, and had the good fortune to shoot them both at one shot. Running to the water-side to pick them up, God only knows the inexpressible joy that filled our hearts when we beheld the water move, and satisfied our senses that we were on the banks of a large river. It was somewhat remarkable that the obstacles I had met with during the last two days, and which disheartened me so much, had yet, by turning me aside from the route I wished to take, been the cause of our falling in with this fine stream so favorable to our wishes. We felt satisfied it must bring us to the ocean, from which, by all appearances, we could not be far removed. My companions were overjoyed beyond measure at this discovery, since we could now make a raft, and descend to the sea without undergoing such severe fatigue as heretofore, not to mention the pleasing anticipation of being daily enabled to procure plenty of food.

On the 6th of June I went out very early with my gun, but finding no game, picked some handfuls of keesletya to make soup for our dinner with the remaining duck, and returned to my companions. A number of fine trees lay before us on the ground. I therefore marked out those which I thought best suited for our raft. The Cossack said he would cut them whilst I should go out in search of food, so that we all might be enabled to work the following morning, and leave that place in the evening. Although I walked a considerable distance during the morning, and saw a deer and several geese, ducks, and gulls, they were all so wild it was impossible to get within shot of them. I returned, quite dejected and tired, along the banks of the river, seating myself in the bushes, about two hundred yards above our tent, where I was determined to stay and shoot something to afford us a dinner on the following day. It was not long before a gull came flying over my head. I shot it, and shortly after a fine duck that fell into the river just before me. Leaning on my gun, I pulled off my boots in order to wade after it. Just as I had got them off, seeing the current seizing my prize, I rushed into the water, fearful of losing it, and forgetting I had a gun in my hand until I was out of my depth and obliged to swim. The weight of my clothes and of the double-barrelled fowling-piece embarrassed me so much that I could not keep myself above water, and, sinking several times, I was at length obliged to let go my favorite gun, and even then with difficulty kept myself from sinking. Luckily, some bushes grew up not far below me, having their tops above the water, which I attained and laid hold of, though I still found myself out of my depth. Here the duck was entangled, and I secured it. There was a bush for every four or five yards between me and the shore, and I swam from one to another, holding the duck in my mouth, and arriving where it was shallow enough to wade before my friends got near enough to aid me. I regretted exceedingly the loss of a gun that had been so useful, but we had two remaining which were sufficient for our purpose. On the 7th we all labored hard to finish our raft, as we had food for that day, and were to trust to our good stars to furnish us on the following. I employed myself in cutting down immediately two large dead trees for the side-pieces ; and before two o'clock in the day we had all the timbers well lashed together, and the raft ready to be launched in the water. After dinner we launched our raft, which to our great joy did not swim too low, and proved in fact everything that we could have wished. It was composed of fifteen lower timbers, of the thickness of a man's thigh, and about sixteen or eighteen feet long, two cross-pieces at each end, to which they were strongly lashed with manilla rope and thongs, and a layer of poles and bushes placed above all to sit on. Thus prepared, we placed our baggage upon it, and committed ourselves to the surface of a fine large river with a current running at the rate of more than five miles an hour. Before quitting this place we all returned thanks to Heaven in the most solemn manner for having conducted us thus far in safety, and prayed fervently for a continuation of the Almighty protection we had so often experienced. We soon discovered a material difference between walking and our present method of travelling, having floated at our ease, before nine at night, a greater distance than we had made during any three days before. We had also the pleasure, for the first time, of being free from mosquitoes and gnats. Just before we stopped for the night I killed a fine large sheldrake that came flying by. I determined to stop every night at ten or eleven o'clock, and start again at four in the morning, being fearful lest during the twilight we might run foul of rocks or trees in the way, and injure our raft so as to oblige us again to go on foot. We encamped this night close on the bank of the river amongst some dry grass, and not far from a mountain called Sunkapskoy, which the Cossack thought he knew he had traversed in the winter, and near to which was a Tongusee tabboon. Between two and three in the morning a swan came floating down the river. I fired at it with my rifle, and missed. Seeing it fly toward a lake at the back of the tent, where we heard another one, I repaired thither and got a shot at it from behind a bush, within forty or fifty yards. The bird rose and flew a little way, and then to our great joy fell dead in the middle of the lake. The Cossack, tying two pieces of old timber together with a thong he had in his pocket, floated himself along on them, and brought the swan safely to shore. This stock of animal food put the whole party in good spirits, and we continued our route on the raft, finding the current increasing every hour, and promising to convey us rapidly to the ocean. During the day I shot another swan and a duck. We soon discovered that the mountain that the Cossack thought he knew was much farther from the sea than he imagined, and after we had floated near it, he did not recollect any of the country around. The river was extremely crooked, sometimes carrying us west, sometimes east, and in fact to all points of the compass. On the 8th, in the evening, we stopped early, and had, for the first time since we left the mountain, what we thought a good supper, though we were still fearful of consuming meat more than once a day, the wild fowl being excessively shy and difficult to shoot.

The weather became so raw and uncomfortable, being accompanied with a drizzling rain, that we stopped earlier than usual, and continued to halt until four o'clock in the morning of the 10th, when we proceeded again, though a chill fog prevailed, and a good deal of wind. We had a most unpleasant time, but, anxious to arrive at the ocean, would not lie by, particularly as the stream had increased in rapidity, and now hurried us along with considerable swiftness. About one o'clock, although we were nearly in the middle of the river, which was here upwards of a verst wide, we were suddenly seized by a whirlpool ; and in spite of our utmost efforts, having nothing but poles to guide the raft, were drawn violently towards the left bank, and forced under some large trees, which had been undermined by the water, and hung over the surface of the stream, the roots still holding them fast to the shore. I saw the danger to which we were exposed, and called out to every one to lie flat on his face and hold fast to the baggage. The branches were so thick it was impossible for all to escape, and there being barely room to admit the raft under them, they swept off the two Chinese, the Karaikee, my tin box with all my papers and valuables, our soup-kettle, etc., etc.

Nothing now remained but a small tea-kettle and a few other things that happened to be tied fast with thongs. The Karaikee and one of the Chinese seized hold of the branches that swept them off, and held their heads above water, but the youngest of the Chinese having floated away with the current, the Cossack and myself had the greatest difficulty in paddling the raft up to him. We came just in time to poke our poles down after him as he sank for the third time. Fortunately he seized it, and we drew him upon the raft half drowned. As the current was running at the rate of six or seven miles an hour, we were carried more than half a verst down before we gained the shore. The other Chinese and the Karaikee crying out aloud for assistance, I ran up the shore as quickly as I could, taking a long pole with me, and leaving the Cossack to take care of the raft and the young Chinese. When I arrived at the spot my Chinese cook informed me he had seized my tin box with one hand, and was so tired of holding with the other that, if I did not come soon to his assistance, he must leave it to the mercy of the current. Whilst I attempted to walk out on the body of the tree, whose branches they were holding, one of the roots broke, and very nearly separated it from the shore. I was therefore obliged to jump off and stride to one that was two feet under water, hauling myself along by the branches of the others, and at length I got near enough to give the Chinese a pole. He seized fast hold, and I pulled him between two branches, enabling him to get a leg over one, and keep his body above water. Thus placed, he tied the tin box with his handkerchief to the pole, and I got it safely ashore. I was now obliged to return and assist the Karaikee, who held by some branches far out, and where there were no others near enough for him to reach, in order to draw himself in. After half an hour's labor I got them both on the bank, neither of them knowing how to swim, and both much exhausted by the cold and the difficulty of holding so long against a rapid current. As the wind commenced blowing very hard, we concluded to stay all that day where we were, it being likewise necessary to dry our clothes, papers, etc., which were all completely wet.

In the afternoon the wind died away, and the sun shone out clear, when I commenced drying my papers, and found many of the most valuable of them totally ruined. The ink in some was quite effaced, and others were so stuck together that they were destroyed in my attempting to separate them. At six in the evening we made an excursion along the banks of the river, to see if we could discover any of the things we had lost, and kill some game. In our rambles we frightened a duck from off her nest, and got six eggs. Shortly after I killed a swan with my rifle, and the poor Karaikee going for it, had the pleasure to find his bundle of clothes that had been swept from the raft. We had lost nearly all our cooking utensils : fortunately our spoons and cups were in our pockets. A small tea-kettle without a cover had to serve for every purpose. The top of my tin box we employed as a dish, pouring our soup into it that we might eat it more conveniently with our spoons. We felt severely the loss of our soup-kettle, being obliged to make our dinner and drink our tea from the same vessel. In consequence of the high wind that prevailed, and its being quite unsafe for our frail bark to proceed, we remained here until four o'clock in the afternoon of the 11th, when we departed, though it was still blowing hard, with drizzling rain, making the weather quite cold and uncomfortable. We became so wet and chilled that we stopped early in the evening. We left our resting place between four and five on the 12th, with a rapid current that conveyed us swiftly along. About mid-day we espied a Tongusee canoe hung up between two trees, and the appearance of some wood freshly cut made me immediately push for the shore, inspired with the hope of finding there some inhabitants. In this expectation we were disappointed, though there was every appearance of persons having visited the spot but a short time before. We were not a little overjoyed to find the canoe with paddles and everything complete. Our raft was much water-soaked and swimming deep, and without the canoe we should have been obliged to remain a day somewhere in order to repair it, and put some additional logs to make it float higher. The canoe we now lashed to one side, put the Karaikee in one end and the Cossack in the other, with a considerable portion of our baggage, and lightened the raft, so that it swam as high as we could wish. We found those two persons with their paddles could turn it more quickly and better than all five of us had been able to do with poles.

We now floated on a fine, deep, and wide river, and, though extremely crooked, beautiful beyond conception, winding down amongst romantic mountains and through large bodies of rich lowlands, interspersed with lakes, rivulets, and meadows covered with fine grass. It appeared a matter of surprise to me that so fine a stream, apparently possessing abundance of game and fish, should be entirely destitute of neighboring inhabitants. We saw numbers of fish constantly playing about us, and contrived a hook with a small nail, but had not the good fortune to catch any of them. The current seemed to increase as we descended, and we set off before four on the 13th to take

advantage of it. About ten o'clock I discovered a jourta
not far from the edge of the left bank, and casting off the
canoe despatched the Cossack and Karaikee to examine
it. They soon returned, informing me it was a winter
jourta of the Tongusees, but was then quite deserted, and
that there was not the smallest appearance of inhabitants
anywhere near. The day was hot and calm, and our visit
to the shore brought off to us a swarm of mosquitoes that
pestered us continually, — an annoyance we had not experienced for some days previously in consequence of the
wind and rain. My companions often complained of not
having meat enough, and seemed displeased at my dealing
it out sparingly. This was, however, absolutely necessary
by reason of the difficulty of killing game, for we perceived that as we descended the river became wider, and
the water-fowl scarcer and more difficult of approach;
besides which it was quite uncertain whether we should
meet inhabitants at the sea-coast, and perhaps, when there,
we might again find game scarce and difficult to shoot.
On the 14th the current increased in rapidity to such a
degree that it cost us considerable pain and labor to guide
our raft in safety, and we felt grateful to Heaven for having fallen with the canoe, without which we could never
have descended this part of the river on so frail a vehicle.

We ran aground three or four times, and twice got
entangled in the trees that hung over the stream, but fortunately escaped without accident. Perceiving a very
dangerous place just below us, and being too near the
shore to prevent the raft's being drawn into the whirlpool,
we pulled in and landed on the bank immediately opposite to us. We then dragged the raft up for about a hundred yards, assisted by the counter current that generally
prevails near the edge of a stream. By this precaution

we got nigh enough to be able to make an offing sufficient to prevent being thrown upon another dangerous place we had seen below, composed of fallen trees, roots, etc., thrown up like an island, over which the water foamed in a cataract. Not long after we had landed I observed the Karaikee examining with great attention the spot where we were and the surrounding mountains, and at length he began to pray and to cross himself with great fervency, the tears running down his cheeks in a stream. I approached him to inquire the cause of his emotion, when he exclaimed: "That is our mountain; our village is not far off, for on this spot I caught some hares last winter. I know that we are now not far from Grebay, a small Yakut village on the sea-coast, at the mouth of the river, which is called Cowvah, and only twenty versts from Towinsk. But a short distance below this is the branch on which Towinsk stands, emptying itself into the bay, about ten versts higher up, and if it had been earlier in the season we might have descended it with a raft, but I perceive the water is now too low to attempt it."

It will be easier for my readers to imagine than for me to express the joy we all experienced at this cheering news. We boiled our kettle and made all the meat we had into soup, determined to have a feast after such a long term of short allowance. This, however, was only a comparative feast, as our whole stock amounted to a third of a swan and a teal. Our repast finished we pushed off our raft with great spirits, paddling with all our strength to obtain the midway channel and avoid the dangers which, like Scylla and Charybdis, threatened us on either hand. The current ran at the rate of eight or nine knots an hour in turbulent eddies that twisted us round and round, in spite of our best exertions. We had, however, the good fortune to escape unhurt, but afterwards ran aground several times, and with great difficulty got the raft off (by all jumping into the water) and that not without injuring it materially. Between two and three o'clock in the afternoon we found ourselves in a fine wide channel, with a moderate current, and on the beach, not far below us, descried a man and two boys mending a canoe. The effect the sight of human beings had upon us is not to be described. Every soul shed tears of joy, and when these people approached with their canoe to assist us it was impossible to resist the impulse, or to answer their questions. Our tears flowed in streams, and we were all so unmanned we could only reply to them by signs. The elder person proved to be a Yakut, whom I had known when I passed before. This good Yakut, when he recognized me, jumped upon the raft, clasped me in his arms, and shed tears in abundance, exclaiming, "Thank God! Thank God! you are all saved." He informed me that the Tongusees having confessed their leaving us on the mountain, the old chief, living near to Towinsk, had despatched his son, with twenty-five head of reindeer, in search of us, and that every one there had given us up for lost, knowing how difficult it was to procure food on those deserted plains and mountains in the spring of the year.

On inquiry we found that had we taken any other route than the one we came we must inevitably have perished!

"Dear Uncle Fritz," said Alice, shivering, "did anything as bad as that ever happen to you?"

"Not for so many days," said he, patting her shoulder

as they walked into supper. "But I have eaten smoked salmon cold with more appetite than I now have for Ellen's hot muffins."

When they were seated at the table, and the decomposition of the muffins had begun, Bob Edmeston followed up what Alice had said.

"You see, Alice," said he, "that the excitement of discovery carries men on. For me, I mourn that nothing is left unknown for the explorers of this age."

They all laughed at his melancholy, and Philip asked him what was the source of Mink Brook, and Laura if he would tell her where the water of the Shannock factories emptied into the sea.

"I will not be bullied," said Bob. "I do not know these things because my education has been neglected. But, alas! some one knows them. They are on the map of Rhode Island. What I thirst for is the unknown, yet not unknowable. Alas! the discoverers have wrested this from me."

"Not at all," said Uncle Fritz. "You have only to ask at the Public Library for the Journal of the Geographical Society, or the Bulletin de la Geographie, and you will see that there is as good discovery as ever going on to-day."

"One comes to love these explorers," said Bertha. "Here I never heard of your Mr. Dobell's wife nor children nor home; but I have been crying, without knowing it, because he was so hungry."

Fergus said, rather seriously, that we always sympathized with men who gave themselves for an idea. It might be obedience to an Emperor, it might be the source of a river,—we were always glad to follow a man in proportion as he was unselfish.

Bob Edmeston, without going into the philosophy of the thing, said there were lots of interesting books on the shelf the Dobell volumes came from.

So there are, and so it happens that the next volume of this series will be

STORIES OF DISCOVERY TOLD BY DISCOVERERS.

Cambridge: Printed by John Wilson & Son.

COLLECTED AND EDITED

By EDWARD E. HALE.

BOSTON:

ROBERTS BROTHERS.

1880.

EDWARD E. HALE'S WRITINGS.

TEN TIMES ONE IS TEN. 16mo. 75 cents.

CHRISTMAS EVE AND CHRISTMAS DAY: Ten Christmas Stories. With Frontispiece by Darley. 16mo. $1.25

UPS AND DOWNS. An Every-day Novel. 16mo. $1.50.

A SUMMER VACATION. Paper covers. 50 cents.

IN HIS NAME. Square 18mo. $1.00.

OUR NEW CRUSADE. Square 18mo. $1.00.

THE MAN WITHOUT A COUNTRY, and other Tales. 16mo. $1.25.

THE INGHAM PAPERS. 16mo. $1.25.

WORKINGMEN'S HOMES. Illustrated. 16mo. $1.00.

HOW TO DO IT. 16mo. $1.00.

HIS LEVEL BEST. 16mo. $1.25.

THE GOOD TIME COMING; or, Our New Crusade. A Temperance Story. Square 18mo. Paper covers. 50 cents.

G. T. T.; or, The Wonderful Adventures of a Pullman. $1.00. "G. T. T." is an abbreviation once very popular, meaning "Gone to Texas."

WHAT CAREER? or, The Choice of a Vocation and the Use of Time. 16mo. $1.25.

MRS. MERRIAM'S SCHOLARS. A Story of the "Original Ten." 16mo. $1.00.

For sale by all Booksellers. Mailed, postpaid, by the Publishers,

ROBERTS BROTHERS, Boston.

HOW TO DO IT.

BY EDWARD EVERETT HALE.

CONTENTS.

How to Talk; How to Write; How to Read; How to go into Society; How to Travel; Life at School and in Vacation; Life Alone; Habits with Children; Life with your Elders; Habits of Reading; Getting Ready.

16MO.   PRICE $1.00.

" The little work is intended especially for the benefit of young readers, but it is equally adapted to give pleasure to the older members of the family circle. It is weighty in thought, of acute observation, versatile in its illustrations and examples, affectionate in tone, and racy in expression." — *N. Y. Tribune.*

" This is a very sensible little book. 'How to Do It' means 'how you are to behave in society,' 'how you are to read,' 'how you are to live with your elders,' and 'how with children,' &c. On all these points Mr. Hale gives very shrewd, kindly advice. The first chapter, with its description and reminiscences of Boston as it was, will charm every reader, and tempt him to go further, when indeed he can scarcely fail to get much good." — *London Spectator.*

" It is a mistake to suppose this charming, amusing, and useful little book is only for young people. It is equally needed by multitudes of people who have less knowledge than years; parents who do n t know 'how to do it' any better than their sons and daughters; men and women, well informed in current matters of interest, but who do not know how to read, or write, or talk, or travel, or go into society, or even behave at church, in a proper manner. Let them get this book, and Mr. Hale, in his quaint, humorous, attractive, and sensible way, will tell them exactly how to do all these things, and more. His pages are crowded with good sense and practical wisdom, and bright with anecdote and story, with pleasant talk and words of cheer, which not only show how to do it, but are sure to teach courage to the timid, and modesty to the self-sufficient, in doing it." — *Universalist Quarterly.*

Sold by all Booksellers. Mailed, postpaid, by the Publishers,

ROBERTS BROTHERS, BOSTON.

OUR NEW CRUSADE.

A TEMPERANCE STORY.

By E. E. HALE.

Square 18mo.   Price $1.00.

From the Southern Churchman.

"It has all the characteristics of its brilliant author, — unflagging entertainment, helpfulness, suggestive, practical hints, and a contagious vitality that sets one's blood tingling. Whoever has read 'Ten Times One is Ten' will know just what we mean. The fact that thirty thousand copies of this last-named volume have been sold gives one some idea of its hold on the popular mind. We predict that the new volume, as being a more charming story, will have quite as great a parish of readers. The gist of the book is to show how possible it is for the best spirits of a community, through wise organization, to form themselves into a lever by means of which the whole tone of the social status may be elevated, and the good and highest happiness of the helpless many be attained through the self denying exertions of the powerful few."

From the Louisville Daily Ledger.

"Mr. Hale thinks, rightly, that this movement of the women of the land to put down an undeniable evil was not a wisely directed one. He is willing enough to have a *Crusade*, but let it be more in the line of women's work, and let it appeal to all the best instincts of our nature, — not the resistant ones. Men are not going to be brow-beaten into being good, especially by the sex that has hitherto been styled the 'gentler;' and we don't much wonder at it. To come and forcibly take possession of a man's place of business, and insist upon praying and singing him out of it, may have, at bottom, a very commendable motive to instigate it; but there is a right and a wrong way of doing every thing. *This* is the wrong way. Now, in his 'New Crusade,' Mr. Hale gives us the clew to a much better, more reasonable, and altogether more popular way of exalting the social status in any given community."

Sold everywhere by all Booksellers.   Mailed, postpaid, by the Publishers,

ROBERTS BROTHERS, BOSTON

9 783337 340025